The Cost of
Victory

CRIMSON WORLDS II

Jay Allan

system 7
publishing

Crimson Worlds Series

Marines (Crimson Worlds I)

The Cost of Victory (Crimson Worlds II)

A Little Rebellion (Crimson Worlds III)
(December 2012)

The First Imperium (Crimson Worlds IV)
(March 2013)

www.crimsonworlds.com

The Cost of
Victory

The Cost of Victory is a work of fiction. All names, characters, incidents, and locations are ficticious. Any resemblance to actual persons, living or dead, events or places is entirely coincidental.

Copyright © 2012 Jay Allan Books

ISBN: 978-0615737508

The problems of victory are more agreeable than those of defeat, but they are no less difficult.

- Winston Churchill

Chapter 1

AS Cromwell
Flagship, Alliance Grand Fleet
Gliese 250 System

There was a battle raging in space. Unimaginably far from Earth, around a massive space station orbiting a gas giant in a binary solar system, squadrons of ships fought each other in a desperate struggle.

In the combat command center of his battle-scarred flagship, Admiral Augustus Garret sat quietly and considered the Western Alliance fleet he commanded. Garret was young for such an assignment, but he was the hero of the Second Battle of Algol and had been in the forefront of a tremendous resurgence in Alliance fortunes after the disastrous defeats of the early war.

Like the rest of the officers busily working around him, Garret wore a tight-fitting pressure suit that allowed him to endure the G-forces he would experience during combat. The suit could also keep him alive if the hull was breached and the control center lost pressurization. That is, of course, if he wore the helmet lying next to his command chair, the one he had carelessly tossed aside.

The command center was cramped, like everything on a spaceship, and it was dominated by a massive screen, currently displaying the locations of the 164 vessels that comprised the fleet. There were 9 large blue ovals, each representing one of the capital ships under Garret's command. They were surrounded by clouds of smaller dots, the support ships and escorts of each battlegroup. On the extreme flank of the fleet was a cluster of small yellow dots, the ships of the allied PRC task group, mostly mid-sized cruisers and squadrons of small attack ships.

The Alliance capital ships were all large and powerful, but the three vessels of the new Yorktown class were something different, each a full two kilometers in length, bristling with weaponry and carrying 4 squadrons of heavy fighter-bombers. This would be the first engagement for these behemoths, and Garret was counting on their firepower to make the difference in the battle now just beginning. He'd considered transferring his flag to one of the new ships, but he'd ridden the Cromwell since the huge victory at Second Algol, and he wasn't going to abandon her now.

Maneuvering a space fleet in battle, with the many variables and tremendous distances involved, was a giant game of anticipating the opponent's moves - a complex exercise in making educated guesses. Augustus Garret was a master of the art, having displayed an uncanny ability to predict his adversaries' intentions.

The system in dispute was Gliese 250, well over 100 light years from Earth, and the battle taking place was large - the biggest ever fought, in fact. Gliese was a vital Caliphate choke point that had been seized in a daring surprise attack when Erik Cain's Marines boarded and captured the giant station. The system had been deep in Caliphate space until an Alliance survey team located a previously undiscovered warp gate, redrawing the strategic map in an instant. The new gate led directly from a major Alliance base to the Gliese system and provided an opportunity to launch a surprise attack on a vital sector the enemy had considered secure.

The capture of Gliese had allowed the Alliance to mount a series of follow-up campaigns against systems on the enemy's frontier, cutting off vital supply sources and dramatically changing the outlook of the war. The Alliance had been losing, but now they seized the initiative and won a series of unanswered victories.

The Caliphate's first attempt to retake the system had been repulsed, and now they and their CAC allies had assembled a massive combined fleet for a second attempt, one which was opposed by every naval unit the Alliance high command could scrape up.

The first group of invaders had come in fast, bursting through the warp gate on a carefully plotted vector that took them directly at their target, the hulking, kilometers long station. Their plan was to gut its defenses with the first task force then fight the defending fleet with a second wave twelve hours behind.

The enemy was coming through the warp gate from Alpha Cephei, which was approximately 80 light minutes from the station. The defenders had good intelligence from the scanners deployed near the gate, which transmitted their data at light speed back to the defending fleet, giving the Admiral a complete report on the enemy first wave seven hours before they entered combat range.

Unfortunately for the attackers, Admiral Garret had anticipated their strategy and positioned his ships for maximum effect. The Western Alliance fleet he commanded was large and powerful, but it was still smaller than the Caliphate-CAC force he faced, and he knew it would take every trick he had to win this fight. Conventional tactics called for meeting the invaders near the warp gate, seeking to hit the enemy before they had time to shake themselves into battle order. But no Alliance ships awaited the enemy as they emerged into Gliese space. Garret had his ships deployed back near the station, waiting. His strategy was to bleed the enemy as much as possible with his fixed defenses and then, with the odds hopefully more even, get right in their faces and fight it out to the death.

The minefields were the first thing the invaders discovered. Far thicker than the attackers anticipated, they were positioned perfectly along the path of the assaulting force. They savaged the incoming ships, which were moving at nearly 0.15c and could not apply enough thrust to evade the ECM-masked fields when they were finally detected.

The mines did not rely on a ship striking them directly, an occurrence of almost infinite improbability. Instead, they released up to 200 individual warheads, small high-thrust rockets blasted out in all directions and carrying individual payloads of up to 500 megatons, creating a large area effect. Even a near miss with one warhead could cause catastrophic damage to a target vessel. A direct hit would vaporize anything manmade.

The minefields tore apart the enemy first wave, mostly cruisers intended to strike the station as they passed, then decelerate to regroup. The attacking vessels plunged right through the most heavily mined sector, and hundreds of the devices were triggered, causing thousands of high-yield warheads to explode in the path of the enemy ships.

Garret watched the scanning reports closely. Ten, at least, of the enemy ships were destroyed outright, and 20 or more suffered significant damage. The force was depleted and disordered when they finally entered range of the station and launched a ragged salvo of missiles. The enemy fire, degraded by the damage from the minefield, was far less effective than Garret had feared, and his defensive countermeasures had been extremely effective. Launched at very high speeds and clearly targeted for the station, the missiles were on vectors Garret had predicted, which made them easy targets for the linked point defense arrays of his defending forces.

He had taken a chance, positioning his entire fleet nearly motionless, in direct support of the station. The resulting combined defense network was extremely potent against missile fire, but it left his ships out of position to engage enemy vessels directly. If the attackers had sent their capital ships in at moderate velocity, formed up for battle, Garret could have been at a disadvantage. But his instincts had been spot on. Missile after missile was intercepted, and in the end only three got close enough to harm the station - mostly surface damage and radiation penetration in outer compartments.

The station did not sit idly by and endure the enemy's fire; it unleashed a heavy missile broadside against the oncoming ships just before they entered energy weapon range. The missiles were launched on a broad spread, timed to disorder and damage the enemy ships before they entered energy weapon range.

The attacker's vector still took them right toward the station, and they attacked with their close-range laser batteries as they closed. Pulses of highly focused energy ripped into the station, destroying surface systems and slicing through armor plating. Lasers are difficult to defend against, though their short effective range tends to limit their effectiveness.

The defenders did have some countermeasures, however. They fired spreads of torpedoes that exploded and filled the space around the station with clouds of reflective metallic particles. Informally called angel dust, it was designed to diffuse and reflect the incoming lasers, reducing their effectiveness against the target. Highly effective when properly targeted, it was a difficult system to use well; the timing and positioning had to be perfect.

Garret was pleased so far. The station didn't have heavy laser batteries, only smaller anti-missile units, so the enemy's close range fire went unanswered. Still, they had hit the enemy hard with their missile volley and, with the damage done by the mines, the attacking task force was down to 30% effectiveness. Even more importantly, it would take them 5 or 6 days just to decelerate. It would be at least a week before they were again a threat. He had the station fire another volley after then as they passed, but it would take those missiles, fired from a stationary platform with no intrinsic velocity, a long time to accelerate and catch the enemy force. It would at least give the enemy something to think about as they decelerated and attempted to re-vector back toward the battle zone.

The Western Alliance fleet, positioned for missile defense around the station, was not formed to fire at the enemy task force as it zipped by, but Garret wasn't concerned. He wanted to preserve his supply of missiles anyway; the enemy battleline would be coming.

With the initial attack on the station repulsed, the admiral quickly shifted his attention to the inevitable second assault. He barked out commands, ordering his group leaders to get their ships moving. The enemy's next wave, briefed by spy drones accompanying the first group, would know his deployments, and he was a sitting duck if he remained where he was. His ships were at a dead stop and tied into the station's defensive network - positioned to intercept missiles, not engage enemy capital ships. Now he needed to build some velocity, and he needed to do it quickly.

Fusion reactors ran at full capacity and beyond, as his battleships and support vessels applied maximum thrust. The crews, wearing protective pressure suits like Garret's own, were strapped into their acceleration couches as their ships' AIs executed full thrust burns, straining to get the fleet into combat formation as quickly as possible. Within moments, the slowest ships in the fleet were accelerating at 12g, and the newer vessels at 16-18, the maximum their drug and technology-assisted human crews could endure for any sustained period.

Attack boats and escort vessels clustered around the capital ships, taking up their support positions. When they were patrolling the frontier or scouting deep space the smaller ships had many uses, but in a major battle they had one duty – support the capital ships.

The vessels of the fleet were executing controlled burns to build velocity, cutting thrust at precise intervals so the crews could physically recover from massive g forces and analyze incoming data. While enduring the pressures exerted by maximum acceleration, even experienced crews could do little but lie motionless on their couches.

"Admiral...energy spike at the Alpha Cephei warp gate. Inbound transit imminent." Lieutenant Simon was young to be communications officer to a full admiral, but she was a rock. The biggest fleet ever assembled was probably going to come streaming through that gate in a few seconds, but her voice was calm, steady.

"Acknowledged." Here they come, Garret thought, then... no, that data's more than an hour old. They are already here. He looked at the plot of the fleet on the main screen and sighed quietly. A lot of his men and women were going to die over the next couple days. "Nelson, engage."

"Engaged, admiral." The voice was emotionless, tinny. The naval AIs didn't have the vaguely creepy soothing voices the Marine versions did, though the tradition of naming the things was shared. Garret's choice was painfully unoriginal. There were dozens of Nelsons, as well as Halseys, Porters, and other wet navy greats among the quasi-sentient artificial intelligence units in the service. "Enemy units now entering system, inbound at

.06c and decelerating."

Garret leaned back in his command chair. His units were currently accelerating at 6g, which was uncomfortable but bearable as long as he remained seated. "I want breakdowns as soon as they are available, Nelson. Raw ship totals and battlegroup formations."

"Yes, Admiral." The naval AIs also lacked the more creative personalities of their Marine counterparts. The navy thought that smartass computers were beneath their dignity.

Garret watched as the plotting screen split into two sections, one showing his own fleet at reduced size and the other the enemy ships emerging into the system, the data transmitted by hundreds of small scanners deployed around the gate. Ship after ship came through, and they kept coming long after they outnumbered the waiting defenders.

"Nelson, project ETA to initial engagement range."

Garret had his AI piped into his headset. "Assuming you elect to continue on our present acceleration plan and the enemy forces decelerate at a constant rate, initial engagement is projected in 30 to 33 hours. I shall maintain an updated estimate based on noted changes in deployments."

More than a day, Garret thought. His own estimate had been pretty close to the computer-generated one, though of course those numbers could change if he or the enemy commander modified their maneuvering.

Naval battles are, in many ways, endurance contests. The vast distance involved creates considerable lag times between points of engagement. When the fleets enter each other's ranges there is an exchange of fire. Ships are battered by nuclear explosions and sliced apart by close-range lasers. Crews die, victims of explosions, radiation, decompression.

Then, unless the fleets are on parallel courses, the surviving ships pass their adversaries and move out of effective range until they can exert enough thrust to re-vector back toward the enemy or attempt to disengage and escape to a friendly warp gate. Hours, even days, can pass between instances of engagement.

Garret's plan was unconventional and therefore unexpected. His ships accelerated at full blast 60% of the way to the projected meeting point, then the capital ships launched their bombers and the fleet itself braked hard, decelerating rapidly while the strike wings blasted toward the enemy. The bomber squadrons accelerated at full thrust, adding to the intrinsic velocity imparted by their launch platforms. Garret wanted his bombers going in hard and fast, so he launched them before he slowed the battleships carrying them. This meant his strike would go in well before his missile volleys, which was counter to the "book." But then, most of what Augustus Garret did was unconventional.

"Admiral, your bio-readings indicate considerable fatigue and low blood sugar. It has been seven hours since you have eaten. I have a stimulant prepared, but I would recommend postponing injection until enemy contact is more imminent." Garret's AI monitored him constantly, working to keep him informed and functioning at peak efficiency for as long as he needed to be. Sometimes that made it a nag, but it was usually right as well.

The admiral didn't answer, but he grabbed a nutrition bar from the small compartment in the command chair and nibbled at it. The high-calorie, supplement-rich bars were designed for crews to eat during sustained combat conditions. He made a face as he took his first bite. *God, I hate these things*, he thought. *Better than what the Marines get, at least.* Ground assault units took meals intravenously for 36 hours prior to a drop. Vomiting in your armor during a rough landing would not enhance your combat efficiency.

The ships were at battlestations, but the crews alternated slumber periods during the approach phase. It's not easy to rest being crushed to death in an acceleration couch with battle imminent, but they did the best they could; if you're tired enough you can sleep anywhere. When they entered the battle zone, the whole crew would be pumped up on stimulants anyway.

The Alliance fleet had nine battlegroups, every one of them built around a single capital ship. Each of Garret's battleships was supported by its own flotilla of supporting craft. There were two, or occasionally three, cruisers in each group, heavily armed and reasonably durable, but lacking the truly heavy weapons and fighter-bomber squadrons carried by the battlewagons.

A destroyer flotilla was also attached, along with one or two squadrons of fast attack ships (FAS). The destroyers were there mostly to defend the capital ship against enemy bombers and attack craft, though they also carried missiles to attack heavier targets. The attack ships were fast and heavily armed, designed to go after the enemy battleships and cruisers. Sardonically called "suicide boats" by their crews, they were heavily armed and fast, but light on defense.

Each Alliance battlegroup also had a single point defense ship, an innovation that had been pushed heavily by Garret earlier in the war. Mostly modifications of older cruiser hulls, these vessels had no heavy weaponry at all, only anti-missile rockets, laser batteries, and angel dust launchers. Pure defensive platforms, they gave Garret's groups a battleship's worth of added point defense capacity.

Garret had his crews brought to full readiness 30 minutes before optimum launch range. Keeping crews sharp and effective during a days-long combat situation was one of the more difficult aspects of fleet command. Garret had a good feel for handling his people, and they were fanatically loyal to their hero-admiral.

The bombers would be hitting the enemy fleet just before the incoming vessels entered missile range. The bombers were likely to take heavy losses since the defenders were not simultaneously fending off missiles and could focus solely on the strike force. But the bomber wings would also inflict their damage before the enemy could launch at the main Alliance fleet.

It was a gamble, one Garret hoped would pay off. Ships went into battle with external racks of missiles to supplement the magazines they carried internally. It was a cheap and easy way to increase firepower, but ships still carrying their racks were at a heavy disadvantage in combat. The missiles were expected to launch before the ships were within range of enemy attack, but Garret's early bomber strike was forcing the issue. If their attack compelled the target ships to jettison the racks, it would cut the enemy firepower significantly - above and beyond any damage inflicted.

"Strike force Alpha, commencing attack run." The com in Garret's earpiece fed him the incoming transmissions from the bomber groups.

"Strike force Beta, commencing attack run." The second group commander echoed the first, followed by the leaders of the Gamma and Delta wings. Four waves of fighter-bombers, 144 ships and 576 men and women running a gauntlet into the maw of the largest space fleet ever assembled.

Into the Valley of Death, thought Garret, recalling an ancient poem about six hundred doomed warriors in a different, yet somehow disturbingly similar situation.

Garret's planning was sound. If his stratagem worked it could save thousands of crew on the ships of the fleet. Missiles jettisoned or destroyed in their launchers couldn't be used to blow his ships apart. But it was a brutal type of calculus that he could perform but never quite stomach. He had known he was sending most of those bomber crews to their deaths, but he did it anyway. They had known too, yet they went unquestioningly. They knew what was at stake.

The bombers were equipped with heavy ECM suites and, not expecting an attack at this range, the enemy was totally unprepared. Garret listened to the reports coming in, knowing they were twelve minutes old when he heard them and wondering if the speakers he was listening to were already dead.

The enemy commander hurriedly ordered his ships to jettison their external missiles and bring their point defense arrays online. Garret's first objective had been attained before his bombers fired a shot. Now they plunged in and, as they had been ordered, ignored all the escorts of the enemy fleet, driving straight to the capital ships. They had one goal, and they targeted all of their ordnance at the launching facilities of the enemy battleships. The Alliance bombers were armed with close-range plasma torpedoes, small sprint missiles that triggered a controlled nuclear reaction just before impact and struck the target as a ball of superheated ionized gas. One of the Alliance's newest weapons, the torpedoes were difficult to target effectively, but extremely powerful. Garret's crews had been practicing for weeks.

"We got in fast, missile fire is light." That was Alpha commander's report, soon reinforced by the others. The enemy had been slow to get anti-fighter missiles launched. Garret's surprise launch had given the bombers a chance to get close enough to make their attack.

The good news didn't last. The bombers were heading straight at the enemy capital ships, and the defensive laser fire from the escort vessels they were ignoring started to take a heavy toll. The bombers were on predictable trajectories, moving at high velocity straight through the enemy fleet. Almost half of them were gone by the time they reached their designated launch points. They fired their torpedoes and then, strapped in their couches, they blasted off at maximum acceleration, trying to outrun the missile volleys sent after them. They had done their job for Garret; now they were working for themselves.

By the time they had cleared the enemy fleet, just under a third of them were left, and they began the slow process of decelerating and vectoring back to the designated rendezvous point. They'd zipped past their targets too quickly to allow for effective damage assessment, so neither the exhausted survivors nor their admiral yet knew that their devastating strike had ravaged the enemy launch bays. Fewer than half of the ships were going to get their own bombers launched and, combined with the loss of external missiles, the enemy's firepower had been degraded as much as 50%. But the cost had been high.

"Entering optimum missile launch range, Admiral." Lieutenant Simon's voice brought Garret out of his guilt-ridden trance.

He put his arm on the edge of the command chair. "Give me a boost, Nelson." He felt the small pinprick as the AI directed the injection of the stimulant cocktail designed to maximize mental clarity and effectiveness. Almost immediately, Garret could feel the drug pushing away the fatigue and the crushing headache. By the time the battle was over he was likely to be a strung-out wreck, but none of that mattered now.

He ordered all ships to flush their external racks in a first volley, and then fired virtually every remaining missile in the fleet in a series of waves, another violation of SOP as outlined in the "book." Only his destroyers kept their small arsenals; every other missile in the fleet was now heading toward the enemy.

His battleships launched 72-96 missiles each, with the gargantuan Yorktowns firing 144. All told, the battleships and cruisers had fired a volley of over 1,000 missiles, each with multiple warheads. His ships were decelerating, and they were moving at a considerably lower rate than the approaching enemy fleet. The lower intrinsic velocity imparted to their missiles meant the incoming volley would hit them before their own salvoes struck, a difference of no particular consequence beyond the possibility that Garret wouldn't still be alive to find out how much damage his attack inflicted.

"Nelson, course change. All ships are to conduct full burns. Thrust plan Vega. Execute in 30 seconds." Garret could have given the order to Lieutenant Simon, but as excellent an officer as she was, the AI would get the orders transmitted to over 160 ships a lot faster than any human could. Garret was conducting evasive maneuvers, trying to position his fleet away from the incoming missile strike. The thrust plan was random, something he'd made up himself, designed to scatter his ships, making them a tougher target. The enemy's weapons were coming in at a fairly high velocity, and they would have a harder time changing course than his slow-moving vessels.

"Incoming missiles. Detonations projected in eight minutes." Lieutenant Simon was still solid, but with a billion megatons of nuclear warheads heading at them, Garret could excuse the slight waver in her voice.

"Full impact procedures, all ships."

"Yes sir." Simon relayed his order on the fleet command circuit.

"Impact procedures require all personnel to be wearing helmets, Admiral." Nelson's voice was as unemotional as ever, but Garret was still annoyed as he reached down and grabbed his helmet. He knew it was irrational, but he hated being nagged, particularly by a machine.

The enemy missiles were blasting hard at 50g, straining to maximize the targeting on his evading fleet. His ships were thrusting full too, but manned vessels couldn't compete with missiles unburdened by the need to prevent human crews from turning into strawberry jam.

"Engage point defense procedures, Plan Delta." Garret gave that order to Nelson, who would implement it immediately. Firing the point defense systems was a computer's game, requiring precise tracking and microsecond targeting. Men and women mostly watched, and waited to see if their computers saved their lives.

Throughout the fleet, cluster-warhead interception rockets launched and short-ranged lasers fired, targeting the missiles whose vectors were judged to be the most threatening. The escorts were positioned around the capital ships, linking their fire with the defensive arrays of their big brothers. Defensive fire was preferenced to protect the big ships. The escort crews knew the deal; they were the shields.

Hundreds of missiles were intercepted, but there were just too many to get them all. In the end, Garret's evasive maneuvers were reasonably effective. The AIs controlling the enemy missiles attempted to inflict maximum damage, splitting the multiple warhead vehicles at the optimum times and triggering detonations as each came as close to a target as its plot indicated it would.

The space around Garret's ships was engulfed in thermonuclear fury as hundreds of miniature suns flared briefly into existence. Seven of the Alliance ships, mostly smaller destroyers and attack ships, were close enough to exploding warheads to be destroyed outright. One of the big cruisers was less than 300 meters from a heavy thermonuclear detonation; the ship just disappeared.

About 20 other vessels took heavy damage from the heat and shockwaves. A few of them were crippled and rendered almost entirely combat ineffective; others had varying levels of damage. Inside the battered hulls, men and women struggled and died. Pressure doors closed, isolating breached sections of the hulls. Nuclear reactors shut down before magnetic bottles failed. Electrical systems overloaded, causing systemic failures throughout entire vessels. Wounded crew filled the sickbays, and ship's surgeons worked frantically to save those who could be saved.

"Damage control report." Garret snapped the order to Lieutenant Simon, who was compiling reports from various ships in the fleet. Garret wasn't asking about Cromwell; Flag Captain Charles would handle that in his own command center. Garret wanted a summary on the whole fleet, and he wanted it immediately.

"Seven ships destroyed, sir. Cruiser Miami; destroyers Sunhawk, Stingray, and Scorpion; attack ships Terrance, Seward, and Clive." She winced a little - her friend, Violet had been assigned to Miami - but didn't hesitate in giving her report. "Data still coming in, sir. It looks like most of the battleline came through it fairly well...except for the Leyte." Short pause. "She is reporting systemic damage. Her weapons are offline and she's running on batteries. They are attempting to get the secondary reactor restarted."

Simon worked her way through the reports as they came in, relaying the information to Garret. By the time they'd organized everything it was clear things had gone fairly well, better than he'd had any right to expect. Only two of the capital ships sustained major damage, and the Leyte was the only one that was combat ineffective. So far they'd gotten off light.

Garret was pleased, but also somber. Every ship destroyed and crewmember killed still hurt. He'd lost count of how many brave men and women had died in his many victories, but at night they visited him, the ghostly cost of his unwanted glory.

Simon's voice interrupted his introspection. "Enemy bombers incoming. Seven minutes out."

Garret smiled. Standard tactics. Right out of the book. "Plan Omega. Execute."

"Launching interceptors now." Garret had held back six

squadrons of fighter bombers and configured them for interception. Now, the launch catapults on six battleships spat
their charges into space with the maximum velocity they could
impart. Launched on a direct intercept course with the attacking
bombers, they strafed the incoming craft with their "shotguns,"
magnetic-powered railguns firing blasts of high-velocity projec-
tiles designed to tear apart the tiny, unarmored bombers.

They only got one pass - by the time they could decelerate
and turn about the attackers would be finished with their bombing run. But they took out half the incoming craft, leaving just
37 to attack, and the combined point defense of the fleet took
most of them out. The entire enemy bombing run scored only
one major hit, though, as luck would have it, that was against the
unfortunate Leyte.

"The Leyte's offline, Admiral. Captain Harris is dead. She's
bleeding atmosphere. Secondary explosions onboard." Simon
was reading the incoming reports directly to the admiral.

Garret winced, grateful for the helmet that hid his face.
He'd known Tom Harris for fifteen years. Like that, he was
gone. The Leyte will be lucky to get through this, he thought.
Rachel Aaron is the ship's exec...at least they're in good hands.
"I want running status reports on the Leyte. If Commander
Aaron doesn't think she can save the ship, order her to imple-
ment Code Y procedures." Code Y was Alliance protocol for
abandoning a hopeless ship.

"Acknowledged."

Garret leaned back in the command chair and sighed softly.
"Nelson, updated projection on energy weapons range."

"At present vectors and rate of deceleration, the two fleets
will be in energy weapons range in 6.5 hours."

"Lieutenant Simon, all personnel not directly involved in
damage control activities are to take two hour rest periods in
one-third intervals. All crew are to be at the ready in 6 hours."

"Acknowledged." Simon relayed the admiral's order through
the fleetcom circuit. "Sir, I can monitor the boards if you want
to get some rest."

"Negative, lieutenant."   He paused briefly, realizing he'd

been a bit abrupt with her. "Though thank you. Please send the damage control reports to my screen. Capital ships first."

"Yes, sir. Reports coming through now." After a brief pause: "Admiral, Commander Aaron reports she believes she can save the Leyte."

"Thank you, lieutenant." Garret sat and reviewed the various reports, occasionally issuing an order, but mostly just monitoring the situation. Damage control was generally within the realm of the individual ship captains. His responsibility was pretty much limited to how to utilize a ship based on its condition.

The fleet had been decelerating, but the Leyte and some of the other heavily damaged ships had lost significant thrust capability. That left Garret two choices - reduce the deceleration rate to keep the fleet together or maintain the thrust levels, allowing the damaged ships to move out of the formation. Since they were decelerating as they approached the enemy, this would be a death sentence for the damaged ships, which would remain at higher velocities and enter weapons range ahead of the fleet. They'd be easy targets, and the enemy would pick them off one by one.

"Synchronize deceleration rate. Maximum thrust that allows the fleet to maintain formation." You're being weak, he thought. Jeopardizing the battle plan to save a few crews. He let the order stand, though.

Commander Jonelle was Garret's fleet operations officer. "Implementing now, admiral." A few seconds later. "Adjusted thrust deceleration level in ten seconds."

Garret lurched back into his chair as the ship reduced its thrust from 4.5g to 1.75g. The reduced deceleration made the crew substantially more comfortable, but it played havoc with his battle plan. "Nelson, prepare a thrust plot for maximum deceleration to implement once the enemy has passed out of energy weapon range."

Garret reviewed the damage reports and checked and rechecked his calculations. "Admiral, energy weapon range in 30 minutes." He had ordered the AI to warn him at the 30 minute mark.

"Begin charging procedure for all weapons systems. All crew are to take a stimulant injection 10 minutes before range." He paused. "Give me mine now, Nelson." He put his arm on the chair edge, wincing slightly as the needle pricked him then inhaling deeply as the fatigue drained away.

His plan was simple. First, a heavy weapons exchange as the two fleets passed each other, inflicting the maximum possible damage to the enemy battleships already damaged by the bombing run. The enemy fleet would continue decelerating as they approached the station, but they expected their first wave to have gutted it. Instead, they would run into a full missile broadside, followed by Garret's returning fleet, ready for another close-range knife fight with energy weapons. It would be a battle of annihilation.

His orders were simple. Hold the system at all costs. Garret stared grimly at the viewscreen. He intended to do just that. Gliese would remain his...or the Alliance navy would die right here.

Chapter 2

I Corps Assembly Area
Columbia - Eta Cassiopeiae II

"Good afternoon, Colonel Cain. I am Captain Peter Warren, your new political officer." The visitor was tall and thin, but
there was something unsettling about him. Cain decided it was
his eyes. They were small and beady, and oddly far apart from
each other. His uniform was spotless and neatly-pressed, but it
was a design Cain had never seen.

Erik wore gray fatigues, and they were anything but spotless
or neatly-pressed. He was young to be wearing colonel's eagles,
and he looked even more youthful than his 35 years. Almost two
meters tall, with close-cropped brown hair and blue eyes, Cain
looked busy, too busy to be concerned with perfect uniforms or
to waste time with officious-looking types sent out from Earth.

"What kind of horseshit joke is this? I don't know what the
hell a political officer is, but I know I don't need one." Cain's
voice was derisive, and it was clear from his body language he
considered the newcomer dismissed. He turned and opened his
mouth to talk to his orderly, but Warren spoke before he got any
words out.

"I'm afraid, Colonel, that you do need a political officer.
New directive from central command. All unit commanders
from battalion level up have been assigned liaison staff. Alliance
Gov has issued a series of new directives designed to improve
conditions and efficiency for our troops. My job is to assist you
with implementation."

Cain turned and looked at Warren with eyes of icy death.
"Captain, I'm going to say this one more time. I do not need
any help seeing to the needs of my men, certainly not from
some bureaucrat they shove into a uniform and send out here to
harass me. You can tell Alliance Gov to sti..."

"Erik! The general wants to see you. Now." Major Darius
Jax ran up behind Cain. Jax was at least ten centimeters taller

than Erik, and his dark skin contrasted sharply with Cain's pale tone. Jax was being technically insubordinate in not addressing his superior as "colonel," but he thought it was more important to intervene quickly. Besides, the two had fought together for years and were close friends.

Cain spun around on his heels and followed Jax without even a word to the stunned officer who stood where he was, staring in disbelief. It was just as well, because if he'd gotten any more words out of Cain, they probably wouldn't have been to his liking. Erik Cain had grown up a gang member in a hellish slum after his family had run afoul of government regulations and been cast out of Manhattan and subsequently murdered. He despised everything to do with the authorities back on Earth, and he was not likely to be patient with a glorified government snitch in a uniform.

"What the hell was that all about?" Erik didn't think it was just coincidence that Jax had been looking for him at this particular moment. Before Jax could answer, Cain turned and shouted back to his orderly, who had been standing next to him when the newcomer appeared. "Anne, tell Major Cantor I'll be with him as soon as I can."

"A new directive from Earth." Jax's voice wasn't quite as corrosive as Cain's, but it was clear he didn't like it much either. "Mine looks like some sort of jacked up cop. Thinks he's hard. Probably piss his armor the first time somebody shoots in his direction." He had a sour look on his face. "We didn't get any warning about this. Not even the general. The first thing he did was send me to find you." He snorted a short laugh. "Guess he figured you were the one to most likely to do something...ah... unfortunate."

Cain laughed, but only for a second. There was nothing funny about this to him. He'd come from Earth's gutter and found a new home for himself in the Corps and on the frontier, and he wasn't about to sit idly by and watch it turn into a copy of that clusterfuck he'd left. "Would it be so unfortunate if there was one less - what the hell did he call himself - political officer running around here?"

Jax laughed. "You see, that's the thing. Everybody would think you were kidding. Except me. And the general. He figured you might just be tempted to use the guy for a live fire exercise."

"We've got a lot of new recruits. They could use the practice. You know what they say...two birds, one stone."

They walked up to a large modular building with two guards flanking the only door. The sentries snapped to attention when the two officers approached. Jax looked up at the facial recognition scanner. "Open."

"Access granted, Major Jax." The security AI's voice was male, not exactly hostile, but definitely businesslike. The plasti-steel door slid open, and Jax and Cain walked into a large room with at least ten workstations, all occupied. There was a large main screen, which currently displayed some sort of numerical statistics on one side and a map of a solar system on the other.

"Major, Colonel. The general is waiting. Please follow me." The general's orderly was an earnest young lieutenant, very low in rank to be an aide to a full general. Lieutenant Raynor had the job because his father had been Holm's friend who had been killed during the disastrous Operation Achilles. The general had been mentoring the son's career ever since.

A second generation Marine was originally a rarity, but it was becoming more common. The Corps did most of its recruiting in the slums of Earth, offering a home to a certain breed of promising misfit. But as more Marines retired and settled on the frontier worlds, the Corps started seeing sons and daughters who wanted to follow in parental footsteps and serve. This was starting to create a subtle shift in loyalties. The oddballs normally inducted into the ranks had no love for Earth, or usually for anything else, and their loyalty tended to focus on the Corps itself. But with second, and even third, generation recruits joining in increasing numbers, there were more Marines thinking of themselves as the military force of the colony worlds. It was a subtle change, but real nonetheless.

Cain and Jax followed the lieutenant down the familiar corridor to the general's office. "Colonel Cain and Major Jax, sir."

Holm was looking at something on an infopad and, without looking up, he said, "Thank you, lieutenant. Dismissed."

Raynor snapped the general a fine salute, then turned and gave one each to Jax and Cain before marching smartly back into the hallway. Cain laughed after the door closed. "That kid's nothing if not a damn fine saluter."

The general was still staring at the 'pad on his desk, so he didn't notice Cain's cursory attempt at a salute, though he'd seen it plenty of times before. "Better than your sorry efforts, Erik. It's a damned good thing you have a few other skills." He finally looked up and they all shared a laugh.

General Elias Holm was one of the true heroes of the Corps. A veteran of the last war, he'd shown himself to be a military genius in this one. Cain and Jax were two of his protégés; the general had been a mentor to both of them since they'd first served under him as sergeants right here on Columbia when the planet had been attacked by a CAC strikeforce.

"I'm just reviewing these final reports on Sherman before I send them up the chain." He motioned toward a table against the wall. "Get something to drink and have a seat. I'll be done in a minute."

Operation Sherman had been a massive campaign intended to liberate systems that had been occupied by the enemy during the early years of the war, when the Alliance had been beaten back. Originally targeting six objectives, the campaign had been scrubbed after three when the attached naval resources were diverted to Gliese 250. Admiral Garret had been the naval commander for Sherman, but Alliance Intel had picked up a lot of chatter about Gliese, and the high command wanted to reinforce the fleet stationed there. Without Garret's battlegroups, Holm's operation was at a standstill, so his battered but victorious forces returned to their staging area on Columbia.

The three battles they had fought had been nasty. Some of the target worlds had been held for eight or nine years, and the enemy had spent that time fortifying them heavily. Garret's ships blasted as much as they could from orbit without wrecking the worlds, but these were friendly populations, so there was only so much indiscriminate bombing they could do. There were still plenty of strongpoints for the Marines to assault.

The invaders had been hard on the occupied populations, and when the Marines got a glimpse of the atrocities that had been committed, they stopped taking prisoners. When Holm got a look, he stopped trying to make them accept surrenders. Two of the battles had gone nuclear, and after years of occupation and nasty fights to liberate them, the colony worlds were in rough shape. Alliance Gov had promised to expedite relief to the worlds, but it was slow in coming. The Marines left the supplies they could spare - mostly extra rations and medicines - but it wasn't nearly enough.

Cain and Jax grabbed bottles of water and sat in the two large chairs facing Holm's desk. Finally the general looked up from the 'pad and managed a smile for his officers, however forced it might have been. "I have better over there than just water if you boys want something a little stronger." Holm was a bit of a drinker, though Cain had never seen him less than 100% sharp.

Cain and Jax both shook their heads. Erik rarely drank, and as far as he'd seen, Jax never did. Besides, Holm had a water sitting on his own desk too, and neither of them would have taken anything if the general didn't.

Holm looked over at Cain. "So I take it that Jax got to you before your new friend? I don't have any reports of a shooting in the quad, so I consider that a good sign."

Erik took a drink from his water. "No, the fool had just introduced himself when Jax came over and interrupted us."

Jax snorted. "Interrupted you from telling him to stick it, I believe." He grinned in Erik's direction. "Where did you intend to tell him to stick it, exactly? Knowing you, there are a number of possibilities."

Holm broke in before Cain could answer. "Look guys, we really need to discuss how we're going to handle this." Erik opened his mouth to say something, but Holm put up his hand. "I'm serious, Erik. I know how you feel about Alliance Gov, but we're stuck with this for now."

He shoved the 'pad across his desk toward his guests. "That's a dispatch from General Samuels about these political officers. I'll let you read the whole thing, but for now let me summarize. We are to accept these liaison officers without causing any problems until he sends me further instructions. Now Samuels is my boss, and I'm yours, so I guess that's all any of us needs to know." Holm spoke to his officers in a relaxed tone, but no one who knew him thought he invited any debate.

Cain leaned back and sighed. He wasn't going to argue. The general was half hero and half father to him; he'd do anything Holm asked. He just wished it was something easier...like charging an enemy bunker with a kitchen knife. "Sir," Cain finally said, "I understand your orders but, if I may ask, what do you make of this whole thing?"

Holm leaned back in his chair and took a breath. "Honestly, Erik, I'm not sure. We all know how things are run back on Earth. It's easy for us to forget just how little of that we have to put up with out here. I suppose it's possible that Alliance Gov just wants more direct information on the war. This is their fight too, and they bear a lot of the cost."

Cain looked skeptical. "Is that what you really think?"

"I just don't know, Erik." Holm shook his head slowly. "The Corps is a lot bigger than it used to be. What was a frontier defense force is now a pretty big army, not to mention the only Alliance ground force that has combat experience. Maybe they are going to try to change the relationship we've had for the last century. I just don't know."

Erik shifted his weight in the chair. He wanted to say something, but he wasn't sure he should.

Holm could see Cain was troubled. "You can speak your mind here, Erik. You should know that by now."

Cain looked at Jax, then at the general. "Well, sir, I don't suppose I know any more than you, but I just can't escape the feeling that whatever we think it is, the truth is probably far worse." He looked at Jax again and back at Holm. "I know none of us talk about our pasts; that's all washed away when we make that first assault. But I know what I saw growing up, and I know what Sar...what some other people went through as well." Sarah Linden was Cain's lover, and she'd told Erik about her suffering at the hands of a government official who'd had her kidnapped when she was a teenager.

Erik was trying to stay calm, but his face was contorted with anger as he spoke. "I remember what I saw when I got sent back there to give speeches and pander to our political masters. That whole system is rotten, sir. Rotten to the core." He stopped, thinking maybe he had said too much.

Holm stood up and walked around his desk, sitting down on the front edge. He leaned forward and put his hand on Cain's shoulder. "Erik, you know you're like the son I never had. There's nothing you can't say to me. But I want you to be careful too. Like it or not, we're being watched a lot more closely than we were. Whatever the politicians are up to, we've still got to win this war, and I don't want my key people distracted. I don't know why General Samuels is going along with this, but he may know things I don't. For now, I'm asking you - not ordering you - not to pick a fight with your political officer. Don't let him interfere with combat efficiency, but otherwise humor him a little. It's probably the best way to keep him out of the loop. Make him suspicious of you, and he'll probably just start snooping around more and causing problems." Holm looked over at Jax. "That goes for you too, Darius."

Erik nodded to the general. "Yes sir. You're right, of course." He looked down and rubbed his hands together.

"What is it, Erik? There's something else bothering you."

"Well, sir..." Cain looked up and locked eyes with the general. "I'm just thinking about the colonies. I mean, you don't think it's just us they're going to pull this with, do you? The colonies have grown too. How much wealth do they produce now? How important have they become to the Alliance economy?"

"You're worried they're going to crack down on the colonial governments?" Holm got up and took his water bottle in his hand.

Erik paused for a second before he answered. "I'm worried they're going to try. And if they do, those people aren't going to put up with it. What are we going to do when they order us to start shooting colonists?"

"You really think things are going to go that far, Erik?" Jax had been content to listen up to now. He was more optimistic by nature than Cain, and he hadn't considered things to the extent Erik had."

Erik almost held his tongue, but he figured if he couldn't speak in front of these two, he couldn't speak in front of anyone. "Yes. I do."

General Holm sat back down behind his desk, and rubbed his face with his hand. "Well, let's hope it doesn't come to that. At least we don't have to worry about it right now. We've still got a war to fight. So let's focus on that right now, and we'll deal with the rest as we go. Whatever Alliance Gov is planning, they aren't going to do it until the war is over."

Cain and Jax both nodded their assent. "Good. So let's talk a little about what comes next. We had to call off the second half of Sherman because we lost our naval support. But we'll eventually get back on track. They can't keep most of the navy at Gliese forever; either they'll be a fight or there won't, but sooner or later they'll send us a couple battlegroups and we'll be able to finish the job."

Cain was relieved to be thinking about something other than the Alliance government. "I suggest we take the time to integrate the replacements we've received into our formations." They had lost about 10,000 troops in the three battles they'd fought, but they'd gotten fresh recruits to bring them back to establishment strength in all units. "We're probably looking at several months at least - just in transit time to and from Gliese - so I'd recommend some war games. Maybe even a couple practice assaults if you can get us the landers and supplies to burn."

Holm smiled broadly. "You're going to have my job someday, Erik. That's exactly what I was thinking." He reached into his desk and pulled out a small box. "First, I need to do some shuffling around of the command staff. You both know General Isaacson was wounded when his lander crashed on Wellington. Sarah's crew managed to keep him alive, but he's got an odd genetic marker, and they've had a hard time regenerating. He's looking at some heavy gene replacement therapy and then multiple regens. Two, maybe three years in hospital."

Cain and Jax both winced. Isaacson had been their division commander and a good officer, popular throughout the ranks.

"So," Holm continued, "I've got to replace him. I don't want to look outside the I Corps for senior officers if I can help it. So, I'm bumping Gilson to command 1st Division. Erik, I want you to take over 1st Brigade, effective immediately." He smiled at Cain's stunned look. "There's no one I trust more."

He looked over at Jax. "Darius, you'll take over the regiment." He tossed him the box he was holding. "Here are your eagles. Congratulations, Colonel Jax. You earned them."

Erik turned to face Jax and put his hand out. "There's no one who deserves it more, Jax," he said as they shook hands.

Holm stood up and walked around the desk again, putting his hand out to Jax as well. He glanced over at Cain. "I'll get you your star too, Erik. But I can't approve a promotion to general rank without an OK from General Samuels. I sent the request this morning." He gave Cain a quick grin. "Another reason I don't want you picking fights with that political officer right now."

After shaking hands with both of them and exchanging congratulatory salutes, he continued. "I want to bump up one of Jax's captains to major and give him the battalion. I'll expect a recommendation from the two of you by 1800 tonight. Try to agree and just give me one pick. I'll approve whatever you guys send up."

"Yessir." Cain and Jax spoke almost in unison.

Holm looked down and poked at his 'pad for a few seconds. "I'm sending you both some operational notes. I want 1st Brigade to plan and execute an assault on Columbia. You'll be taking on 2nd Brigade, which will be defending. We'll do a simulated bombardment, and then you'll hit the ground, Erik. Review the notes, and we'll discuss again tomorrow, say 1300 hours." He glanced back down at his desk. "Dismissed."

The newly promoted officers stood up and snapped salutes

to the general, Jax's sharp and crisp, Erik's a little ragged. They turned and walked toward the door.

"Oh, and gentlemen?"

They turned to face the general. "You have both seen a force assault Columbia. See if you can do better than they did, ok?"

Chapter 3

Western Alliance Intelligence Directorate HQ
Wash-Balt Metroplex, Earth

The conference room was large and extremely plush; the polished walnut table alone cost enough to feed a hundred starving Cogs for a year. The soft leather chairs surrounding it were no less expensive, and in these comfortable seats there were a number of well-dressed men and women. To the side of the table was a large credenza covered with platters of food. This was a lunch meeting, and the group assembled here quietly picked at their plates and fiddled with their 'pads while the waiters finished serving everyone. Finally, the last of the staff departed wordlessly, and the heavy glass doors slid shut, the clear panes turning opaque as they closed.

The room had an old look to it, with its real raised panel wainscoting and antique oil paintings on the walls. The paneling alone was noteworthy - wood of any kind was an expensive commodity, and walnut of this quality was almost priceless. There were few forests remaining in 23rd century America, and almost none with the old-growth trees needed for this type of craftsmanship. The illusion of some ancient manor home's drawing room ended abruptly, however, at the single wall of floor-to-ceiling windows, which offered a kilometer-high panoramic view of the southern Washbalt skyline.

"We have a number of items to discuss, and time is short. I have to brief our British friends on the status of our operations; my transport leaves in three hours, so let's not waste any time." The speaker was a tall man, perhaps sixty years of age, his black hair sprinkled lightly with gray. His name was Gavin Stark, but only a few people in the room knew that. To most of them he was simply Number One, the head of Western Alliance intelligence and one of the most feared men on the planet. "Let's start with the Epsilon Eridani initiative. How does the excavation proceed?"

A woman seated at the opposite end of the table responded. She was tall and trim, perhaps a few years younger than Stark, though there was more gray in her hair. "Operations are almost back on schedule. As you are all aware, thirteen years ago, just before the war, CAC intelligence discovered what we found on EE-4. They launched a surprise attack and took control of the planet. We were able to divert a detachment from 1st Marine division to retake the world before they could dig in or reinforce. Or, of course, get any heavy intel from the excavation site. The battle was small - neither side was heavily mobilized at the time. In the aftermath we were able to substantially upgrade the system's defenses, and a naval battlegroup has been posted there since."

Stark put up his hand, an impatient look on his face. "Yes, Number Ten, we can bypass the history lesson. Let's focus on the implementation of the Directorate's most recent operational plan."

Mildly chastised, the woman cleared her throat softly and continued. "Yes, Number One. At our last Directorate meeting it was decided that, with the discovery of several additional excavation sites, the colonial population had become an unacceptable security threat to the overall operation. Removal has been completed in accordance with that finding."

"Has there been any blowback from the implementation?" Andres Carillon was designated as Number Three in the Directorate. He was tall, well over two meters, with white blond hair and pale skin. To look at Number One, he could have been an accountant or a college professor; Carillon, on the other hand, was everyone's image of an evil spymaster.

"No, sir." Number Ten paused to clear her throat. Carillon made her nervous. He made everyone nervous. "As per plan, we utilized our new variant of the G-11 virus family, which has a considerably higher mortality rate than the original. Unlike the versions used during the Unification Wars, this new strain carries a specific genetic marker rendering it impotent against anyone who has received the companion vaccination. Of course, only our personnel were given the injections."

Carillon's usual grim expression gave way to a slight smile, which was somehow even more unnerving. "Was the virus 100% effective?"

"Actual mortality among the population was in excess of 94%. The rest have been liquidated through conventional methods, though we have officially attributed all deaths to the virus. We have also utilized the plan to remove the Marine garrison. Their mortality rate was lower, approximately 50%, mostly because the commander responded quickly and put biohazard procedures in effect almost immediately. Nevertheless, the outbreak gave us the perfect cover to have the Marines ordered offworld. Carson's World is now occupied by two battalions of our new Directorate troops. A planetary quarantine is in effect. The orbital defenses remain manned by naval personnel, and there is a reinforced battlegroup permanently assigned to system defense." She glanced down at her 'pad for an instant. "Currently, the AS Sheridan and her group are on station, reinforced by the 3rd Cruiser Squadron."

Carillon looked like he was about to say something further, but Stark spoke first. "Security seems well in hand." He turned slightly. "Number Six, what is the status of the actual excavation?"

"Progress has been slow. As you all know, this is a very sensitive project from a technical perspective." Number Six was a woman, younger than Number Ten. Indeed, she was the youngest person present. Tall, with long blond hair and blue eyes, Alex Linden had risen faster than any agent in the Directorate's history. It didn't hurt her rise that she was drop-dead gorgeous and willing to use it; before she had been appointed to the Directorate she had been the lover of two of the men and one of the women in the room. But she was brilliant too, and cold-blooded. As well as the affections of a roster of highly-placed officials, she also possessed many of their secrets. Alex was a big believer in using both the carrot and the stick to get what she wanted.

"We all know the difficulties involved, Number Six." Stark was amused at how differently he reacted to her than anyone else in the room. It was involuntary, and he found it interesting how difficult it was to suppress. Not that he would ever allow that to interfere with his decisions. But he realized he wasn't *entirely* immune to her charms. "I think what we need is a reliable estimate on when the shipment will be ready. We are going to need the maximum possible security on that. A full battle-group, at least."

Alex's smile was brief, barely perceptible, though Stark saw it as she had intended. "Number One, I am confident that the first shipment of items will be ready for transit within six months. With your permission, I will go to Epsilon Eridani IV myself to supervise the final security measures."

"Yes, that is a good idea. You may leave as soon as you are ready." He paused for a few seconds. "Be careful out there." He doubted he would have added that if he were speaking to any of the others. Honestly, he wouldn't really have cared if most of the others made it back. But he'd miss Alex. He'd probably have to get rid of her one day, he thought, but for now he enjoyed having her around. "Number Ten, please clear Number Six through your onsite security and arrange a suitable cover that affords her any access she requires."

"Yes, Number One. Consider it done." She kept her voice even and professional, for which she was pleased with herself. Number Ten hated Alex Linden. Bitch was the nicest thing she called her in private.

"Very well. Let's move on. Number Four, what is the current status of our Marine Corps initiatives?"

Number Four was the only member of the Committee not present, represented instead by a hologram of a professional, middle-aged man in a stylish suit, which was likely not at all what the individual in question really looked like. Stark was the only one in the room who knew the identity of Number Four, and he intended to keep it that way for now. Not even pretty little Alex had been able to charm it out of him, though she'd tried with commendable enthusiasm.

"The plan is underway, but progress is slow." Number Four's voice sounded normal - too normal. A regular crowd wouldn't notice the perfection of the tones, but this was a room full of spooks, and they all could tell it was a fake. But it wasn't in any of their interests to push for information Number One didn't want to share. Not in the open, at least. "The political officers have been assigned to units currently in base. It is not practical to interfere with the command structures of deployed forces while they are on campaign."

"What response have the political officers received from the Marine personnel?" Stark had a pretty good idea, but he wanted to hear it anyway.

"There has been considerable resistance." The hologram moved naturally as Number Four spoke, turning to face who-ever had asked the last question. "As you know, the Marines are recruited from among those who least fit in with the normal population. Their training builds on this, and the result has been an extraordinarily effective fighting force. The Corps fills a void in their lives, which creates a very high level of morale and élan. However, loyalty is largely to the Corps itself and not Alliance Gov. In fact, most Marine personnel harbor a level of resent-ment, at least against the system in general if not the govern-ment in particular."

"Yes, yes, we are aware of all of this. It is the primary reason we have initiated this plan." Number One found himself look-ing at the hologram as he spoke. Damn, those things are realis-tic, he thought as he forced himself to turn away. "But what is the status of implementation?"

"Few of the officers have truly accepted the attachment of political overseers. Instances of true insubordination have been rare, but there has been tremendous resistance to integrating the new officers into the command structures. Among the Marines themselves there has been considerable grumbling. To date, we have not implemented any disciplinary measures. In fact, with virtually the entire officer corps of one mind on this matter, it will prove to be extremely difficult to impose any serious penal-ties. At least conventionally."

Stark reminded himself not to look at the hologram. Not for any particular reason other than it made him feel foolish talking to a laser-generated phantom as is it were a human being. "Do we have any reports regarding the impact on the operational efficiency of the units in combat?"

"Negative." The hologram looked back at Stark as it answered his question. "Although some units with assigned political liaison staff have been deployed to campaigns, none of these operations have reached a decisive point as of yet. We do have reports that officers are generally keeping the political officers out of the chains of information and command wherever possible. Whether this is the result of multiple instances of individual resistance or a more orchestrated campaign of noncompliance is not yet evident."

"I'd like to interject something into this debate." The gray-haired man sitting next to Stark had been silent until now.

"Yes, Number Two, what would you like to add?" Stark paid close attention to everything Number Two said. The old man would have been Number One himself, but he felt he was no longer up to the demands of the job, and he'd asked his protégé Stark to leapfrog him and take the Chair.

"First, let me make clear that I am in complete agreement that something must be done about the Marine organization as well as the colonial governments, so what I say now is only intended in the context of how best to tactically execute the needed changes in the near term." He looked around the table as several of those present nodded their understanding.

"I have some concerns about implementing these measures too quickly at this time. While the war has unquestionably taken an upward trajectory from the disastrous early years, it is far from over. I am extremely hesitant to do anything that might impair the combat effectiveness or morale of our forces until victory is assured.

"We have managed to keep the empire out of the current conflict by an effective campaign of bribery and blackmail. However, if I understand Number Seven's report" - he looked briefly over at that operative, who nodded in response - "General Santiago has been removed from command and may, in fact, have been executed. In any event, he is certainly no longer in a position to sabotage Imperial combat readiness in return for the stipend we have been paying him. We know the Imperial high command is planning attacks on several of our colony worlds. I agree with our decision to withhold warning from our field commanders - the outrage caused by a surprise attack will be quite useful as a propaganda tool, both in terms of focusing the attention of the military and instilling a useful amount of fear and nationalism into the civilian populations. Overall, it is clear the war is escalating, not winding down. I must question if now is the time to tinker too significantly with the military."

"Do we need to do this at all?" asked Number Ten. "It was relatively easy to maneuver the Marines off of EE-4. Perhaps we can handle things in a less sweeping manner. Maybe we don't need to completely eliminate the Corps. They are a very effective fighting force, and that is useful as long as we can maintain the requisite degree of control."

Number Two took a drink of water and cleared his throat. "The Corps must be replaced by a more, ah...pliable organization, at least eventually. We all know our history. For nearly a hundred years, the current system has served to remove troublesome elements from Earth and turn them into a valuable resource off-world. The very nature of the system makes the entire force uncontrollable. If we were able to select their officers we might be in a position to work with the current structure, but they all start as privates. It is an interesting system from the perspective of the fighting man or woman, and I can think of no historical force where the officers were as loved and respected by the foot soldiers. There is no reasonable way to infiltrate and control the organization from outside. If we tried to sack the existing officer class and replace them with political appointees, we would face a force-wide mutiny.

He paused for a breath. "We know why things were set up this way. The Unification Wars had just ended, and the government was in utter disarray. There was no choice but to deal with the military and negotiate the structure of the off-world service, and the resulting flow of military settlers helped build the early colonies. But our colonial presence was a fraction of what it is today, and the Corps was small....fewer than 10,000 during the First Frontier War. Even fifteen years ago there were only 40,000 in total. Now there are over 250,000 active duty personnel, armed with state of the art equipment and nuclear weapons. They have become too strong a force for us to allow outside of our control."

He tapped a few times on his 'pad. "I just sent you each a dossier containing a watchlist of political trouble spots in the colonies. You will note the length of the list and the fact that almost every vital resource-producing world is on it. There are retired Marines settled on most of these worlds, creating an incestuous relationship we can no longer ignore. The Corps is extremely effective at combating foreign enemies, but if a colonial world rebelled, would they execute an order to crush the revolt?"

He paused to let them consider what he had just said. "I am also sending you all an economic impact study that shows just how important our colonies have become to the nation." He poked at the 'pad again. "This war has been extremely expensive, and our economy, which was already precarious, has been pushed to the breaking point. If we were to lose the resources of the colonies, or even suffer serious disturbances, we could face total economic collapse within three years.

"There is no doubt that we must take steps to insure our unquestioned control of the off-world military. But we cannot risk defeat in this war. Therefore, I counsel that we proceed with our initiatives, but slowly. If we experience pushback, indulge it for now. When the war is won there will, of course, be a significant demobilization of the Corps. That will give us the chance to make a more substantial move to take control...or simply to replace the entire structure."

The room was silent for a moment. Some of the people present were thinking about what Number Two had said; others were simply hesitating, not wanting to express an opinion until they saw what Number One would say.

Stark just sat quietly, amused by the fact that they all waited for him to express an opinion. Let them wait a while, he thought.

They assumed we was stewing on what Number Two had said, but the two of them had already discussed the topic thoroughly, and they were both were on the same page. What Stark was really thinking about was Alex's legs. Specifically, some of the more interesting ways they'd been wrapped around him. She was wearing a very short skirt, something she'd made sure he noticed.

Finally, he broke the silence. "I agree with Number Two's conclusions. We will proceed with the deployment of the political officers, however no coercive or punitive measures are to be employed until the war is nearing conclusion. We will push very softly on the Marines until they have won the war for us." He paused for a moment. "However, we might as well do some prep work. Instruct the political officers to compile a list of troublesome Marine personnel. When the time comes, we will deal with them first. Perhaps we can cut off the head of the snake, so to speak."

He stood up and walked over to the window, looking out over the skyline as he continued. "I do, however, think this is an excellent time to step up the implementation of our program to establish greater control over the civilian governments of the colonies themselves. They have had far too much leeway in the past. I want each of you to review the dossier Number Two prepared. When we meet back here next month, be prepared to discuss the specifics for deploying Directorate enforcement personnel to colony worlds, beginning with the most trouble-some ones. The war gives us an excellent opportunity, espe-cially on the planets most vulnerable to enemy action - and the projected Imperial surprise attacks will only help in this regard. The pretext of improving defensive capabilities will allow us to established enhanced civilian monitoring in a clandestine man-ner. Let's also develop a plan to assign a Directorate supervisor as advisor to each of the colonial governments."

Stark looked around the table to see everyone present nod-ding in agreement. "Lastly, Number Five, what is the status of our training program for our Directorate military units?"

Number Five cleared his throat. "We have graduated two

battalions, which have been assigned to Number Ten's EE-4 security operation. As we reviewed at our last meeting, we are still having difficulty with the powered armor training. The Corps has had a virtual monopoly on elite powered infantry for nearly a century, so we've had to start from scratch on our efforts."

"What is the feasibility of ramping up the magnitude of the program?" Stark was looking down at his 'pad as he spoke. "We're going to need to move more than two battalions through at a time if we're going to replace the Corps within the next 5-7 years."

"Sir, there are some difficulties we will have to overcome before a massive escalation of the program is possible." Number Five was always nervous when he had to tell Number One something he didn't want to hear. Troy Warren had been a corporate magnate and not a political academy graduate like the others. Even though he'd worked his way onto the Directorate, he wasn't a career intelligence operative, and he sometimes felt like the odd man out. "Our instructional regimen is already substantially accelerated from the standard Marine curriculum. Our casualty rate during training is over 200% of that of the Marine course, despite the greater intensity of their program."

Number Three scowled. "Are we overly concerned with casualty rates? It's not as if we are likely to run out of cogs any time soon."

"It's not the recruits; it is the wasted cost and program capacity used on trainees who are going to end up in bodybags and not the battlefield." Warren was annoyed, but he tried to hide it. He was almost as scared of Number Three as he was of Number One. We already have to start with 4,000 recruits to graduate two battalions. If we could cut down the loss rate to parity with the Marines, we could more than double our output of combat-ready units."

Number One made a face. "Are they really combat ready?" He started to turn to the hologram, but stopped himself again. "Number Four, you've reviewed the reports on our first two battalions. Would you characterize them as combat ready?"

The laser-generated image turned toward Number One. "It depends on how you define the term." The Number Four projection paused for a second, then continued. "Against planetary militias or armed rebels I am certain they would acquit themselves satisfactorily. They have a substantial advantage in equipment over second rate or reserve units and would likely be used in situations where we had total local space superiority."

There was a moment of silence before Number One spoke. This time he forgot to catch himself, and he turned to face the hologram. "And against better adversaries?"

The image coughed twice before speaking. Wherever the real Number Four was, he had a dry throat. "If they faced a Marine assault force or Caliphate front line units they'd get cut to pieces unless they had a substantial numerical advantage."

"How substantial?" The hologram turned around. The question had come from Alex, who asked it mostly because she knew that's what Number One wanted to know. It never hurt to remind him what a good team they made.

"At least three to one. More if they are facing real combat veterans. Their unit tactics are simply not good enough to go up against elite troops. But the worst problem is the lack of any blooded veterans in the organization. Not the non-coms, not the officers. We don't have anyone at all in the formations with combat experience. We're recruiting cogs as footsoldiers and pulling the non-coms and officers from the terrestrial army, but these guys haven't fought a war in a century. They're glorified internal security."

"Thank you, Number Four." Stark spoke up more quickly this time, before Number Six could say anything else. He enjoyed Alex's games...to a point. But he had to get moving, so it was time to wrap things up. "I want the training program ramped up now so we're moving six battalions through at a time. Number Five, I want you to consult with Number Four on how to improve our training program. In five years, seven outside, these troops are going to have to be able to take on any enemy - the CAC, Caliphate, even our existing Marines if they resist demobilization."

Number Five was going to argue, but he decided against it. "Yes, sir."

"Number Six, I will be in London until tomorrow. I have a mission for you after you finish on EE-4. Let's discuss tomorrow night before you leave." He looked out over the table. "If there's nothing else..." He knew there wouldn't be; he'd already signaled the meeting was over. "Thank you ladies and gentlemen. I will see you all in a month."

Chapter 4

Control Center
AS Pendragon
In orbit around Columbia - Eta Cassiopeiae II

Cain wasn't sure what he thought of the new Gordon II landers. They were bigger, which not only allowed one craft to carry a whole squad instead of just a fire team; it also increased the storage space available. Remembering back to his squad leader days, he was sure he would have liked having all his men with him during an assault. As an officer, however, he wondered if it wasn't better to have a squad combat loaded on two separate craft. In a pinch, a team could fill in for a squad, at least for a while, but if you lost the entire unit you had a hole in your line.

But battles had gotten bigger. The first time Erik Cain stepped into the launch bay of a troopship, he was part of an assault with two companies. His most recent battle had seen 18,500 troops hit the ground, 1,400 under his direct command. Larger landers helped get more troops planetside, and the enhanced storage capacity was useful for the sustained campaigns that were becoming the norm.

The escalation in the scale of war was everywhere. Erik's early drops were made from the AS Guadalcanal, a fast troopship that carried a single company and about 60 sailors. During Operation Sherman, his regiment had been billeted on the Pendragon and two of her sister ships, massive kilometer-long transports, each carrying a full battalion with heavy weapons and an atmospheric fighter squadron, plus 280 naval crew and supplies for a protracted campaign.

He smiled wistfully as he thought of the Guadalcanal. He'd served on a lot of ships since then, but he still had a soft spot for his first posting. She'd been blown to plasma in the final stages of Operation Achilles, the worst military disaster in Alliance history, but she'd gone down fighting and taken a couple enemy ships with her.

He was standing in the control center staring at a bank of monitors, watching the activity in the bays of the Pendragon and the other five transports holding his brigade. His first wave was about to launch. As always, it made him uneasy not being bolted into one of those landers, but he'd been told in no uncertain terms that a colonel did not go down in the first assault. He didn't suppose it was any different now that he was filling in as an acting brigadier general. He obeyed General Holm's orders, but it still pissed him off to be standing there when his men were going into battle. Even simulated battle.

At least that political officer was leaving him alone. Cain did his best to do as General Holm had asked, and he'd actually managed to get along with Captain Warren or, more accurately, he pretended to get along with him. Warren was full of suggestions on how to better handle the troops day to day, but he seemed willing to step aside when they were actually fighting...or pretend fighting at least.

Cain sighed. These were only wargames, but men and women would die anyway. You didn't land 3,600 troops from space under combat conditions - even simulated combat conditions - without taking losses. Accidents and mechanical failures would claim their toll. He knew this training session would save lives later, when his troops were attacking enemies that fired back with real weapons. He knew it intellectually, but that wasn't going to make it any easier when he got the first fatality report. Erik Cain had led thousands of troops, but he still had trouble dealing with the ghosts of those who didn't come back. Sleep was a sporadic thing for Cain, and it was at night he usually hosted his old comrades. They held a place for him in Valhalla; he knew that. One day, brothers, he thought grimly. One day when there is less work to do.

His eyes were fixed on the monitors, but he needn't have bothered - he knew by heart what was happening in those bays. First, the troops would stand there, armor deactivated, the crushing weight held up only by the locking bolt attached to the lander. That's when the claustrophobia is the worst. Even those who aren't bothered by tight spaces are uncomfortable encased in several tons of Osmium-Iridium polymer hanging there like dead weight.

Then the nanotech nuclear plants that energized the armor would come alive, and power would flow into the various circuits and systems of the suit. The Marine was still bolted in, but now the servo-mechanicals were working, and the crushing feeling of weight around you was gone. Armor looks bulky and cumbersome but, the truth is, a well-trained Marine is fairly comfortable in his suit.

The bolted in Marines would be getting updates from the ship's battle computer. In Cain's early days this voice was mechanical, electronic. But the newer ships had human-sounding AIs, just like the Marine armor itself. Erik wasn't sure he didn't prefer the old electronic voice to the new human-sounding ones - either in the bay or from his own wisecracking AI, Hector.

Just before the bay depressurized and the doors opened, the Marines bolted into the Gordons would be pressure coated with heat-resistant foam specially designed to protect against the high temperatures of atmospheric landings. Cain was watching it all unfold right in front of him, but his mind was eons away, in other launch bays with long-dead Marines.

The last update was given by the ship's captain, a tradition Cain was glad had survived the escalation of the war. Alliance skippers always wished the strike force good luck and, soldiers being superstitious, it was considered a bad omen if some mechanical problem prevented the captain's message from being relayed to the troops.

Cain watched the bay doors open and then heard the whining hum as the catapults powered up and launched the landers out into the upper atmosphere of Columbia. This "real" simulated attack had been preceded by a completely fake bombardment that had inflicted considerable phantom losses on the defenders. Cain's target selection had been brilliant and unorthodox. He was attacking an entrenched enemy with no numerical advantage, a no-win scenario. The point of the exercise wasn't for Cain's forces to win, but rather to see how far they could get.

But Erik Cain wasn't wired that way. If he was going in, he was going in to win.

He watched the initial wave descending to the surface, taking simulated losses from hidden ground-based weapons. His theoretical warships scanned the surface aggressively, targeting any emplacement that fired on the landers and blasting it immediately. He had two full simulated battlegroups supporting the landing.

They won't know what to make of it, he thought with wry amusement. General Holm, maybe, but nobody in 2nd Brigade. His landing was as unorthodox as his bombardment, and he was sure it would give Brigadier Slavin fits which, of course, was just what he wanted.

It looked like everything was going according to plan, so he turned away from the monitors and headed down to the launch bay to suit up. The general had forbidden him from landing in the first wave, but he hadn't said anything about the second...

Cain's command post was a beehive of activity. Communications were coming in from all over the field. Slavin's forces, which were supposed to be defending, had been maneuvered into counter-attacking, and they were throwing themselves against Cain's hastily dug trenches.

His first wave had been small, and he'd landed them in an unexpected area, beyond the ridge north and east of the capital city of Weston. Erik knew those canyons well. The last time he'd led troops on Columbia he'd eaten a nuke just a few klicks east of the LZ. He'd survived by the thinnest of margins and spent a year in the hospital recovering.

The second wave he held back for a long time, and when he finally launched, he landed them right in the broad plain in front of Weston, a glaringly obvious point of attack, and the one the CAC had used eight years before when Cain was a sergeant and Elias Holm a colonel in command of the last ditch defense of the planet.

But Erik didn't attack. He ordered his forces to establish a defensive line stretching between the northern and southern ridgelines, and he began to dig in. He set up every heavy weapon he had and started to return the fire the enemy had been dishing out since the landing.

The defenders had been deployed almost entirely in front of the city, and when Cain's first wave hit the ground on the other side of the steep ridgeline, General Slavin sent a battalion through the pass and then back west to meet them. But Cain's main landing had cut them off in the canyon, and he sent a force to hit them from behind. Pinned between his two groups of attackers, they were cut to pieces.

Several of Cain's landers in the first wave had suffered apparent guidance errors, and a number of ships went off course, landing in seemingly random locations as far as 5 klicks from the designated zone.

The defenders disregarded them, assuming they were just the victims of malfunctions, but Cain had sent his elite company with the first wave, and out of the errant landers climbed squad after squad of his specially trained infiltration unit. In small groups they followed their tactical plan, making their way over the mountainous ridge and into the city itself, unnoticed by the defenders.

The third wave of attackers landed behind the south ridgeline, opposite the LZ of the first group. Cain now had the defending position bracketed, his main force hastily entrenched in front of them, and flanking forces advancing over the ridgelines on both sides. Worse, General Slavin started getting communications from Weston; Cain's special action teams had infiltrated the city. There were armored Marines standing around in front of power stations, data centers, and every other vital facility. No one had anticipated any attacking units reaching Weston, and the parameters provided to the AI running the wargame had not included directives for this eventuality.

Along the ridgelines, Cain's flanking forces set up positions to fire down upon the defenders, who were now attacking the main invasion force in the plain attempting to break out of the trap. Cain's troops along the ridges raked the flanks of the enemy, and simulated casualties mounted quickly. All through

Slavin's forces, Marines were told by their AIs that they were casualties. The armor of the "dead" Marines initiated a partial shutdown, leaving them lying motionless to await the end of the battle.

General Holm had been watching the action unfold from his headquarters, and he tried to stifle a laugh. Cain was his protégé, and everyone knew it, but it wouldn't do for the commanding general to appear to be taking sides. Still, he couldn't help but be amused as he watched Erik's forces run circles around Slavin's defenders. Holm had given permission for Cain to create the special action teams from his veterans, but even he had never thought about how effectively they could be utilized.

Simulated losses were less than 550 for Cain's attackers, while the defenders had lost 1,700, almost half their number. Holm was going to put a stop to the exercise, but he figured he'd wait for the AI to call it. When that happened a few minutes later, Holm got on the comlink and addressed all of the participating troops.

"To all personnel participating in the exercise, this is General Holm. The strategy AI has called the battle, awarding a decisive victory to the attacking force." Decisive indeed, he thought with a small laugh. How about a rout? "I want to congratulate and thank everyone who participated. Those who have been immobilized as casualties should have suit power restored within five minutes. At that time, battalion commanders are to direct the return of troops to billets. Command personnel from battalion level up, we will have a briefing tomorrow at 1000 hours and review the exercise. Holm out."

Holm switched his com to a direct link to Cain. "Erik, did you have to smack them around so badly?" He laughed again. "Seriously, that was an outstanding performance."

"Thank you, sir." Cain sounded tired

"Come see me after you stow your gear and grab a shower. I want to discuss a few things, including your special action teams. We can have some dinner sent in. No rush, though. I'll be here late, so take your time."

"Yes sir."

Holm flipped off the comlink, still trying to suppress his smile.

Cain walked across the quad toward the general's HQ. He was freshly showered and dressed in a clean pair of fatigues. It was dark already, maybe 2300 local time. He was starting to get used to the 27 hour local day. He'd just gotten the casualty figures - the real ones, not the simulated ones. Three dead from accidents during the exercise, another two seriously wounded. The fact that all three were from General Slavin's group didn't make him feel any better.

Lieutenant Raynor was expecting him. Cain smiled and wondered, does this kid ever sleep? Holm's orderly led Erik back to the general's office, and with a quick salute he ducked out into the hall, closing the door behind him.

Cain gave the general his own salute, which was actually a pretty good one for a change. Holm was talking into a small comlink, but he waved over toward the small table in the back corner, which was laid out with a light dinner. Erik nodded and walked over, taking one of the seats.

A few seconds later, Holm finished his call and walked to the table. Erik started to get up, but the general motioned for him to sit. "So what did Lieutenant Raynor scrounge up for dinner?" He reached over and pulled the top off of one of the trays as he sat down. It was filled with some sort of grilled fish. The Columbian seafood was excellent, and the general loved fish. There were also plates of vegetables as well as a local growth that resembled Earth mushrooms. "I told him light. I figured he'd go find some sandwiches."

Erik smiled. "I'm trying to remember if I was ever that young and earnest."

"Oh, you were. I remember a very young and memorable sergeant I ran across some years back." Holm smiled and speared a large chunk of fish, dropping it on his plate. "And you, my friend, are still every bit as earnest as anyone in this corps."

Erik laughed softly, taking a piece of fish for himself, smaller than the one the general had picked. "So am I in trouble for exceeding mission parameters? I'll have you know that there was nothing in the mission book that precluded an infiltration of Weston."

Holm snorted just as he was taking a drink. "Under a different commander, you'd be in trouble on a semi-permanent basis." He wiped his mouth with his napkin. "I, being a glutton for punishment, wish I had five of you." He took another bite, swallowing before he continued. "Erik, your special action teams looked great out there. I'm glad you badgered me into letting you train them."

"I was happy with them as well. I felt I had a range of options for using them." His eyes narrowed as he looked at the general. "Especially when I'm given an exercise I'm supposed to lose."

"You should know more than anyone, not every situation is a fair or reasonable one. God knows, you've been in a few hopeless fights yourself, yet here you are."

Erik looked wistful. "Yes, here I am. But a lot of the guys who were there with me aren't."

The general sighed. "Erik, we talked about this before. You can't carry the guilt for every soldier that gets killed under your command. Have you ever thought about how many of them you've pulled through a tough fight? They'd be at war with or without you. But I suspect a lot more of them would be dead on some desolate planet if they hadn't had you." He stared over at Cain, trying to stress his point. "Anyway, we'll discuss this further another day. For now, I want to fill you in on some intel I just received."

Cain stopped chewing and looked up at the general. "New intel?"

"Yes. I finally have some idea why we haven't had to deal with the South Americans yet. Apparently, Alliance Intelligence managed to get a double agent inside their command structure and really mess up their logistics. The agent's been compromised, but Intel estimates a minimum of six month's prep time before the empire can launch any major offensive."

"Well that's good news." Cain put his hand up and rubbed his mouth. "I just wish we weren't sitting here playing games while we have this window. We could finish Sherman in less than six months if we had the naval support."

Holm smiled broadly. "I have one more bit of news." Cain looked over expectantly. "I am going to make an announcement tomorrow, but I'll let you in on it early. The Caliphate and CAC launched a massive attack on Gliese 250."

Cain felt his stomach tense. Losing Gliese would really set them back. Erik himself had led the surprise attack that had seized the huge space station, and subsequently General Holm had conquered several chains of systems leading out from there. The Gliese attack, and the subsequent campaigns, had been the turning point of the war.

"Admiral Garret smashed the attack. From the preliminary figures it looks like he took out around 40% of their strength. It was a rout." Holm smiled broadly.

Cain's face changed rapidly from apprehension to shock to gratification. "That's great news, General." Then more somberly. "How bad were his losses?"

"That's the best part. They were heavy for sure, but nothing like what he inflicted. He didn't lose a single capital ship, though it sounds like the Leyte is pretty close to a writeoff. Some of the escort squadrons took it hard, and it sounds like the station took some bad hits in the final stages of the battle."

Cain was speechless. He knew Garret was a great naval commander, but it sounded like he'd taken on all that two Superpowers could throw at him and wrecked it. If the victory was as complete as it sounded, the Alliance just might be able to win this war decisively.

"Admiral Garret is putting together a scratch task force from the less-damaged fleet units and leaving Gliese for Columbia immediately. He'll be here in seven weeks. In eight we're restarting Sherman."

"That gives us four months," Cain said. "Four months for three planetary assaults. It's tight. You think we can do it?"

Holm smiled. "I've been working on the revised schedule for the past two hours. I think we can just make it."

"I'll get started on prep for the brigade tomorrow." Cain had lost interest in dinner. He was ready to get back to his own office and start working.

"No, Erik." Cain looked up with a start. "I don't want you to get mired in details. Let Jax handle the prep for both regiments. We've been ready for months; there isn't that much to do. I want you to spend the next two months expanding the special action teams. You've got a company of them. I want you to expand it to a battalion."

Cain was surprised. "General, I don't have nearly enough veterans for that. If I strip that many experienced men from the brigade it will impair combat efficiency."

"Which is why I have authorized you to appropriate personnel from any formation in I Corps, even the British and Oceanian formations. Just don't take too many from any one battalion. But get yourself enough for two more companies. And find a good captain you want to bump to major to put in direct command of the whole crew."

Cain's mind was racing. The special action teams were his pet project, and now he was going to be able to expand it to a size that could really make a difference in battle. "Warren's going to object." The political officer had questioned why Cain had a specially trained elite company with no authorization from the high command. He had suggested, with considerable insistence, that training an elite force to a high level of proficiency was demoralizing to the rank and file. Erik couldn't have disagreed more, but he kept his comments to himself.

"Don't worry. If he gives you a hard time just tell him you are following my orders. He'll whine to my babysitter, and I'll figure out a nice way to tell him to go fuck himself."

"You should have been a diplomat, sir."

Holm laughed. "Maybe after the war."

Chapter 5

CAC Central Committee HQ
Hong Kong, Earth

Liang Chang paced nervously on the polished marble floor outside the Central Committee Hall. His dress uniform was almost absurdly ornate, green with gold epaulettes and braid. CAC field gear was generally practical and utilitarian; their formal uniforms, however, were quite theatrical.

Liang was the supreme field commander of the Combine's interstellar navy, a post he wasn't at all sure he'd keep for more than the next few minutes. Truthfully, he wasn't sure he'd keep his head. More than one CAC commander had found his way to an unmarked grave after a defeat, and Liang had just presided over the worst one in living memory. Fortunately, it was more of a Caliphate defeat than a CAC one; his forces had been an allied contingent under joint command.

At least they want to talk to you, he thought. He wouldn't have been surprised if the internal security men had grabbed him right off the transport and dumped him in the harbor. He glanced at his chronometer and was shocked to realize he'd only been waiting five minutes. It felt like he'd been there much longer.

The gold-plated doors slid open suddenly, and a Committee Guard in a spotless red uniform walked out into the foyer. "Admiral Liang? The Committee will see you now." He stood aside and gestured for Liang to enter.

Liang took a deep breath and marched into the room. There was a massive semi-circular desk spanning the distance halfway around the outside edge of the room. Seated in the twelve spots were six men wearing various military uniforms, five clad in expensive civilian attire, and one woman wearing a finely tailored, moderately masculine suit. Liang walked over to the seat in the middle of the room and stood beside it, rigidly at attention.

"Admiral Liang, the Committee has summoned you to report on the events of the recent battle in the Gliese 250 system." The speaker was one of the civilians. Not good, thought Liang. Protocol called for one of the officers to address him first.

"The combined Caliphate-CAC forces engaged significantly outnumbered the defending Alliance fleet, did they not?" There was an edge to the questioning, but not outright hostility. I'm not lost yet, Liang thought.

"Yes, Your Excellency." It wasn't the time for excuses. Not yet. "We had an advantage of 45% in tonnage and 42% in hulls."

"And yet we were not only defeated, but apparently suffered a loss factor more than double that of the defenders." A new questioner this time. Lin Kang, the naval chief of staff. Liang's commander.

Liang wondered, is he feeding me a lifeline? "Much of that differential resulted from the difficulty in re-vectoring our ships back to the Alpha Cephei warp gate after Admiral Al'Assar ordered the retreat." Liang was nervous. Trying to shift the blame was risky.

"Admiral Liang, we are well aware that Admiral Al'Assar was in overall command." The civilian again. Liang couldn't tell if the guy was trying to save him or bury him. "The Caliph has already rendered his judgment. Admiral Al'Assar met his fate in the airlock of his flagship." The speaker paused. Liang tried to stand steadily, but he could feel the tingling in his legs. "Nevertheless, we would like to know from you exactly what transpired."

Liang started to speak, but his mouth had gone dry. He'd been in battle dozens of times; he was no coward. But standing here waiting for these old men to decide his fate called for a different sort of courage. He cleared his throat. "Your Excellencies, I would like to begin by stating for the record that our officers and crews fought with great bravery and distinction. That the battle was lost is in no way attributable to the devotion of our naval personnel."

"We understand that our forces serve with distinction at all times, Admiral." The civilian again, more impatient this time.

"However, we are concerned with the command decisions that resulted in the defeat and the loss of over half the committed force and 28% of our entire active naval capacity."

Liang shifted his feet nervously. "Yes, Your Excellency." They aren't going to let you evade this, Liang thought. "Admiral Al'Assar insisted on stripping the cruisers from the combat groups and sending them in as a first wave. I objected strongly to this plan. Many of our officers can bear witness to this."

"There is no need for that. The Committee is not questioning the honesty of one of its senior commanders." Admiral Lin again.

A good sign, Liang thought hopefully. Though he may just be defending the honor of the service. "Yes, Your Excellency. The cruisers were sent through the warp gate well ahead of the main attack force. Admiral Al'Assar wanted the initial assault to go in at very high velocity. The attack date was delayed nine days to allow the first wave to reposition and accumulate the required velocity before transiting." Liang paused and scanned the Committee members.

"Continue, Admiral."

"Yes, Your Excellency. The cruisers went directly at the station, intending to zip past the defending fleet and launch an overwhelming missile strike, rendering the installation combat ineffective before the balance of our forces engaged the enemy fleet. However, the enemy was not deployed in a conventional defensive array; the entire Alliance force was positioned near the station instead of formed up for a warp gate defense.

Admiral Al'Assar's tactical plan was blunt, a straight line advance from the warp gate to the station. Unfortunately, Admiral Garret had vastly increased the density of the protective mine belts, and our force went right through the thickest section. The task force suffered catastrophic damage, and the command structure was severely disordered. By the time the ships were able to launch, their attack was significantly weakened, and the entire Alliance fleet was linked into the station's point defense array. The missile barrage was almost totally ineffective. Worse, our cruisers took even more hits from the station's missile volley."

Liang paused to take a breath. "We did manage to inflict some damage to the station with energy weapons as the task force passed, but the window of fire was brief because of our high velocity. The cruisers immediately began to decelerate, however they needed at least six days to get back to the combat zone, which meant they were effectively out of the battle."

"Tell us what occurred when the main force began its assault." This was a different civilian member of the Committee - a man, about 60 years of age, very well dressed in a stylish black suit. Liang recognized him as Wu Xilong, the head of internal security. A dangerous man, even more so than most of the others.

Liang described the events of the battle as succinctly as possible. The Alliance bomber squadrons had surprised the fleet and inflicted enormous damage. He squarely blamed Admiral Al'Assar for unreadiness, though he had been caught flat footed too. Making things worse, the attack had forced the CAC-Caliphate ships to jettison their external missile racks. Between the loss of the hull-deployed missiles and the damage inflicted, the fleet's barrage was significantly weakened, while Admiral Garret's was well-planned and perfectly plotted.

By the time the two sides engaged at energy weapons range, the Alliance force was still outnumbered, but fewer of its ships were heavily damaged. The fleets savaged each other with laser fire as they approached, and when they passed, the ships spun about and continued to fire. He credited his weapons teams with a strong performance under difficult circumstances, and tried to attribute the disappointing results to the damage they had suffered.

"After the energy weapons exchange," he said, "Admiral Al'Assar ordered maximum deceleration. Unfortunately, it proved impossible to adequately change the fleet's vector before we reached missile range of the station which, unfortunately, was still fully operational. Worse, many of our ships had been damaged and were unable to produce maximum thrust, so the formation degraded. A number of heavily damaged ships could not maneuver away from the station's missiles. Isolated, with their point defense seriously degraded, many were destroyed."

"Is that when our fleet attempted to flee?" A woman's voice. There was only one female member of the Committee, Liang thought with a chill. Li An, First Minister of C1, the main intelligence agency of the CAC, and one of the most reptilian members of the human race ever to draw breath. The CAC did not make it easy for women to advance to the upper levels of power, and how many bodies she'd disposed of during her climb was a matter for the most circumspect conjecture.

"Your Excellency..." He was trying hard to stay calm, but Li made him even more nervous than he already was - she made everyone nervous. "...it was at that point that Admiral Al'Assar ordered the individual fleet elements to retreat at their best speed." Despite a major effort to remain calm, his voice cracked a bit. "Unfortunately, at this point, Admiral Garret was able to target numerous isolated elements of the fleet, inflicting additional losses before the surviving ships were able to reach the warp gate and transit to the safety of Alpha Cephei."

Li put her hand up. "Enough, Admiral Liang." Her tone was icy. "While I will acknowledge that Admiral Al'Assar was in overall command and that he displayed a level of incompetence greater than your own, I cannot overstate the Committee's disappointment at your performance in this sorry affair." Liang didn't dare respond, but he couldn't help fidgeting under her frosty gaze. "You have presided over one of the greatest military disasters in the history of war in space, and you have handed the Alliance an enormous victory...one that has seriously jeopardized our position in the war as a whole."

I'm not going to leave this room, Liang thought. He stood as still as he could, but he was beginning to panic. Li An did not allow procedure or ceremony to interfere with efficiency. If she wanted him dead he would never see it coming. He kept imagining a shot ringing out, hitting him in the back of the head. He could feel the sweat trickling down his neck.

"Do you know why you are here, Admiral Liang?" Had her voice softened slightly?

"Yes, Your Excellency. To provide a report on the events of the battle and to answer for my part in it." Maybe I will get out of here yet, he thought.

"Wrong, Admiral."

My God, it is Li An who had me brought here, he thought. Why? What does she want with me?

"Your ineptitude in the recent engagement is quite apparent to us." Her merciless eyes bored into his. "Had that been the only factor, I can assure you that things would have been dealt with below this level. Your actions are unpardonable; you very well might have shared Admiral Al'Assar's fate."

There's a but coming. Maybe I have a chance after all, he thought.

"However, there is a way that you can atone for your failures and serve the state." She punched a button on the desk, and the large viewscreen at the front of the room activated, displaying photos of two Alliance officers. "Our recent reverses have been almost entirely attributable to these two enemy commanders, General Elias Holm and the newly promoted Fleet Admiral Augustus Garret."

She paused briefly. "The fortunes of war, as they say, are sometimes unpredictable. Though we were well-prepared for the conflict and, indeed, enjoyed almost uninterrupted success during the initial phases, fortune has taken an ill turn. It would appear that our enemies have not one, but two bona fide military geniuses in their service, while we..." - she looked at him contemptuously - "...have nothing of the sort."

Li motioned to one of the men standing along the back wall of the room, who walked toward Liang. "Admiral Liang, you are indeed fortunate, for we have prepared a plan to rid us of Admiral Garret once and for all. Through no small efforts, we have penetrated Alliance Intelligence and obtained a copy of Admiral Garret's most recent orders. He is still in the Gliese 250 system, attending to fleet repairs. However, he will soon depart with a taskforce bound for Eta Cassiopeiae."

Liang was uncomfortable with Li's aide standing behind him, but he remained still and managed not to turn around and look.

"You will leave here immediately and transit to the Capella system to take command of the force assembling there. You will intercept and engage the Alliance force bound for Eta Cassiopeiae. You will target and destroy Admiral Garret's flagship. Regardless of the outcome of the battle, you will eliminate Admiral Garret, whatever steps you must take. If you succeed, your poor performance in the recent combat will be pardoned, and you will retain your rank and perquisites."

Here is comes, he thought nervously.

"However, if you fail, you will be punished as a traitor." He didn't think her voice could get more intimidating, but he was wrong. "I trust you understand what that means, not only for you but for your family as well."

He imagined his wife, his children, even his aged father strapped to a bare metal chair in a soundproofed plasti-crete room in the sub-levels of C1 headquarters. Those rooms were the stuff of nightmares - cold and featureless, other than the drains in the floor for washing away the blood and other fluids.

"I will not fail, Your Excellency." Then for good measure he added, "Thank-you, Your Excellencies, for the chance to redeem myself."

"Good, Admiral. Agent Deng will brief you fully. You leave within the hour."

"Yes, Your Excellency." Liang bowed to the Committee and turned to follow his new companion into the outer gallery. One chance, he thought. I cannot fail.

Li An sat at a large mahogany desk sipping a drink. Although the CAC cultural ministry encouraged citizens to embrace Asian traditions, Li favored bourbon, smuggled, at great cost and effort since the war began, from the Alliance. Behind her there was a wall of windows with a panoramic view across the harbor to Kowloon. The glass was special, not only strong enough to stop a mid-sized rocket launcher, it was reflective on the other side, which allowed Li her view and her privacy at the same time.

Most of the government buildings were west of C1's head-quarters, in the main business district, but Li preferred the lux-

ury and slightly less frenetic pace of the Wan Chai neighbor-
hood. And Li An usually got what she wanted. No one in
the CAC's multi-tentacled government knew as many secrets as
she did. Infighting and plots were common among upper level
functionaries, but no one wanted Li An as an enemy.

Though she frequently worked late in the solitude she
enjoyed, tonight she had two guests ensconced in the buttery-
soft leather chairs opposite her. Wu Xilong sipped at small glass
of Maotai. Li couldn't decide if he really enjoyed it or just liked
the image of the traditional state drink. She and Wu were generally rivals - technically she had jurisdiction over external affairs
while his covered all internal security matters. In actual practice,
they frequently stepped on each other's toes. Tonight, however,
they were of like mind. It was in no one's interest for the CAC
to lose the war, and they were far closer to that unpleasant eventuality than anyone below their rarified heights knew about.

Her other guest was Lin Kang, though he had discarded his
naval uniform for non-descript civilian attire. Like Li, Lin Kang
preferred his liquor imported, usually vodka, though in this
instance he had accepted only tea.

"If fortune is with us, our friend Admiral Liang will succeed
at his mission." She drank the last few drops in her glass. "He
is now well-motivated." She grabbed a crystal flask and poured
herself a refill. "The intelligence that enables his effort was difficult to obtain, but it is highly reliable."

"I am concerned about the naval resources we are providing
to Liang for this mission." Lin Kang was a worrier by nature,
but he had good cause to be concerned. Liang was taking well
over a third of their depleted strength to attack Garret's fleet. If
he suffered another defeat they would be in a great deal of the
trouble, with no significant new naval construction scheduled
for completion for at least two years. "Perhaps we are being too
aggressive."

"Admiral Lin, I believe that we are short on options." Wu
spoke softly, politely, not wanting to offend Lin with what he
was going to say. "With all due respect to your military organization, can you honestly state that you have anyone in your com-

mand structure that can defeat either Admiral Garret or General Holm? At least without significant numerical superiority that we are not currently able to provide?"

Lin felt a flush of anger, but he stifled the urge to mount a kneejerk defense of the military. Wu was very clearly trying to avoid provocation. Besides, he was right. None of Lin's officers could outfight the Alliance's devil commanders. Fortune had favored the Alliance dogs and given them not one, but two military masterminds. "No," he finally said. "Though we have many fine commanders, I do not believe they are the equals of Garret and Holm."

If we had so many fine commanders, Li An thought bitterly, we would not be at this pass. "Whatever the skill levels of our command personnel, I believe it is an inescapable conclusion that our path to restoring our fortunes and winning this war begins with eliminating these two adversaries." She leaned back in her chair, her eyes darting between her two companions as she spoke.

Lin saw the need for the proposed course of action, but he didn't like it. Li and Wu were spies - they were just as pleased if their ends were served by bodies dissolved in acid in the dark as by military victory in the open. More satisfied, in fact, for they considered such a solution to be expedient. But Lin was a career soldier, and while he despised the Alliance and had spent his entire life fighting them, he also respected them as worthy enemies. He wanted to destroy them, but he wanted to do it in battle and not by thinly-disguised assassination. Still, he knew that Garret and Holm represented a true threat to the overall war effort. Grudgingly, he had decided to go along with the plans.

"My staff will brief Admiral Liang further, and assist him in organizing his new command. He must be underway quickly, or he will arrive too late to complete the plan." Lin tried to sound positive, but he was still unhappy, and he doubted he disguised it completely.

"Very well. We will leave it in your hands." Li An knew Lin had reservations, but she was confident he would do his best to execute the plan. "Now, let us discuss our intentions with regard to General Holm, who is no less of a threat." She paused to allow her guests to interject, but both remained silent and waited for her to continue. "I have developed a plan of some complexity. If we are able to execute it, we will not only rid ourselves of General Holm, but we will also inflict a major military defeat on the Alliance forces. Indeed, there will be ancillary benefits as well, which I shall disclose to you shortly."

She took a sip of her bourbon and leaned back in the plush desk chair. "The resources required for the execution of this plan have been in the works for some time. As both of you are aware, we were able to agree to the terms of a treaty with the South American Empire quite some time ago. The provisions of this alliance are rather complex, but fundamentally, we have agreed to aid them in conquering five specific colony worlds, four from the Alliance and one from the CEL. These systems will provide the empire with two points of access to the rim, something they currently lack."

Wu listened intently, rubbing his temples silently as Li explained her plan. She knows something I do not, he thought. It made him uncomfortable to lack information, and it annoyed the hell out of him that she'd obtained intelligence he had not.

Li continued. "What you are not aware of, is that C1 has been conducting an ongoing operation with the Red Bureau...an effort to deceive Alliance Intelligence." The Red Bureau was the South American Empire's intelligence agency. Not as capable as C1 or Alliance Intelligence, the Bureau was more of a brute force rather than the rapier of its CAC or Alliance counterparts. "We have allowed the Alliance to bribe General Santiago to interfere with Imperial preparations in order to delay the South Americans' entry into the war." She paused for a few seconds. "What they do not realize is that the general has been part of our plan from the beginning."

Li smiled. She particularly enjoyed putting one over on Gavin Stark. The head of Alliance Intelligence was a worthy opponent, one who was rarely fooled by anyone. At first, Li was surprised that her plan had not been discovered, but later she became aware that Stark was distracted and deeply immersed in several unknown initiatives. It made her nervous not to know what he was up to, but she was glad at least to be working against one of his cronies on her op.

"General Santiago has been duping the Alliance all this time?" Wu sounded surprised.

Li looked over at him. I love that he has no idea what I have been doing, she thought. "No, General Santiago is greedy, and he was actually flipped by Alliance Intelligence. However, we were aware of the entire operation from the start."

Wu interjected. "But Imperial intervention has been delayed for months because of Santiago's disruptions. If you were aware of his status, why didn't you inform the Bureau?"

She smiled. "We did inform them." She enjoyed Wu's renewed look of surprise. "Monitoring Santiago's activities was a joint operation. We allowed his sabotage to occur in order to continue the deception. The Alliance now believes that the empire will not be able to initiate hostilities for at least six months. General Santiago has imposed significant delays on their supply chain. It was necessary to allow him to actually cause damage to convince the Alliance that the empire's lack of readiness was factual."

"But it is factual." Admiral Lin had been listening quietly until now. "I have seen the reports. It is not possible for them to mount a significant offensive operation until they have resolved their supply issues. And I think six months is a very optimistic projection."

"Indeed, Admiral, your analysis is correct save for one fact. My agency has been conducting an operation to secretly provide supplies and support to the empire. Admittedly, this has been a strain on our own logistics, and hiding that has not been easy, but I can state unequivocally that the Imperial forces can be ready to launch a major offensive in as little as two weeks."

Wu and Lin both reacted with stunned surprise. "Is that possible? The Alliance cannot be expecting an attack so soon. We must coordinate with the imp..."

"Please, Admiral," Li interjected. "Allow me to continue, as

I have only advised you of the first portion of the plan." Lin was annoyed at the interruption, but he leaned back. He was curious what else Li An had to say.

"The Alliance expects the empire to attack one of the obvious target worlds along their line of advance to open space. However, I have obtained the emperor's approval for an alternative operation. Indeed, he has placed most of the available Imperial military resources at my disposal for this operation."

She cleared her throat before continuing. "To understand what I now propose, we must review some back story. Early in this conflict, before the war was even officially declared, we became aware of a significant discovery made by the Alliance on Epsilon Eridani IV." She placed a data chip on the desk. "This chip contains a summary of what the Alliance found on that world. Before you leave tonight, you will both view the information on my secure terminal. The data chip will self-destruct after this single viewing." She paused, clearly uncomfortable about having to disclose the secret. "Please understand that this is classified at the very highest level. Most of the Committee is even unaware of the contents of this chip. I must stress that you cannot speak of this or record anything to do with it by any means." She looked at them both with a feral gaze. "Are we agreed?"

Lin nodded immediately. He had already considered it unwise to cross Li An, but one look at her current expression was enough to freeze his blood. Wu paused for the briefest moment, not happy to be taking something like orders from Li, but he too nodded his agreement.

Li acknowledged their acceptance with a nod. "You will recall that we launched a pre-emptive attack and took control of the Epsilon Eridani system. Unfortunately, the Alliance was able to respond more quickly than we projected, and they retook the planet before we were able to reinforce." At least they made it easy on us in one way, she thought. Angry that the invaders had employed chemical weapons against the militia, the Alliance had wiped out the CAC troops who had been on the planet, saving her from having to do the same to maintain security.

"The Alliance has reinforced the planet and stationed a battlegroup there in defense." She leaned forward in her chair, hands on the desk. "We will attack Epsilon Eridani IV and again seize control of the planet."

Lin was startled. "Minister Li, we do not have the resources to launch such an assault. Epsilon Eridani is three transits into enemy-held systems. We would need an enormous force to fight our way there and then engage and defeat the defending battlegroup and planetary defenses. It is impossible, at least until Admiral Liang's mission is completed."

"Indeed, Admiral," she said, smiling. "This operation would seem to be impossible and so the enemy will never expect it. Surprise will aid us in fighting our way to the target. The intervening systems are lightly defended, and we will not be attacking any populated worlds. However, what truly makes the mission feasible is the assistance of our allies."

Wu blurted a response this time. "The Caliphate? They are crippled after the battle in Gliese 250, and their logistics is in a shambles since they lost their rim worlds and the vital supplies they provide. What help can they give?"

Li flashed a catlike grin. "I do not speak of the Caliphate, though I have secured a small supporting force from them for the operation. I refer to the emperor, whom I have convinced to commit virtually the entirety of his naval forces to the campaign."

Wu and Lin gasped in unison.

"And to Europa Federalis," she continued, "which has agreed to provide a battlegroup and a cruiser squadron to the effort."

They looked back at her blankly, too stunned to answer.

"As I mentioned previously, one of the systems the emperor demands as the price of his support is held by the CEL. The need to meet this requirement forces us into eventual war with the League, which makes an alliance with Europa Federalis inevitable. By moving up the timeline we gain the element of surprise as well as support for this operation. The Alliance defenders in Eridani will not expect an attack, and they will be faced with a combined fleet and overwhelmed. Meanwhile, Admiral

Liang will have eliminated Admiral Garret, creating a command vacuum in the Alliance navy."

Her two guests sat in stunned silence. They were shocked at the amount of preparation Li had managed to complete in total secrecy. Finally, Wu spoke, trying to keep the anger out of his voice. "We should have been briefed on all of this much earlier."

"These were C1 operations undertaken for the good of the state." Li An spoke evenly, her expression calm and non-provocative. She really didn't care if Wu or Lin liked what she had done, but her plans were likelier to succeed without petty rivalries interfering. "Of course, the alliance with Europa Federalis will have to be ratified by the Committee, which is why I have called a special session for tomorrow." She held up another data chip. "I have here the Europan ratification of the treaty. The Consulate met in secret session two days ago and approved both the alliance and the plan to provide support to our Eridani operation."

Now I will make them feel a part of this and cut off any foolish resentment, she thought. "Admiral Lin, Minister Wu, it was my intention to fully brief the two of you in advance of that meeting, which is why we are here now. To date it has been necessary to maintain the highest possible degree of secrecy, however if we are to achieve success and redeem the fortunes of the war, we must work together."

Wu was still clearly annoyed, but she could see that she had successfully appealed to his vanity by placing him and Admiral Lin above the other members of the Committee. What they didn't know - didn't need to know - was that she had similarly met with a number of other Committee members. Li An left as little as possible to chance, and when she called a Committee meeting she made sure she had the support she needed before anyone entered the chamber.

"You should have advised us sooner." Wu found it necessary to complain a bit more, but Li was pretty sure he was onboard. Lin didn't even argue. He understood the military situation, and even if he didn't want to admit it, he was well aware they were now losing the war. Li's bold moves had an excellent chance of dramatically changing the strategic situation.

Li relaxed a bit and leaned back in her chair. "Please note the table of organization I have provided." She motioned to two small 'pads on the desk. "This is a proposed partial order of battle for a ground force to occupy Epsilon Eridani IV. It includes most of the Imperial mobile forces as well as a small contingent from Europa Federalis." She looked at Lin. "Admiral, you will find suggested formations from our own ground forces to add to the operation. I would be most appreciative if you would review these and make whatever modifications you feel are required. Overall integration of the allied contingents with our forces is your responsibility."

Lin nodded acknowledgement, his face blank. He picked up the 'pad and began to scan the information on the screen. He glanced over briefly and saw that Wu was doing the same thing. My God, he thought, how did she put all of this together? On the 'pad in his hand was set forth the greatest land army ever assembled for an off-world operation. The table included most of the mobile assault forces of the South American Empire as well as contingents from both the Caliphate and Europa Federalis - tens of thousands of troops. After the allied contingents was a list including dozens of CAC units drawn from every colony or base within a reasonable transit distance to Epsilon Eridani IV.

Lin was about to question how so many troops were to be shipped to the Eridani system when he flipped to the next screen and saw a detailed manifest of transport assets. Troopships from four superpowers, plus list after list of civilian transport ships to be commandeered.

Li smiled as she saw his question answered before he could ask it. "You will note that we have completed a significant amount of prep work on securing sufficient transport. The actual assault force to take the planet will consist of approximately 10,000 troops. The rest are being sent as part of our overall plan to trap General Holm." She paused, waiting for them to look up from the 'pads and pay attention. "The Alliance will do anything to take back Epsilon Eridani IV. Most of our fleet will withdraw to the outer reaches of the system and go dark, waiting." She saw that she had the complete attention of her guests. "General Holm is the natural choice to mount an assault to retake the planet. We want him to land. We will leave a small naval contingent near the planet to put up a cursory resistance. This force is largely sacrificial. They must be defeated for the plan to proceed."

Wu continued to listen, untroubled by what Li had said. Admiral Lin looked less happy, and while he had sent thousands to their deaths in battle, he didn't like the way she was casually using CAC warships as bait. Still, he remained silent and listened.

"If our counter-intelligence efforts are successful, General Holm will have no idea that he will be facing almost 100,000 troops. Most of this force will be landed after we secure the planet and kept hidden in reserve. The planet has significant heavy metal deposits, and troops deployed in and around the primary mountain ranges will be undetectable from orbit. When General Holm has landed along with the bulk of his forces, we will commit the entire army to a full scale battle of attrition. Simultaneously, our hidden fleet units will move back in-system to engage and destroy the Alliance naval forces, while Holm is overwhelmed and crushed on the ground.

Lin and Wu just sat in stunned silence. The scope of Li's plan was shocking, yet they could see the potential. The operation would not only eliminate General Holm, it would inflict enormous land and naval losses on the Alliance, especially if Liang was also successful in his attack. Combined with the entry of the empire and Europa Federalis into the war, the operation could be the climactic battle. It could swing the fortunes of the CAC from near-defeat to total victory.

There was just one thing bothering Lin. "Your plan is impressive, Minister Li. You are to be congratulated. However, the entire plan is dependent upon the Alliance reacting immediately and committing everything they can to retake the planet. How can you know they will respond so aggressively? While it is well within their sphere, the planet is unremarkable."

She stared right into Lin's eyes. "Now I would like you both to review the contents of that data chip. It is time you knew the secret of Epsilon Eridani IV."

Chapter 6

Classified Excavation Site Z
Epsilon Eridani IV

Alex picked her way through the rubble-strewn excavation site and brushed the reddish dirt from her fatigues. Things had been going even more slowly than she had feared. Someone was going to pay for dragging her out to this forsaken dustball.

The site was beyond just classified; no other secret she knew of had ever been so carefully guarded as this one. That made it hard to move things quickly. The workers were expendable at least; they didn't realize it of course, but none of them were ever going to leave Carson's World. But the supervisory personnel had to be drawn from the highest levels of Alliance Intelligence, and there wasn't a big cross-section between that group and excavation experience. Not beyond burying bodies, at least.

She was having trouble getting equipment here too. She wasn't used to dealing with such mundane problems - a member of the Directorate pretty much had a blank check. But this was specialized equipment, and you couldn't buy too much of it too quickly without drawing unwanted attention.

Her cover was Christine Cole, an engineer and trouble-shooter brought in to expedite the operation. She had revamped the procedure and reviewed every aspect of the timetable. She'd promised Number One that the first shipment would leave in six months. It had taken her almost one of those months just to get here. She started making changes immediately, adding two additional hours to each shift, and shaking up the supervisory staff. They'll grumble, she thought, but what are they going to do about it? She was going to keep to her schedule whatever it took. Even if she had to stay here for the next five months and manage the operation herself. This was the most important op anywhere in human-occupied space. If she could pull this off, she'd be the odds on favorite to replace Number Two when the old man finally realized how ancient he was and died.

This planet had been full of miners, she thought wistfully. Once we'd decided to eliminate them, we should have gotten some work out of them first. They would, of course, have done that, except for the damned Marine garrison. And the only way to get rid of them was the epidemic that killed all the miners. They'd blamed that on some local pathogen, but if it got out that it was a GX-11 variant, people would go crazy. GX-11 was manmade, just one more hellish invention from the Unification Wars. Though the Directorate's new strain was new and improved and a lot more controllable than the original.

Now, courtesy of the virus there was no one on Carson's World but her and her people. The planet was safe, even to the unvaccinated. GX-11 couldn't live without a host, and all of the carriers on the planet were dead. Nevertheless, it would be regarded as a plague planet for some time which, she thought, would probably prove useful.

I wonder who Carson was, she pondered. Guy named this whole planet after himself, but I bet he had no idea what he really had here hidden below the surface. She wondered how many third or fourth generation Carsons were among the eleven thousand civilians she'd killed to keep this planet's secret.

She thought about her meeting with Number One before she'd left Earth. Not the Directorate conference, the one in her bed the next night. They'd discussed some interesting things. Alex preferred to deal with Number One on as close to her own terms as she could manage, which was usually her naked and on top. She knew her charms and just how far she could go with them. Most men - and a lot of women too - would do just about anything for her. But Gavin Stark was different. She could push him only so far, and she knew, if it served his purpose, he'd snap her neck without a second thought. He'd miss her; they were good together, and some of the things she did to him he'd find hard to replace. But he'd never let that get in the way of his best interests.

She laughed softly. They were all so scared of Andres Carillon, mostly because he was so creepy. But Stark was far more dangerous. Brilliant, ruthless, soulless. If Alex knew one thing, she knew how to pick her allies. It pissed off Carillon when she rebuffed his advances, but he'd never dare give her a problem. Not while she was allied with Stark.

She found it hard to believe what he had told her. My sister, she thought, could she really still be alive? When Stark first brought it up, she'd had a momentary flash of excitement. Her family had been gone for a long time...she tried to picture her sister's face, to wonder what it would be like to have family again.

But then the anger came back. Alex had been eight years old when her sister was offered a place as a concubine for the son of a very highly placed politician. If she'd have gone along with it, the whole family would probably have benefited. But she refused, and they all suffered. Worse, after the hired thugs came and took her despite her refusal, she managed to kill her admirer and escape. When they couldn't find her, they came after her family. Their parents were questioned with very aggressive methods and, when it was obvious they didn't know where their renegade daughter was, they were expelled from Manhattan into the crumbling slums across the river west of the city.

Her parents were broken by the torture they had suffered while in custody, and her mother died within a few months. Her father hung on, desperately trying to protect her, stealing food, finding shelter. Somehow he survived for three years before he too died, and Alex was alone. She'd repressed all of those memories, but now they came flooding back. Life was not easy in that urban hell for an eleven year old girl on her own. She was no one's weakling, but even she couldn't bear to think of what she'd had to do to survive. She thought bitterly, all the people who think I am such a rock hard bitch should live through what I did...do the things I had to do.

She hated to show any weakness, but she'd lost her composure that night with Stark, and she was angry with herself for the lapse in her iron control. She couldn't imagine how pleased he was with himself...to have found the chink in the ice queen's armor.

"So, sister dear...we may meet again." She spoke softly to herself, her words dripping bitterness and hatred. "If you'd just spread your legs for that pig, mother and father would still be alive. And I wouldn't be what I have become. What you made me."

Alex woke up to the frantic buzzing sound of her com. "What is going on?" She was groggy and irritable, but her mind was still sharp.

"We have received a transmission from the garrison task force. Enemy ships transiting into the system from YZ Ceti. No data yet on numbers or breakdowns."

YZ Ceti was an Alliance-held system. A backwater with no real garrison, but not the place she'd expected an invasion to come from. She hadn't expected an invasion at all.

But Alex was not one to ignore reality because it seemed implausible. If the enemy was here it was because they were after the same thing she was here for. And they knew as well as she did the strength of the defending fleet. If they didn't have the force to beat it, they wouldn't be here.

She barked at her AI while she hurriedly dressed. "Get me Colonel Evander. Now!" Evander was the commander of the new garrison of Directorate troops. *Your men are going to get their test, Colonel,* she thought. She hoped they were up to it, but she doubted it.

"Evander here." His voice was tinny on the com, impatient.

"Colonel, I need to discuss the dispositions of your troops as soon as possible."

His response was arrogant and dismissive. "I do not take orders from an engineer. You are not to disturb me again."

"Colonel!" He had been about to cut the line, but her voice had become commanding and bone-chillingly icy. He hesitated while she continued. "I have come from the undiscovered country from whose bourn no traveler returns." She had to force back a smile as she uttered the code that identified her to him as a member of the Directorate.

"Ah...my apologies, Director." His voice was high-pitched and cracking with fear. "I beg your forgiveness, Director." She was silent, enjoying the man's squirming. "I am at your command, of course."

She let him sweat a few more seconds and then said, "Be at operational headquarters in 30 minutes, ready to give me a full briefing." She cut the line without waiting for his response. Pompous ass. She hated these Political Academy bottom-feeders. The ones with real power were bad enough, but this guy's father was probably a magistrate in New Wichita.

She sat on the edge of the bed and sighed. This ass and his rookie soldiers are all we have here, thanks to the Directorate's decision to get rid of the Marines. They were well-trained, at least reasonably so...she knew that. But she also knew in her gut that if there were Janissaries or CAC stormtroopers on the way they would cut through Evander's newbies like a knife through butter.

She commed the excavation supervisor. We've got to get this stuff hidden back in the caves, she thought. The enemy's coming.

Admiral Josh Franklin sat in the control center of the AS Sheridan, reviewing incoming data on the enemy force now emerging into the system. There were sensors deployed near the warp gate, as there were near every active gate, and they flashed information back to the fleet at the speed of light. The enemy's escort vessels would try to destroy them all and blind the defenders, but the scanning devices were numerous, small and well protected by ECM.

As more ships transited into the system he began to realize he wasn't going to be able to hold them back. Sheridan was his only capital ship, and the enemy had at least five battlegroups, possibly with more to come. Normal doctrine called for an evacuation; the navy didn't usually throw away task forces in hopeless battles. But his orders were clear...hold at all costs.

He'd have to fight a close in defense, combining the ships and the planetary fortresses and defense satellites into his combat net. It would expose the planet to enemy attack, but there weren't even any colonists left down there, so Franklin wasn't concerned about it as he would be in a more populated system.

Maybe they could inflict enough damage to convince the enemy to withdraw. He knew better, but hopefully it would give his crews some hope. He intended to make the enemy pay dearly for the system.

"Starting to get capital ship IDs, Admiral." Lieutenant Commander Stone had just arrived a few weeks before, but Franklin already considered the communications officer indispensible.

"Feed it to me as you have it, commander." Unless these were new ships, the battle computer would have a complete breakdown on armaments and capabilities. He needed to figure out any weaknesses as soon as possible.

"Admiral..." Stone paused, staring at his screen in startled disbelief. "Three of the capital ships have been identified as the Bolivar, the Emperador, and the Caracas." He turned to face the admiral. "The South Americans are here in force, sir."

Franklin nodded acknowledgement. He wasn't surprised the empire had finally jumped into the war, but he couldn't understand why they were here in Epsilon Eridani. He didn't even know why he and his ships were here. Carson's World was the only useful planet in the system and, while it had been a fairly rich mining colony before the epidemic, it was nothing that rated a reinforced battlegroup permanently stationed in defense.

"Admiral!" Franklin could hear the surprise in Stone's voice. "A sixth capital ship has transited. Scanners indicate it is the Prince de Conde."

Franklin swore quietly, under his breath. "Europa Federalis? So we've got two new enemies." But he couldn't get the thought out of his head...why are they here? "Commander, we need to get this data to Fleet Command. I assume the interstellar net to YZ Ceti has been cut." Epsilon Eridani had only two warp gates, and the second one led down a dead end path. His mind raced - how am I going to get a report through?

"Affirmative, sir." Stone turned to face the Admiral. "The relay station broadcast Code Z protocols before transmission ceased." Code Z meant the imminent destruction of a ship or station that was beyond hope of saving or even abandoning.

The interstellar transmission system consists of a network

of small stations positioned as closely as practical to each warp gate. Communications are flashed at lightspeed within the system, so a transmission reaches the station in a matter of hours or minutes. Messages are then downloaded into a robot drone and sent through the warp gate. Once the drone has transited to the destination system, the messages are transmitted to and from the station on the other side before the robot ship reenters the gate and returns. Priority messages can travel at an effective speed of 4-12 hours per system.

"I want twenty priority dispatch drones launched, full ECM suites." The drones would take AI-generated evasive paths around the enemy fleet, attempting to transit to YZ Ceti. The onboard AIs would then determine the best way to get their messages through - most likely through the warp gate to Kruger 60, which was the most secure route through Alliance-held space. As soon as a confirmed Alliance vessel or facility was identified, the encrypted priority message would be transmitted. The drones were large, sophisticated pieces of equipment, and Franklin was expending all of his in the hope that at least one would get through. He figured the odds at 50-50.

"Acknowledged sir." Stone barked orders into his com, then worked the controls at his board. "Drone programming sequence underway. We can begin launches in four minutes."

Franklin nodded. "All drones are to be launched when ready." He looked down at his screen. "Send data from the warp gate scanners to my console. And get a schematic of the enemy fleet dispositions as soon as we have it...up on the main screen."

"Yes sir." Stone's fingers flew over the keyboard. He could have told the AI what to do, but Stone was old school, and preferred to enter his data manually. "Warp gate data coming to your console now, sir. Initial projection on enemy fleet formation in..." He paused to listen to something on his earpiece. "... two minutes, thirty seconds."

Franklin glanced down at the data now coming to his screen. The enemy had come in slow, so they'd have to build velocity to traverse the distance to Carson's World. The warp gate was not a distant one, much closer to the primary than most, but it would still take at least two days for the enemy to reach the planet.

"Hal, prepare a course to bring the fleet into supporting position of the Carson's World defenses." Franklin typically relayed orders to Stone; it was more formal to go through a subordinate officer, and the admiral was a bit of a martinet. But Stone was busy working on the enemy fleet projections, so he went right to his AI.

"Yes, Admiral Franklin." The machine's reply was cold, unemotional - something Franklin liked. The fact that he'd named the thing after a fictional insane computer from ancient literature was an odd concession to humor from an officer who was known, with some affection and some grumbling, as "Ramrod" among his crews. "Course prepared, Admiral. Estimated time to arrival and full task force deployment 7 hours, 40 minutes."

Franklin looked up from his console, to the main screen where Stone was just starting to display projected enemy fleet dispositions. "Transmit instructions to all ships. Execute in two hours."

"Yes, Admiral Franklin. Displaying countdown to maneuver on secondary chronometers."

"Commander Stone, schedule a video conference with the ship captains in 30 minutes. I will address the fleet in one hour."

"Yes, admiral."

Franklin stared up at the screen as formation after formation was added to the enemy force. Yes, he thought, I will address the fleet. But what will I say? How will I tell them they're all going to die in four days?

Chapter 7

Space Station Tarawa
Gliese 250 System

The aftermath of battle was in and around the mammoth space station. Damaged ships, floating debris, the twisted, irradiated wreckage of entire sections of the station itself. And of course, people.

My people, Garret thought grimly as he walked down the corridor from the station's main med facility. They looked to me to lead them. They died following my orders. They were wounded, broken, and burned manning the positions I gave them.

They were hailing Garret a hero, saying he'd covered himself in glory and won the greatest victory in interstellar history. One day I wish I could feel the glory, he thought, but all I ever see is its terrible cost. If only they knew how much I hate this.

People tend to think combat in space is somehow cleaner, less brutal than its messy ground-based cousin. But Garret's ships had been buffeted by massive thermonuclear barrages, multi-megaton warheads detonating all around. A direct hit meant death, even for the largest ship, but most of the missiles were near misses, miniature suns exploding a few kilometers away. Ships were ripped apart piece by piece from the shockwaves and armor-plated hulls melted from the atomic infernos.

Men and women operated these ships, and their bodies, not being made of reinforced plasti-steel or high-density ceramic armor, were not built to withstand such forces. Crews from outer compartments were sometimes exposed to radiation so intense the victims could actually feel it, a strange tingling sensation that meant imminent death. Others were crushed under collapsing structural members or seared by the extreme heat of nearby nuclear explosions. Their pressure suits helped a little, but you couldn't operate a space ship wearing Marine power armor, so the protection was limited.

The corridor was dimly lit; the station had taken heavy damage in the final stages of the battle, and one of the reactors had been scragged. Garret had ordered strict conservation measures for all non-essential functions. And for now, essential meant medical, damage control, and prep work for getting his task force ready to leave for Columbia. A few high-ranking functionaries who'd been caught on the station complained about the inconvenience, but Garret had told them not only to go fuck themselves, but specifically how to do it. One persistent gasbag had harassed him so much he'd almost ordered one of his officers to draw a diagram of the anatomically challenging suggestion he offered the self-important fop.

The Admiral spent a lot of time in the med centers and sick bays after a battle. He considered it a core part of his duty, and no crisis, no VIP, no pressing project would keep him from it. He would make the time to pay his wounded their due and to personally insure they were getting the best care possible - they deserved nothing less.

The battle had been a hard one, and it had taken days to reassemble the fleet and organize care for the wounded. Men and women died on heavily damaged ships, waiting to be transferred to vessels with functioning med facilities. Damage control parties worked throughout the fleet, slowly beginning the process of recovery.

There had almost been another fight after the battle. The enemy had fled back through the warp gate, but the cruisers of their first wave were far in-system, still decelerating when the retreat orders were given. By the time they had started back toward the warp gate, Garret's forces were already there, having pursued the retreating enemy battleline. The taskforce commander tried to negotiate terms, offering to transit back to Alpha Cephei without further hostilities, but Garret would accept only unconditional surrender. For a few minutes it looked as if the fleets would engage, but the enemy commander blinked first, and 14 cruisers surrendered. No enemy vessels remained at large in the system, save two.

On the far side of the primary, two CAC cruisers hurtled into deep space, beyond detection range. Their engines destroyed, they were unable to decelerate; their communications knocked out, they couldn't call for help. Spacefarers had few fears more intense than ending up on one of these "ghost ships," a prison first then, when the life support finally fails, a tomb. No one knew just how many missing ships from man's wars in space were hurtling into unexplored darkness, their frozen crews transfixed at their posts.

But now was not the time for introspection; Garret had other work to do. The fleet had been hard hit, but things could have been much worse. Most of the ships had taken serious damage, and putting together a scratch force that could depart in seven days was proving to be difficult. He stepped into the lift, shifting ships on and off his mental list as he barked at the AI to take him to the control center. The lift was operating at reduced speed, victim of his own power management orders, and he was impatient to get back to work.

"Status report on the Cambrai?" Stepping off the lift, he snapped out the inquiry without preamble.

"Captain Arlington advises she will be ready to depart in ten days." Lieutenant Simon had transferred over to the station along with the boss, and she cringed as she passed on Arlington's report. She'd been with Garret long enough to know what he was going to say.

"Unacceptable. Advise Arlington that she has five days. On day six she will be ready to maneuver into formation for departure."

"Yes sir." Simon really hoped Captain Arlington didn't argue. She'd seen the results of that before, too.

"Other reports?" Garret dropped hard into the command chair. They were on the station, not on the ship, so he'd discarded the pressure suit for a set of well-worn duty fatigues.

"The Cromwell will be ready in 24 hours. Captain Charles reports he'll have all main systems at 95% or greater operational proficiency by then." Byron Charles had been Garret's flag captain for five years; twice he'd turned down promotions to flag rank to stay and command the Cromwell for the admiral. "The

Saratoga will be ready in one day as well, though Captain Krill advises that the landing bays will still be non-operational until she can get the ship to a space dock." The Saratoga was one of the big new Yorktown Class monsters, the only one with light enough damage to make Garret's tight departure schedule.

It's not like we've got the fighters anyway, Garret thought bitterly. Only 20% of the fleet's fighter-bombers had made it back in the end, though their daring attack had played a huge role in the victory. He couldn't understand why the survivors didn't hate him, but they knew how desperate the situation was, and they were aware just how much their sacrifice had bought.

He hated to abandon the more seriously damaged ships of his battered fleet to someone else's command, but he doubted the enemy would be back soon, and he had promised to return and complete Operation Sherman. Garret had forged a kin-ship with General Holm, and they both agreed that their people had been under occupation long enough. He too had seen the reports, the images...he'd even met some of the survivors. He simply could not allow those types of atrocities to continue a day longer if he could do something about it. The force he was taking to Columbia included every decently functional ship in the fleet - three capital ships plus cruisers and escorts. They were depleted and low on missiles and other supplies, but Garret had sent his instructions ahead; the supply ships would meet his force at Columbia. Normally he could refit at the base at 12 Ophiuchi, but that facility had been stripped bare to support his defense of Gliese.

The trip to Columbia was fairly long, with five transits and several long cross-system legs in between. Just one of those systems had warp gates leading to enemy possessions, but he intended to be cautious; the task force was in no condition to fight, not until he could resupply.

Lieutenant Simon sent the updated order of battle for the task force to his console. He'd be light on cruisers, which he didn't like. The enemy had stripped their battlegroups of their cruisers to assemble their first attack wave, but the loss of heavier supporting firepower proved decisive when the battle-

lines fought it out. He didn't like the idea of exposing himself
to turnabout, but he only had two cruisers in good enough repair
to make the trip. So two would have to be enough. Otherwise,
the OB looked good, or at least as good as it was going to get, so
he pressed his thumb against the reader on his command chair,
approving the document. He sent it back to Simon so she could
get started relaying orders to the ships of the force.

Garret's mind had wandered back to the med center, to the
wounded and the dying - though most of the ones that had gotten there still alive would make it no matter how badly they were
wounded. They might have a long recovery, but once they got
help their chances were good. How many died at their posts,
unable to get medical attention in time he didn't know. Simon's
voice finally brought him out of his trance.

"Sir?" She paused. Simon was a very proper officer, and she
disliked addressing the admiral other than to respond to him or
provide him with information. But she knew he'd been up for
days. "I am starting to worry about you. It has been several days
since you slept."

Garret smiled. Technically, she was being insubordinate, but
he knew she was genuinely concerned. Ah, my dear Jen, he
thought, if only you knew how very long it has been since I truly
slept. "There will be time for sleeping later, Jen." He hoped his
voice was sympathetic and appreciative; she was a good kid. He
poked at the small screen adjacent to his command chair. "For
now, I'd like the updated repair schedules for the station. I want
the defense grid up and running before we leave and take half
the fleet's remaining firepower with us."

There will be time, Jen, he thought...time enough for sleep
when our work is done.

The fleet decelerated hard as it approached the warp gate
to 12 Ophiuchi. They'd had a long trip across the Gliese system - the Ophiuchi gate was well on the far side of the Gliese
primary - so they'd accelerated halfway at 8g to build velocity,
then decelerated most of the rest of the way. They were going
through the gate slowly; they had a hard course change right

after the jump, so any velocity would have worked against them once they were in the 12 Ophiuchi system.

Garret had done his best to put together a fleet on an impossible timetable. No task force had ever set out for a campaign less than two weeks after fighting a major battle. His ships were battered - there was no way to repair all of the battle damage so quickly, not even to the most lightly hit ships. Only a few ships had missiles, and they only had a tithe of their normal supply. Garret had left most of the paltry supply of missiles, and all of the fighter-bombers, with the remaining fleet units. These vessels, mostly the ones too battered to leave with the departing task force, would have to defend the Gliese system in the unlikely event the enemy was able to mount a new offensive, and Garret wanted them as ready as they could be. Just in case.

He felt the feeling of relief as the deceleration abruptly slowed to 1g. At 8g, the crew really couldn't do much except stay in their couches and try to breath. The ships' AIs did all the work. But now the crews sprang back into action and none quicker than Jennifer Simon. "Lead vessel insertion in 90 seconds, sir."

"Very well." Garret voice was hoarse. He was tired, bone tired. After the jump was done and the course to the next gate was set, he'd grab a couple hours of sleep. Or at least lying on his bunk; sleep was a more problematic project. The warp gate from 12 Ophiuchi to HD82943 was not far from their entry point, so they wouldn't be maneuvering at more than 2g. That gave him a fighting chance to at least doze off for a while.

The fleet deployment was standard for an unopposed warp gate transit. The first vessels through would be escorts, mostly fast attack ships, followed by the heavier escorts and then the capital ships. In an assault situation, a screen of escorts would go in first, followed immediately by cruisers to give the forming line some firepower. The battle groups would then come through in formation, minus those elements detached for the initial wave.

Garret had lost count of how many transits he had made, though his AI could have reminded him it was 373. They all felt the same, not painful exactly, but not pleasant either. Civilians and first-timers usually found the experience very unsettling, but to veteran spacers it was a minor annoyance.

Though utilized for over 100 years, warp gates are an occurrence only partially explained by 23rd century physics. The gate itself forms around a naked singularity, a phenomenon the existence of which was only theorized until an unmanned British space probe passed through one of the Sol system's two transit points and initiated the age of interstellar exploration.

Warp gates generate gravity waves, very slight under normal circumstances, but building as successive transits are made. One or two ships going through need only move into the transit horizon, which ranges from 30-300 kilometers in known gates, and they emerge into the connecting system, with their exact entry velocity and mirrored vectors.

However a task force or large fleet moving through a gate generates increasing gravity waves, which not only cause considerable turbulence, but also require the application of thrust to counter the effect and maintain the formation. The calculations involved are enormously complex and left to the ships' AIs.

Normally, a warp gate gives off no detectable energy. However, as multiple transits are made, the space around the transit horizon emits a faint blue glow. By the time Cromwell was entering the gate, the halo was visible to the naked eye - if you knew just where to look. Garret had the projection up on the main display; he considered it one of space's rarest and most beautiful images. Warp gates had opened the universe to man's exploration and colonization. Of course, he thought, we turned them into a new way to wage war.

He felt the tingling, not quite an electric shock, but close. The nausea was a passing feeling for a grizzled spacehound like him, though rookies were frequently incapacitated the first few times they experienced it. Then the flash, which seemed to come from inside his head and, when his vision recovered, the fringe of the 12 Ophiuchi system was laid out before him, the distant primary no brighter than the full moon in Earth's night sky.

It did take time to traverse the gate itself, and the time increased with the distance between systems. The nanoseconds involved were imperceptible to the human mind; indeed, it was some years before the computers on transiting ships were able to measure the miniscule time expended.

Garret had never become jaded about the miracle of the warp gate. In an infinitesimal fraction of a second, his ship had traveled 13.9 light years. If he were to find Gliese 250 twinkling in the inky blackness he would be seeing light that left almost 14 years before. His own ships, state of the art human technology that they were, would have taken over a century to make the trip conventionally.

Once the last of the ships flashed into existence and the fleet's course was set for the next gate, Garret rose and walked toward the lift. "Lieutenant Simon, notify me if anything requires my attention."

"Yes sir."

Garret smiled. She's glad I'm going to get some rest. He was still thinking about what a wonder the warp gates truly were as the doors closed and the car began to move. He was amused that with all he had seen, with all he had done, he could still be amazed by anything. He was grateful for that.

Chapter 8

Western Alliance Intelligence Directorate HQ
Wash-Balt Metroplex, Earth

Stark held his glass up to the light, admiring the caramel color of the fine single malt scotch. Luxuries like this were available to a privileged few, and he was glad to be one of those. The Cogs were animals to him, necessary labor to do the dirty, dangerous, and unpleasant jobs perhaps, but nothing more. Poorly paid and completely replaceable people could do some jobs cheaper than machines. He considered that an interesting anomaly in a technologically advanced society.

The middle classes, gutless, joyless, clinging in fear to their meager existences, were beneath his contempt. The Cogs, at least, were uneducated and knew no better. But those in the middle, living in places like Manhattan's Protected Zone and the WashBalt Core, they had no excuse. They'd been given just a taste of a decent life by their political masters, and they were so ruled by fear of losing it they did what they were told without question.

It had been Stark's biggest surprise as he rose in the intelligence community that maintaining internal security had proved to be a minor task. Of course there were troublemakers - that's what those rooms down in Sub-Sector C were for, but there were remarkably few.

In space, of course, the opposite was true. The colonies, full of troublesome types, seethed with discontent, and they resisted every effort by Alliance Gov to tighten the leash. The scope and ferocity of the war had put those problems on hold - neither Alliance Gov nor the colonies themselves wanted the Caliphate or CAC to end up controlling the frontier. But he knew the problem was still there, waiting to re-emerge once the war was over.

He felt he could control the colonists because he understood them; he comprehended them in a way most of his associates

never could. Gavin Stark had the arrogance of a man born
into power, but he had not been. Most of the other members
of the Directorate had their spots in the Political Class through
accidents of birth. Places in the Academy were their birthrights,
and they were assured of high positions in their careers. But
Stark's path had been a different one, far more difficult and less
common.

He'd been born into the lowest strata of the middle classes,
and he was only a clerical worker when he began his career. But
random fortune had placed him on the junior staff of a powerful politician. In his youthful optimism, he'd hoped the Senator
would mentor him, but the one time he'd approached the great
man all he'd gotten was a beating from the bodyguards...a lesson
in learning his place in the social order.

But espionage was in Stark's blood and, not content to
meekly accept his place along among the sheep, he set about to
find another way. That way turned out to be evidence of the
Senator's graft, which was so vast in scope it exceeded even the
considerable level of corruption that was a de facto perk of his
position. The Senator had stolen from general funds, of course
– they all did that. But he'd also stolen from other politicians,
including a few even more powerful than he was. Stark didn't
hesitate to blackmail the man, and the second time he spoke
with the Senator, things turned out quite a bit differently. Stark
was granted admission to the WashBalt Political Academy, the
first of many "favors" he would enjoy from his new political
sponsor.

Eventually, the Senator exhausted his usefulness, and Stark
was never one to leave a loose end he could tie up. His unwilling
benefactor ended up in Sub-Sector C, never quite understanding how it had happened. And the Senator's replacement owed
Stark a big favor for clearing his way to the newly vacant Seat.

"Mind if I interrupt this daydream?" The old man stood in
the doorway. Jack Dutton was Number Two at Alliance Intelligence. Indeed, he could have had Stark's job but, old and tired,
he'd deferred to his protégé instead. Dutton was the consum-
mate professional, with a lifetime spent as a spy, but he no lon-

ger had the drive and killer instinct he saw in his younger ally. He was content to remain Number Two and deflect the burdens of the top job to Stark.

Stark looked up and smiled. The old man was his only real friend - or the closest thing to a friend a reptile like him could have. "Please. The diversion would be welcome. Quiet introspection is overrated." He motioned to the credenza along the wall. "Have some of the single malt. It's top notch."

"Have you read the intel on Li An's plot to take out Admiral Garret?" Dutton walked slowly over to the side table and poured himself a drink. "She's got Liang Chang so scared shitless he may just pull it off out of sheer desperation."

"Yes, her plan is interesting." He took another sip from his Scotch and put the glass down. "I'm a bit concerned about how much intel she seems to be getting from Alliance sources. I'm going to have to take a closer look at the Directorate."

Dutton dropped tiredly into one of the soft leather guest chairs. "Yes, she does seem to have a fair number of sources... certainly more than the ones we feed her intentionally." He rubbed his forehead. "I've been tangling with that miserable bitch since before you started your climb up Senator Harper's back." He took a drink then looked at the heavy cut crystal glass approvingly. "You're right. It is excellent."

"I'll send you a case. Let's call it a birthday present. I never have been able to uncover when you were born...assuming you were born and not hatched or something. Sometimes I think you've just always been here." He looked up with a wicked grin. "I guess the records don't go back that far."

Dutton laughed and took another drink. "So what do you want to do about Li An's ambush of Admiral Garret? Change his route? Or hit Liang with another force?"

Stark paused. "I was thinking about doing nothing."

Dutton wasn't surprised by much, but he wasn't expecting that response. "Liang's got a good chance to succeed if we don't intervene. Garret's ships are depleted; we stripped the base at 12 Ophiuchi to supply his fleet in Gliese. He won't be combat ready until he gets to Columbia and resupplies. And Liang will target everything on Cromwell. He's terrified of ending up in one of Li's little rooms if he fails."

Stark just sat silently, leaning back in his chair. Dutton's eyes widened in realization. "You want to get rid of Garret?"

"Just a thought." He gave Dutton a hard stare. "We both know we're going to have to do something about him sooner or later. This last victory has made him almost a legend. He owns the navy...none of them will refuse him anything. Can we really trust a guy with so much power?"

Dutton looked concerned. "You know I agree with that generally, but the war isn't over yet. Li wants Garret dead precisely because she doesn't think they can win as long as we have him. Do we really want to give that up?"

"Yes, I know what Li is thinking. But I have my own set of scenarios. Tell me what you think of this. We send a rescue force to intercept Liang, but we make sure they don't get there until after he has engaged Garret's ships. Liang probably takes out the Cromwell and kills Garret, but we both know that depleted or not, the admiral's going to go down fighting. Liang's going to take losses, probably heavy ones. Wouldn't that be an amusing time for our rescue force to burst onto the scene, just in time to avenge their beloved admiral?"

Dutton's face brightened slightly. "We'd take out a huge portion of the rest of the CAC fleet." He smiled. "And if Garret manages to fight his way out, it still looks like we backed him up and sent him help. Either way, Liang would still be hit by both forces."

Stark was leaning back in his chair with a self-satisfied smile on his face. "So? What does the old master think?"

Dutton paused, thinking. "I like it. Or rather, I want to like it. But I'm still a bit concerned about the prosecution of the war. If things go as planned, the CAC will be in bad shape for a while, but we still have to deal with the Caliphate. And you know the South Americans are going to be a factor too. We had a good run with General Santiago and his sabotaging their supply net, but now we're going to have to fight them. And it's not like we haven't suffered losses too. None of them have anyone who can face Garret, but without him, who knows? The odds are still too even to risk our big advantage."

"You are, of course, familiar with our classified shipyards in the Wolf 359 system?

"Of course." Dutton nodded quizzically.

"What would you say if I told you I'd used some, shall we say, aggressive management tactics to encourage productivity?"

Dutton snorted a short laugh. "I'd say it sounded like you."

"Then what would you say if I told you the four Yorktowns under construction there will be ready to launch in 30 days and not a year?"

The old man look startled. "What did you do? Roast them over a fire?"

"Not too many of them." Stark grinned. "Just one, really. I needed the shipyard CEO to resign so I could quietly replace him. We discussed it down in Sub-Sector C. He whined a lot at first, but by the time we were done I think he understood my point. Too bad he died in a yachting accident right after he stepped down."

"That was us?" Dutton looked a little annoyed. "You didn't tell me anything about this op."

Stark sighed. "Look, Jack. I didn't mean to cut you out, but we need those ships, and I know you're a little soft on these political and corporate types."

"Gavin, you need to be careful." Dutton looked at the younger man with concern. "These are powerful people. You can't treat them like Cogs. They have certain rights under our syst..."

Stark put up his hand. "Relax, Jack. I haven't declared war on the political class; I just do my job. We need those ships, and to get them we needed someone kicking ass over there, not some inbred corporate magnate who thinks he has a birthright to take up space. The fat fuck was sitting in a suite at the Willard with three female acquaintances when my men picked him up. So what the hell was he doing in WashBalt when he was supposed to be out at Wolf 359 managing a vital 500 billion credit war contract?"

Dutton sighed. "Fool. Do they think this war will win itself? And you replaced him with?"

Gavin knew where the old man was going with this. "He's someone I found. Someone with more to gain than the imbecile he replaced."

"I know you're ambitious, Gavin." Dutton leaned forward and looked at his companion intently. "Be careful. Don't make too many powerful enemies. The Political Class is protective of its position. If it got out that you'd disposed of a high-ranking Corporate to replace him with a nobody - and that's how they will see it - there's going to be hell to pay."

Stark smiled. "Don't worry, my friend. I may have come from the wrong crowd, but I'm no crusader. I don't care where someone comes from if they serve my purpose. But we need those ships, and now we've got them. And Garret already arranged for field repairs and conversions on all the captured CAC and Caliphate ships in Gliese. For the first time in the war, we've got the clear advantage."

"Which means we don't need Garret anymore?" Dutton looked grim, unsure.

"It means we can do without him." Stark's voice was superficially decisive, but Dutton knew him well enough to sense the uncertainty. He was gambling. "If Li An and Admiral Liang want to rid us of Garret and serve us up most of the rest of the CAC fleet in the process, I think we need to let her." He paused. "I know Garret would be helpful in winning the war, but do we really want him to have even more stature? What would a few more victories do? You know we're going to have problems with the colonies after the war. Have you considered what would happen if Garret sided with them?"

Dutton swallowed the last of his Scotch and got up to refill his glass. "The whole navy might follow him. Or at least a good part of it." He paused, his glass in one hand, the crystal flask in the other. "It's dangerous either way."

"War is dangerous business. But we need to make decisions based on logic and strength, not fear." His eyes narrowed and he looked right at Dutton. "But I want you with me on this. If you don't agree, I'll scrub my plan and we'll warn Garret and change his flight plan."

Dutton paused, making a soft noise as he blew air out his mouth. "I'm with you. If you think it's the right move, I'm behind you." He paused again, started to say something, and then stopped, putting the flask down on the table.

"What is it?"

The old man sighed again. "I'm just worried that Li An's got something else up her sleeve. Something we're missing. She's a tough adversary. Don't underestimate her, Gavin."

Stark leaned forward. "I know." He continued with a touch of uncertainty. "But we don't have any intel on anything else. If she's got something coming, she's done a hell of a job keeping it under wraps."

The two were silent for a minute. Finally Stark spoke. "So what do you say? What's your final opinion?"

Dutton put the newly filled glass to his lips and drained it in one gulp. "Do it."

Chapter 9

AS Cromwell
Flagship, Task Force Tecumseh
AD Leonis System, en Route to TZ Arietis Warp Gate

"What the hell are they doing here?" Garret scolded himself
for the surprised outburst. Normally he was very circumspect
in front of his crews. "I want full data as soon as possible, Lieutenant Simon."

"Yes, sir." Simon's voice was strained. They hadn't expected
to encounter any enemy presence here, two transits deep in Alliance space. They are definitely CAC scanner buoys, sir. We've
picked up two of them so far. Already transmitting." A brief
pause. "I may have a third....and a fourth. They seem to be
deployed in their standard pattern"

"Very well." Garret's mind was racing - why are there CAC
forces in this system? "Let's get the computer working on projected fleet locations based on buoy patterns. They know where
we are; we need to know where they are."

"Admiral, we have located eight total scanners. The buoy
distribution strongly suggests they were expecting a transit from
our entry warp gate." Lieutenant Commander Barton was one
of Garret's tactical analysts. Barton was the best at what she
did; she breathed, ate, and drank spatial patterns. "Computer
analysis confirms. Heaviest concentration appears to be along
vectors consistent with an anticipated target transiting from AB
Doradus on course for the TZ Arietis warp gate." She looked
up from the screens her eyes had been fixed on and over to Garret. "They knew we were coming. I'm sure of it, sir."

"Nelson, compute a course change for the fleet." Garret
paused for a few seconds, considering where to go. We can't
keep our original course, he thought, but what to do? "I want a
vector change toward the primary. Calculate a slingshot course
around AD Leonis to bring us back to the TZ Arietis gate at
high velocity." Instead of moving straight toward the exit warp

gate, Garret was going to head for the star, using its gravity to help his ships make an abrupt vector change back toward their destination. Hopefully the enemy, who was probably waiting along the direct route to the TZ Arietis warp gate, would think he was heading for another exit and try to pursue. At the very least, it would take his ships away from the course most likely seeded with enemy detection devices. They knew he was here, and they knew what he had, but he was damned if they were going to watch his every step.

Garret sat in his command chair, his face grim. He hated running from a fight, but his ships had almost no missiles - they'd be at a huge disadvantage in a battle until they could resupply. He also knew he was unlikely to get out of the system without a battle. In the end he had to get through the TZ Arietis warp gate, and the enemy knew that too. Hopefully they'd deployed well in-system, but if they were near the warp gate, none of his maneuvering would matter.

" Commander Barton, all ships are to launch probes. You are to assign search sectors to all vessels. I want to know where the enemy is, and I want to know now."

"Yes, sir." Barton leaned over her station, working out plotting solutions. The probes were small drones, equipped with massive thrust capability and sophisticated scanners. A solar system is a massive volume, and a spaceship, even a kilometer-long battleship, is infinitesimally small in that great empty vastness. Shipboard scanners had limited effective tracking range, depending on the power output of the vessels to be detected. If they were blasting at full thrust they could be located from a considerable distance, but if they were on low power, laying in wait, it was a different matter.

A defender typically utilizes a matrix of scanners pre-deployed around each warp gate, providing information on the composition of incoming forces. The attacker, lacking an equivalent data feed, relies on his intel on the system and the knowledge that a fixed target, such as an inhabited world, tends to compel the defensive forces to remain within a predictable range of locations. However in a situation like this, an ambush or a meeting engagement, knowledge of the enemy's where-abouts and force composition is a massive advantage. Garret had to assume his adversary knew where he was and what ships he had, while he had no idea what was waiting in the system.

"Probes launching now, sir." Barton's voice was a little har-ried; she had rushed to prepare the plotting solutions as quickly as possible. The tactical AIs prepared a starting point, and could mathematically calculate the most effective plan in a purely spa-tial sense. But there was intuition to this as well, and a skilled tactical officer could almost divine the location to search for an enemy in a way a computer could not. "All drones set for maximum thrust."

Garret glanced toward Barton. "Thank you, commander. You prepared that plot with commendable speed." Garret wasn't one who particularly craved praise, and he had to keep reminding himself that his staff, like most people, did. His team was a finely honed blade, and he wanted to keep them that way. "Report any contacts immediately." He leaned back, quietly staring at the main screen, currently displaying the schematic of this normally uninteresting system. Who the hell are you, he thought, and where are you lurking out there? And how did you know we would be here?

Liang sat in his own command chair considering his next moves. The data on Garret's forces matched the information Li An had provided him. He wondered how she had gotten such precise intel; her order of battle and timing had both been almost exact. Everything was perfect. Except Augustus Garret.

Liang had expected Garret to proceed on a straight line course to the TZ Arietis warp gate, but instead his forces had made an abrupt course change. "Garret is a sorcerer. How can he always know what is coming?" Liang spoke under his breath, for no one's ears but his own. He could feel the sweaty clamminess on the back of his neck. If Garret escaped, Liang knew he was finished. He wouldn't even be able to kill himself, because Li An would target her retribution on his family. God, that woman is evil, he thought. I must not fail.

He watched the final update on Garret's force as it moved out of range of his last scanner buoy. "I want the enemy's course adjustment analyzed immediately. Have the computer generate likely courses based on the observed data." Liang was a competent commander, but he completely lacked the intuition and gut instincts that made an admiral like Garret so formidable.

"Admiral Liang, sir." Commander Deng was Liang's operations officer. "Is it possible they are changing course for the 111 Tauri warp gate?"

Liang considered the idea. He could only assume that Garret had detected his scanner buoys and was reacting accordingly. Still, even if he knew there was a threat, he couldn't know what or where yet. Liang's forces were dark, sitting motionless 30 light minutes from Garret's presumed exit warp gate. There was no way he could have picked them up.

"111 Tauri is a dead end." Liang was skeptical. "If he is heading there he is planning to go dark and hide in the system." *That doesn't sound like Garret*, he thought. *If he goes in there we can blockade him at the warp gate, and he's got no way to resupply.* "I do not believe Admiral Garret will flee like that. He would be cut off with no means of resupply."

"He knows we cannot stay here indefinitely, sir." Deng's voice wavered slightly. He wasn't disagreeing with the admiral exactly, but he was pressing his point more aggressively than CAC officers usually did with such highly ranked officers. "He may feel he can outwait us."

Deng was a good officer, and Liang tended to take his advice seriously. But he just couldn't believe Garret was going to turn tail go dark in a dead end system. And it wasn't Deng who would end up being dissected by Li An's inquisitors. "No, Admiral Garret is not going to run and hide. One way or another, he is planning to go through the TZ Arietis gate. This is an evasive maneuver, and nothing more." He stood up and stared at the large viewscreen, which displayed the plot of Garret's ships as they left the range of the scanner buoys. "All ships are to power up immediately." He turned to face Deng. "Plot a course back to the TZ Arietis warp gate. I want the fleet to assume an intercept position directly in front of the gate. Prepare a spread of probes positioned out from the gate extending our detection range." I'm not taking your bait, Liang thought. You are still planning to go to TZ Arietis, and I'm going to be right here waiting for you.

"Dammit, they are getting smarter." Garret had intended to speak quietly to himself, though his words came out louder than he'd expected. The task force had used the gravity of the AD Leonis primary to slingshot around and change its vector, allowing it to approach the exit warp gate with far greater velocity than would otherwise have been possible. It was a complex maneuver for an entire fleet, and only Garret's crack team could have managed it. But in the end it was just a fancy way of rushing toward the warp gate right through anything that stood in the way.

The first spread of probes had found the enemy positioned along the straight line course Garret's force would have taken had they not stumbled on the enemy scanner buoys. They'd been sitting motionless on minimal power, so the probes missed them at first, but then they powered up and began to exert thrust. Suddenly, five of Garret's drones were transmitting a steady flow of information - location, force composition, thrust direction.

Garret now knew he faced a substantial CAC task force. The enemy outnumbered him, but not by so much that he'd run from the fight. If he had missiles and bombers that is, which he didn't. There was no way he could take on a superior force with almost no missiles. His ships would be ravaged by unanswered volleys before they were in energy weapon range. The only option was to race them to the warp gate. His slingshot maneuver had him coming in at a much greater velocity than the enemy, but he also had farther to go. It was going to be a close race, but he was going to lose it. He'd hoped the enemy commander would chase him in-system, but his adversary didn't take the bait.

Now he was going to have to go right through the CAC

force at high velocity and take whatever they dished out. The inevitable missile barrage was going to hurt, even more so because his ships were packed tightly together. At this velocity they were going to have a limited ability to quickly change vectors, and his formation was constrained by the need to insure that all his ships would pass through the transit horizon of the warp gate. Any ships that missed the gate would be left alone in the system and, presumably, hunted down and destroyed by the enemy fleet.

He was still troubled at the enemy presence in the system. There was no strategic reason for them to be here. He couldn't imagine how they could have known that his force was coming this way - his departure had been a closely guarded secret. All communications and travel to and from Gliese had been suspended to insure that his fleet would be well away before any leaks could occur.

"Sir, the enemy forces have reached their position. They have decelerated to nearly a dead stop, directly across our path to the warp gate." Simon's voice was tense and labored. They were all on edge, he knew...and it wasn't easy to speak at all with the g forces they were currently experiencing.

Garret was frustrated. He was accustomed to having the initiative in a combat situation, and his crews were used to it too. But this time he was most definitely reacting, choosing the least-bad strategy since there really weren't any good options.

"Understood, lieutenant." He took a deep breath and exhaled...not an easy thing to do at this level of acceleration. "All ships are to continue in accordance with the thrust plan." Garret had ordered the fleet AI to generate a plan to allow for maximum thrust until transit. All ships directly on a line for the warp gate would thrust full the entire time. Vessels further on the flanks of the formation would alter their thrust angles to reposition their vectors for warp gate insertion. They'd have a lot of ships going through very close to each other, but Garret didn't see any other options. As usual, none of this was by the "book," but he thought it was the best way to save his people.

"I want all ships on full defensive alert. All crews are to

focus on anti-missile defense." Even his heavy batteries would be targeted on incoming missiles. They weren't terribly effective for that kind of fire, but Garret wanted anything he could get. "Full damage control procedures." For the most part these orders were designed to make his people feel engaged. The fleet was accelerating at 10g, and the crews were pretty much stuck in their couches, uncomfortable and sluggish. But it helped if they felt they were accomplishing something. Their course was highly predictable, but there was no way around that...not if they were going to get through the warp gate.

"Entering missile launch range now, Admiral." Simon paused, struggling to lift her head to look at her boards. "Sir, it does not appear that the enemy fleet is launching."

Garret wasn't sure why the enemy was holding fire. Unless they were also low on ordnance, they could launch multiple unanswered volleys before his ships zipped past them and entered the warp gate. Not that it mattered. He'd done everything he could. His ships were blasting hard and heading for the warp gate. The AIs were ready for missile defense, and his crews were suited up and strapped into their couches. It was time to run the gauntlet.

"We are well within launch range, sir." Commander Deng's voice was urgent. The enemy fleet was approaching them at high velocity; they were only going to have a brief window for missile barrages before their targets raced past them and through the warp gate. Yet Admiral Liang had held back the launch order.

"I am aware of that, Commander Deng." Liang's tone was abrupt. He didn't like having his orders questioned under any circumstances, but there was more at stake here than Deng could know. This was no normal battle; in a sense, it wasn't a battle at all. Liang didn't care what damage he did to the Alliance fleet or even how badly his own ships were hit. All he cared about was killing one man...Augustus Johnson Garret. "I want Cromwell targeted as soon as the enemy is close enough for scanners to ID her."

The Powers had extensive records of each others' naval

rosters, particularly capital ships. When the range was close enough, the computers could easily ID individual vessels...and Liang intended to throw everything he had at one enemy ship. Normally, he wouldn't have the luxury of holding fire this long; in a normal engagement the enemy's first volleys would have reached him already, forcing him to jettison his external racks if he hadn't launched them. But Liang was facing an adversary with little or no capacity to launch a missile attack, so he could afford to wait for his target.

"We have Cromwell identified, sir." Deng paused briefly as he scanned his readouts. "94% probability."

Liang smiled. Good enough. "All ships are to activate external missile launchers. Fire plan codename silver dragon." Liang had programmed his own fire control directive into the computer, overriding standard target selection protocols.

Deng's hands raced over his boards, control the flow of information to the various ships of the fleet and instructing their fire control computers to download the specified targeting directives. "Fire plan silver dragon locked into the fleet AI." He glanced at his screen. "All ships ready to launch. Awaiting fleet command order."

Liang stared up at the main screen, where a partial schematic of the Alliance fleet was displayed, ships being added as they were scanned and identified. He took a deep breath, something he'd hardly been able to do since that day he stood before the Committee. Now he was on the verge of success. Without turning his head, he uttered a single word. "Launch."

"Enemy launches detected! Multiple platforms." Lieutenant Simon's tone was excited, but she spoke slowly, deliberately. At 10g, that is the best she could manage.

Nelson was telling Garret the same thing through his earpiece, but he let his crew go through the motions. He wasn't planning to reduce the acceleration rate, which meant his crew was basically out of the battle, stuck in their couches with little to do. But it would relieve the stress and fear somewhat to feel like they were busy, so he indulged it while the AIs did the real work. "Very well, Lieutenant. Keep me advised."

"Admiral, I am detecting an unconventional pattern on the incoming missile strike." Nelson's voice was calm and unemotional as always, untroubled by the crushing g forces. "Analyzing now."

Simon was a few seconds behind Nelson. "Sir, we are detecting a stran..."

"Hold that, lieutenant." Garret was waiting for Nelson's follow up. He didn't know why they'd waited so long to launch, and now he was trying to determine what they were up to.

Nelson continued after a few seconds. "Incoming missile spread is abnormally focused." Another short pause. "Analysis of thrust patterns indicates continuing shrinkage of target area." Garret was just coming to a conclusion when Nelson confirmed his developing thought. "Admiral, it appears that the entire incoming volley is targeted at Cromwell."

Again, Lieutenant Simon was a few seconds behind Nelson. "Admiral, the entire strike is targeting us...I mean Cromwell." Simon had tremendous poise for so young an officer, but he could hear the stress in her voice now.

Garret forced another deep breath. Is that it, he thought...is this just a glorified assassination attempt? There was definitely an intelligence leak somewhere.

"Admiral Garret..." Flag Captain Charles' voice followed Nelson's in Garret's earpiece. He closed the visor on his helmet so they could speak privately.

"Yes, Byron?" Garret knew what was coming.

"We have to get you off the ship, sir." There was extreme urgency in Charles' voice. He knew his ship was unlikely to survive the coming fight.

"That's out of the question, Byron."

Garret's tone had left no room for argument, but Charles wasn't dissuaded. "Sir, you know there's a good chance we won't get through this. You are giving the enemy what they want." He paused to take a labored breath. "There is still time to get you off the Cromwell before the barrage hits."

"Byron, there is no way - no way - I am going to abandon

this ship and crew to run and save my own skin."

"But, sir..."

"That's the last word, Captain Charles." Garret's voice was stern. Abandoning his flagship just wasn't in him, and leaving the crew behind to die while he ran away was utterly unthinkable.

"Now detecting a second wave of missiles, Admiral." Nelson paused a second, then continued. "Preliminary analysis indicated a similar pattern to the first volley."

So that's it, Garret thought. They're expending an entire fleet's ordnance just to kill me. I suppose it's flattering, he mused with grim humor. Though the thought of everyone on Cromwell dying because of him drove away even dark amusement.

"Nelson, I want a plan to fire what missiles we have in defense of Cromwell. Maximum coverage timed to intercept the enemy first wave." He didn't have many missiles, but all of them were multiple warhead weapons. Every 200 megaton bomb would destroy any incoming missile over a 10 kilometer radius. The key was timing the launches and subsequent detonations to catch the enemy missiles in the blast zone.

The fleet AIs couldn't modify the fleet's thrust plan without jeopardizing the ability of some ships to hit the warp gate, but they did reorder targeting priorities and combine the entire force in a single defensive array around Cromwell.

The missiles were fired first, detonating along the projected path of the incoming attack. The enemy missiles were bunched together as they closed on their single target, and the Alliance fleet AIs were able to take out over half the first wave, the incoming weapons consumed in the thermonuclear fire of Garret's limited defensive barrage. Point defense rockets and lasers tore into the remaining missiles, and only five got close enough to Cromwell to have an effect.

The ship shook violently as it was impacted by multiple shockwaves. Only one missile got near enough to cause serious damage, but that one was close indeed, and it tore into the starboard side of the ship, ripping open compartments and knocking out the control system for one of the reactors.

Garret lurched forward out of his couch as the Cromwell's

engines shut down with the power loss and the intense g forces of acceleration abruptly stopped. He was already getting damage control reports from Nelson. Normally, he left Cromwell to Captain Charles and concerned himself with the overall condition of the fleet. But Cromwell was the only fleet unit currently under attack.

"Enemy second wave incoming, sir." Simon's voice was somber. "Estimate to detonation range, 3 minutes."

It was going to be worse this time, Garret thought. He had no missiles left and would have to rely entirely on conventional point defense. And they weren't going to get their engines back online in three minutes, which meant his course was even more predictable than it had been - straight ahead at a constant velocity. Cromwell couldn't have been an easier target.

Garret was about to order all personnel to abandon non-essential outer compartments when he heard Captain Charles issue the same order. "Ok, Byron, it's your ship," he was muttered softly to himself.

"Admiral, I insist that you leave the ship at once." Charles again in his earpiece. His voice was almost frantic. He knew the chances Cromwell had of coming through this.

Garret was about to answer when Lieutenant Simon had the same idea. She stood up and turned to face his command chair. "Admiral, you have to leave the Cromwell."

He spoke to both of them at once. "Under no circumstances am I going to leave the ship. We will get through this attack." A slight pause. "Now we all have better things to do, so return to your posts immediately."

"Thirty seconds to projected enemy detonations." Nelson, at least, was remaining on point, Garret thought. There was nothing else to do, so he sat quietly, watching the readouts on the effect of the fleet's point defense on the incoming missiles. They were doing well, but not well enough.

All around the Cromwell, space erupted into atomic fury as warhead after warhead exploded. At least ten were close enough to cause significant damage, and the Cromwell shook violently. Power flickered, then failed as the second reactor was destroyed.

Entire sections of the ship were torn away, the men and women stationed there killed immediately or blown into space. Their pressure suits would keep them alive for a while, but the fleet was not stopping to conduct rescue operations so they had little hope of survival. Even if there was a chance of rescue, the space around Cromwell was an unhealthy place for an unprotected person, and many would be exposed to massive heat waves and high radiation levels. Along the port side, an entire chunk of the ship was torn off, four decks and over 30 crew members tumbling off into space, powerless and out of control.

The flag bridge was dimly lit, the reserve batteries providing limited power to run the vital systems. Debris was strewn about, and life support systems were failing. Garret's people were still at their stations, working feverishly, though there was little they could truly do. They were still in the middle of the second barrage, but their scanners showed the third one seven minutes out. They might survive the current attack...barely. The third was a death sentence.

Garret was about to direct Captain Charles to order all non-essential personnel to abandon ship...and he was going to tell his people to go too, though he doubted they would obey. His action was cut short by the detonation of one of the last missiles of the second wave. The warhead exploded less than 8 kilometers from Cromwell. The shockwave smacked into the foundering ship, sending it spinning violently. All through the Cromwell, structural members failed and entire sections of the ship collapsed.

Garret was strapped to his chair when the huge plasti-steel girder gave way and crashed to the deck. He couldn't remember it hitting him...one minute he was in his command chair and the next we was lying under the massive beam. He didn't feel any pain, only the taste of blood on his lips. Around him his people struggled and shouted as they tried desperately to somehow control an uncontrollable situation.

He was vaguely aware of people talking to him, straining to try to move the debris that pinned him to the deck. But all that seemed distant, ephemeral. His mind filled with strange thoughts, old memories. He was a cadet again, newly arrived at the Academy. He could almost smell the rose bushes in the admiral's garden. She was there too...the girl he'd left for the service, her long red hair blowing in the gentle breeze. Young Augustus Garret wanted glory - and he'd gotten more than his share. But what had he lost....what had he left behind? His mind drifted slowly, steadily, until the growing darkness took him.

Chapter 10

I Corps HQ
Columbia - Eta Cassiopeiae II

"But Epsilon Eridani is a backwater. It was a moderately productive mining colony, but from what I hear it was shut down completely by some plague. Why the hell would they scrap the rest of Sherman to send us there?" Cain's voice was strained. He was trying to control his anger, but it had been a frustrating morning.

General Holm sat at the head of the conference table, his expression blank, unreadable. The general was wearing his poker face and not letting anyone know what he was thinking. The discussion had been subdued, mostly because the damned political officers were there too. They'd more or less been staying out of the way until the previous day. Clearly, they'd gotten their own orders regarding this entire Epsilon Eridani matter, and they'd been stuck to their assigned officers like glue ever since. Cain was the closest to boiling over, but a lot of the others were getting sick of it too.

"Erik, we don't know everything yet. We have to assume there is a good reason." He stared briefly at Cain, not long enough for anyone else to notice. Erik Cain was a great soldier, maybe the best Holm had ever seen. But no one was about to assign him to the diplomatic corps. Blunt, direct, and incredibly stubborn, Cain simply would not, in his mind, lower himself to consider the politics of a situation. He considered politicians something he'd scrape off his boot with a stick - and maybe he'd wear a glove when he did it. Holm was just grateful that Cain's political officer hadn't ended up in a ditch somewhere.

"Indeed, Colonel Cain. The general is correct. It is not our purpose to initiate matters of grand strategy or question orders from the high command, but simply to execute those directives as effectively as possible." Captain Peter Warren was the political officer assigned to "assist" Cain, a job he'd found to be challenging to say the least.

Cain flushed with anger, but he'd understood the general's brief glance, and he bit down hard on his rage. "Understood, general. I can assure you that 1st Brigade will be ready to execute its orders." He looked right at Holm, ignoring the political officer as if he didn't exist.

"I want all of you to have your units ready to begin uploading in five days." Holm tapped on his 'pad briefly. "I have transmitted berthing assignments for all formations. There have been some changes, so I want everyone to review these within the hour and contact my staff with any questions or concerns. Now is the time to address any issues, not in five days."

Holm looked back at Cain. "Erik, your brigade is 100% ready, so you should have some free time. Major Linden will be returning this afternoon; her ship just entered orbit. She's going to have a tight schedule getting her people ready in five days from a standing start. I'd like you to assist in any way possible." Holm had a good poker face, but he couldn't hold back a tiny smile. Most of the officers at the table were well aware that Cain and I Corps beautiful medical chief of staff were lovers.

"Yes, sir!" The sour expression he'd worn all morning softened considerably.

Holm's eyes scanned the seated officers. "Very well. I will want to meet with each of you individually to review your unit statuses. Lieutenant Raynor will get back to you with schedules. In the meantime we all have work to do, so let's get to it. Dismissed."

The assembled officers rose, snapping off salutes to the general before heading to the door. Holm allowed himself a passing grin as he watched Cain walk out. He must be happy, Holm thought. He even managed a textbook grade salute!

Cain walked briskly across the quad, and for the first time in quite a while there was a smile on his face. Sarah Linden had been the executive officer of medical services for Operation Sherman. When the campaign was suspended, she accompanied the wounded to Armstrong, the Marines' hospital planet, personally supervising the care and transfer of over 6,000 injured men and women. Cain had personal experience with just how good a doctor Sarah Linden truly was, and he couldn't imagine how many lives she'd saved.

Now she was back, and Erik couldn't wait to see her. It had been over six months and, though they were used to long periods apart, Erik had actually gotten accustomed to seeing her frequently on the campaign. Rank has its privileges, and if shuttling over to the med ship a few times was one of them, no one begrudged him. Not with his combat record.

Sarah was billeted in the support services section of the camp, a fairly long walk from Cain's quarters adjoining 1st Brigade HQ. He figured she'd just gotten in, but why waste any time? He walked up to the entry and identified himself to the AI, and a few seconds later the door opened.

Her quarters were large, not as plush as his now that he was a pretend general, but very nice nevertheless. Neither one of them would have anywhere near this much room once they boarded ship...though again, his acting-general status would get him a few extra square meters.

He walked through the door as she came running up from the back room and threw her arms around his neck. "God, I missed you." Her voice was happy, but also tired.

"I'm going to need to have you assigned as my personal doctor." He laughed softly as he held her tightly. "The separations are getting too hard."

"Touching scene." Erik was startled by the voice coming from the darkened doorway to the back room. A familiar voice.

Sarah smiled. "I have to tell you, I've been seeing another man." She giggled and stepped back as General Holm walked into the light.

"I can't tell you two how haunted by guilt I am to interrupt this reunion." He grinned. He was joking, of course, but he did feel a little bad about his timing. "However, I *am* the closest thing to a matchmaker you two have. Except, of course, the nuke that sent you into her tender-loving care in the first place." Holm was, in fact, largely responsible for their relationship. They'd met when Sarah had nursed a badly wounded Erik back to health, but it wasn't until they spent six months together on Earth that they really became inseparable. And it was General Holm who'd gotten Sarah Linden assigned to that trip.

"Don't be silly, sir." Cain began a sloppy salute, but Holm waved him off.

"Don't try to salute, son. I'd hate to have you hurt yourself." They all laughed. Cain was a notoriously poor saluter. Despite his exemplary record in the Corps, deep down he had a major resentment of authority, and it came through in his salutes. Fortunately, Holm had been his CO for quite some time, and the general didn't give a rat's ass whether Cain snapped him a sharp salute or not.

"Erik," Holm continued, "I really am sorry to disturb you both tonight, but I need to talk to you privately, and I figured even Captain Warren wasn't dum enough to follow you here."

"I'll give the two of you a few minutes." Sarah smiled and started to walk toward the back room.

Holm put his hand on her shoulder as she moved by. "Stay. Private does not mean without you around." He paused and looked back at Erik. "It means without our minders listening in." She nodded and sat down quietly. "Erik," the general said, "there is something strange going on."

Cain frowned. "What gave you that idea? That we can't go to the head without a spy from WashBalt tagging along?" His voice was sarcastic, of course, but also serious and concerned.

Holm took a seat at the small table and motioned for Cain to sit as well. "It's more than just the political officers. I sent a message to General Samuels several days ago expressing my concern that the political officers have their own communication nets. It's an obvious security risk in an op. You know how tightly scrambled our communications are during a campaign. We have no idea about their networks...how they are secured, to whom they are connected."

Cain nodded. "You know I agree, sir." He looked disgusted. "These guys are a whole world of problems. Just like the cops back in the MPZ. Whatever you're worried about, I guarantee the truth is ten times worse."

Holm rubbed the back of his neck. It had been a long day. "I'm sure you are right, Erik, but that's not what's really bothering me. General Samuel's response was, well...strange. He didn't seem to see my point or have any real concern about the political officers. He dismissed my concerns rather abruptly. It almost felt like a reprimand for even bringing it up."

Cain looked surprised. Elias Holm was the great hero of the Corps, the man who'd commanded in every major victory of the last five years. He couldn't imagine anyone disregarding the general's concerns. "You think there is a problem with General Samuels? Maybe his transmissions are being watched."

"Or maybe someone is controlling him." Holm sounded uncomfortable even discussing such possibilities. "Could someone be exerting some type of influence over him in some way?"

Cain's expression was icy, focused. "I wouldn't put anything past our friends in Alliance Gov, sir." He paused, not sure if he should say what he was thinking. "General, I would not be surprised if the government made some sort of attempt to exert more control over the Corps. It's not like them to be comfortable until they control everything."

Holm looked troubled. He wasn't an overly trusting man, and he certainly wasn't naive, but he lacked Cain's deep cynicism. Erik Cain automatically assumed the worst, while Holm just allowed for it as a possibility. "Erik, the Charter has governed the relationship between the Corps and Alliance Gov for a century. Do you really think they want to destroy that now?"

Cain hesitated again. This was a dangerous conversation. But he was alone with the two people he trusted most in all of human-occupied space. "Yes." He paused to emphasize the definitiveness of his answer. "I think they want us to win the war, certainly. But look around you when you leave here. Do you realize how large and powerful the Corps has become? There were 280 of us on my first assault, from two small ships. The last time there were 45,000 of us. I think we've become too big for their comfort."

"But the Corps has never given reason for concern." Holm

was still trying to temper Cain's pessimistic view.

"Sir..." Erik cleared his throat and shifted his weight in the seat. "These politicians...their minds work in a different way. The whole system was set up for them, to keep them in a position of power and privilege. And they see threats to that everywhere. It's not that they think the Corps is a threat; it's that they think it could become one."

"As much as the Corps has grown," Holm replied, "it's not like we're capable of invading Earth and seizing power. We're still dependent on them for support, industry...almost everything."

Cain's eyes narrowed. "An ambitious Marine commandant and a cooperative fleet admiral could set themselves up as rulers on the Rim. That's how the politicians see it. Because that is what they would do if they were able." He paused and looked right into Holm's eyes. "You and Admiral Garret could probably do it. Don't fool yourself...they think of you both as threats."

Holm snorted. "That's crazy. I'm just a Marine, and I do my duty. I'd never do something like that. And neither would Garret."

"I'm saying that's how they think, sir." Never say never, Erik thought as well, but that he kept to himself. "I spent six months alongside these people when you sent me back to Earth. Their sense of entitlement is something we can't even understand. They hate and fear anything that threatens their order." Cain waved his arm, motioning upward. "These colonies...have you ever seen anything on any of them that is even remotely similar to how the Cogs live on Earth? There is a different culture out here, and some of these politicians - the smart ones - are starting to realize they are not going to be able to push the colonists around as easily as they do the folks back Earthside. They're figuring they are going to have to stomp them eventually, and the last thing they want to worry about is which side the Corps is going to choose when that happens."

"When?" Holm looked startled. "Do you really think it's inevitable?"

Cain let out a sigh. "I don't know what I think, sir. But I know it is possible, probably likely." That was a lie. Erik knew in his heart he was right. "The last few years I've thought a lot about the day we get an order to start killing our own people."

"He's right, sir." Sarah had been sitting quietly, just listening. Now her voice wavered with emotion. "My family was destroyed because of the whim of a politician's son. They will take whatever they want, and they will destroy anyone who gets in their way. It may have been opportunistic when the system was initially created, but now these people believe they are entitled to behave this way. If the worlds out here resist any directives from Earth, Alliance Gov will try to crush them. No other response would even occur to them."

Cain and the general both turned to look over at Sarah. She sat in the edge of the chair, her eyes moist with memories of old pain. Erik knew just what she had gone through before she'd found her way to the Corps, and he rose from his seat and walked over to stand next to her, placing a gentle hand on her shoulder.

Holm looked down at the floor, thinking about everything they had discussed. Finally he took a deep breath and stood up. "I don't know what is going on, and I certainly don't know what is going to happen. If General Samuels is being blackmailed or coerced in some way, we have a major problem...one I don't know how to address."

Erik and Sarah listened quietly, the side of her faced pressed against his arm as he stood next to her. He looks very sad, Erik thought to himself. He wants to believe better of things; he wants to be positive, but he's realizing the truth. Cain was sympathetic, though he did not share the general's emotions. He had never believed in anything except the Corps and generally expected the worst from people outside that sphere.

"We're not going to solve this problem today, but I think we need to be careful moving forward." Holm spoke slowly, deliberatively, as if he didn't want to say what he knew he had to. "We need to be able to communicate with each other without the political officers being aware of it. Erik, I want you to help me put together a list together of officers you think should be part of this discussion. If something crazy happens, I want more than one or two of us in the loop."

Erik thought for a minute. "Jax, of course. And Anne Dela-corte." He paused briefly again then rattled off several additional suggestions. Finally, he added, "How about the division commanders? They've been with you a long while."

"Yes, I will have to speak with them. Honestly, if someone is coercing General Samuels, they could target another senior officer as well." He paused, clearly uncomfortable with the entire conversation. "I need to know if anything out of the ordinary is going on in I Corps."

Cain rubbed his face with his hand. "General..." He paused until Holm looked over at him. "You know I'm very concerned about Alliance Gov and the future. But not about I Corps. Every man and woman in this outfit is 100% on the team. I am sure of that." He made a face. "Except these damned political officers. How are we going to communicate with them following us around everywhere? There's no way we're going to get two or three senior commanders together without at least one of their babysitters coming along."

Holm twisted his lips into a troubled expression and looked over at Sarah. "We need a go between. Someone the officers can speak with who can relay messages. Sarah? I hate to involve you in this, but you would be perfect. You'll need to consult with them all regarding medical staffing for their units anyway, and that's just the kind of insignificant thing the political officers will ignore. And they don't seem to have assigned political officers to medical staff. You can transmit messages back and forth."

Cain opened his mouth to speak, but Sarah motioned for him to wait. "General, I'm already involved in it. I'm a Marine, and the only people in the universe I care about are in it too. Whatever I can do, I will."

Erik looked down, into her eyes. "Are you sure?"

"Erik, love, if those people have their way and turn these colonies into replicas of Earth, what place is there for you and me? For any of us? You more than anyone should know I would do anything to stop that."

"Thank you, Sarah." Holm's voice was warm and genuinely appreciative. "It's just about secure communications...a precaution until we can figure out what is going on." He looked over at Cain. "Erik, before I get the hell out of here and give you two some privacy, I wanted to ask you about Carson's World. Privately. You fought there, didn't you?"

Cain turned to face the general. "Yes, general. It was my first assault. I'm afraid I was paying more attention to not tripping over my own feet than checking the place out. What do you want to know?"

Holm exhaled loudly. "Can you think of any reason the place is worth all this effort? It's one transit off a dead end, and it's not even populated anymore."

"Not really, sir." His brow was furrowed as he tried to remember his first assault. It seemed so long ago. "The locals fought like hell; they really impressed me. It's a shame what ended up happening there." He paused again. "The place was a pretty successful mining operation, but nothing all that irreplaceable."

"That's what I figured." There was definite concern on Holm's face. "Someone has a reason to send a force as large as I Corps to a seeming backwater. I keep thinking abo..."

"There was one thing!" Cain had spoken with startled recollection then realized he'd interrupted the general. "Sorry, sir. I didn't mean to interrupt."

"C'mon, Erik." Holm flashed a grin. "You've got to know me better than that by now. If you have something useful to say just tell me the shut the hell up and say it!"

Cain nodded. "Well, sir, I don't know what it means, but the CAC troops were using gas to hunt down the militia. Back then the locals really didn't have much protective gear, and the nerve gas was pretty effective. Remember this was before the war was even official, and way before it went nuclear." Cain closed his eyes and paused for a few seconds, thinking. "I remember how surprised the experienced guys were. There were some unwritten rules in those prewar skirmishes, and not using gas was one of them. When the battle was over and some of the

CAC troopers tried to surrender, we just shot them down. I remember how odd it seemed that they would use that kind of weapon on a backwater raid. They had to know it meant no quarter if things went bad." He looked quizzically at the general. "Why were they so desperate to finish off the militia? It's not like the locals could have held out that much longer anyway. What was so urgent?"

They stood there silently for a few seconds. "Whatever it was," Holm finally said, "I suspect it is the same thing at work here. I wasn't in the chain of command for the op you were in back then, but I remember the reports that the CAC had raided Epsilon Eridani IV." He snorted. "I guess 'raid' was what we called an attack before the politicians made the war official. I fought in half a dozen of those 'raids,' and the responses to them, and when my troops got shot they were just as dead. I wonder if they felt better or worse in their last minutes because we weren't really at war." He looked down at the table, lost for a moment in old thoughts, then he shook his head. "I'm getting off subject. As I was saying, I remember being surprised that the CAC went after EE-4, especially before hostilities had widened. It's not really strategic to them at all. It seemed very random, just like it does now." Another pause. "There's something about all of this we just don't know. But someone does. Is that General Samuels, I wonder? Or someone who is pulling his strings?"

Cain sighed. "I don't know, sir. But I guess we're going to find out."

General Holm put his hands on the arms of the chair and slowly rose. "I guess you're right, Erik. We can overthink this right now. Let's take things a step at a time." He walked toward the door. "But I think the war just got a lot more complicated."

"Yes, sir. I think so too."

Holm walked up to the door and motioned for the AI to open it. He turned back and smiled. "Well, I've intruded here far too long. You two have better things to do than discuss government plots with me." And with that he slipped out into the night.

Chapter 11

Marine Earthside HQ
Camp Puller
Near New Houston, Texas

General Raphael Samuels walked down the long corridor to his office, his polished boots clicking loudly on the bare steel floor. The spotless white walls were sleek and utilitarian, the framed oil paintings of past Commandants the only concession to decoration. He wore a crisply-pressed gray duty uniform, with silver braid around the collar and four platinum stars on each shoulder. Samuels was a full general, second in command of the Marine Corps, and he was usually surrounded by a cluster of orderlies and assistants. But now he was alone, and the outer office was deserted, the staff very deliberately sent away on various errands.

He barked at the AI to open his private office, and he walked in quickly, the door sliding shut behind him. His office was large and luxurious, as would be expected for the workspace of so lofty and celebrated an officer. The furniture was all antique, which was mildly anachronistic alongside the sleek walls and banks of computer equipment. He walked around the expensive, carved wood desk and dropped hard into the massive black leather chair. The seat creaked slightly under his great bulk - Samuels was a big man, tall and broad shouldered, and in the years since he'd last donned armor and crawled into a landing craft he'd put on considerable weight. Leaning back in the chair, he sighed and ran his hand through his mop of hair, mostly gray now, with just a few strands of black remaining.

He glanced at the chronometer. Ten more minutes, he thought, as he turned his chair and looked out the large window at the massive Marine reservation sprawling out before him. The modern Corps - the spaceborne Corps - had been a huge experiment. In the early days, battles were small and strike forces operated independently, far from any reinforcements or support. It took a certain type of individual to excel in those types of campaigns.

The system created was unorthodox, but it actually worked. Recruiting misfits, square pegs who weren't able to find their round hole in terrestrial society, produced a breed of rugged, independent, and resourceful soldiers. But the real surprise was the psychological effect of providing a place in the world for this cadre of troublemakers, which forged a tremendous loyalty and esprit de corps. Where one might have expected indiscipline and rebelliousness, there was excellence and morale. Because their officers were all plucked from the same gutters, and had all donned powered armor and made their first assault as privates, there was a strong connection between the enlisted men and their commanders. Any private could rise all the way to a general's stars based solely on merit. This was virtually the opposite of normal Alliance society, where birth or patronage was required for any advancement. Marines have traditionally been rabidly loyal to the Corps, which was the only home, the only parent, many of them had ever known.

Times were changing, though. In the First Frontier War there were operations were a single platoon was dispatched on a mission, and the lieutenant in command was the only officer deployed...the only officer within light years. There were battles where senior privates ended up in command, yet in virtually all cases the units were still able to function. The tooth to tail ratio in these early conflicts was astonishingly low for a high tech fighting force.

But man's presence in space had expanded massively, and the wars he fought to preserve and expand that foothold had grown as well. Today's campaigns had become substantial affairs, with taskforces of warships and combined arms on the ground. Samuels had lived these changes. He'd been a private once, a lifetime ago. He'd come up in the years just after the First Frontier War, and despite the formal peace there was still plenty of fighting to do back then. He still remembered his first assault, the fear, the anticipation, the determination to become a real part of the unit. Oddly, what he recalled most vividly was how cold the launch bay was when he was squeezing his naked body into his armor. There were about 100 troops in that assault, and they were transported to the target world on a single unescorted ship.

Samuels wondered if the Marines' unique method of recruitment and training was outdated. Certainly there were those who thought so. To many in the government, a tiny frontier security contingent composed of an eclectic group of rebellious types was tolerable, but the demands of the Third Frontier War had expanded that small force into an army almost 300,000 strong, equipped with every manner of weapon. And that army existed almost entirely outside the control of the political class, something the politicians found increasingly unacceptable.

He watched a group of recruits as they moved into his field of view on the training ground. They were heading out on a run, probably part of physical training for a batch of new arrivals. Marines chosen for assault units spent six years in training, but they all started the same way, running until they ended up doubled over, heaving up their guts, sergeants dogging them the whole time. Most of the recruits who came here thought they were tough, and job one for their instructors was showing them what tough really was.

Samuels lost track of time gazing out the window, and he was startled by the AI's gentle, human-sounding voice. "Incoming communication, General Samuels."

He took a deep breath and turned away from the window, laying his hands on the desk. "Establish link." A slight pause. "Encryption, code Matahari."

"Link established. Encryption code Matahari in effect."

Samuels found himself looking around the room, even though he knew he was alone. Satisfied, he picked up the headset and strapped it on. "Number Four, checking in."

The Directorate conference room was quieter than usual. There had been bad news, and everyone present was concerned how Number One would react. As always, the mysterious Number Four was represented only by a hologram and altered voice.

At the end of the table, on one side of the laser-generated image, sat Jack Dutton, quiet and impassive. He was the only person besides Stark who knew that the shadowy Number Four was actually General Raphael Samuels, though even he didn't know how Stark had managed to flip a Marine of such high rank.

The seat on the other side of the hologram was empty. Alex Linden was on Epsilon Eridani IV, personally supervising the crucial excavation there, though with recent developments it now appeared she was in serious trouble. There had been no word from her for several weeks.

Sitting across the table from Dutton, Andres Carillon sat quietly, his face impassive. He wondered how Alex was handling the situation on EE-4. Maybe the snotty bitch finally got what she deserved, he thought with just a little malice. Alex had rejected his advances several times, and he hadn't taken it well.

The door slid open, and Number One walked in briskly. "Please accept my apologies for my tardiness. I'm afraid with the current situation it couldn't be helped." He slid the chair back from the head of the table and sat. "I assume you have all been briefed on the CAC's assault on Epsilon Eridani IV." He scanned the table, noting the general nods of assent.

"I'm afraid we have very little information beyond that contained in Admiral Franklin's drone." He moved his eyes around the table as he spoke. "The lack of any follow up communication does not suggest a favorable outcome. The admiral indicated he was heavily outnumbered, though he acknowledged his hold at all costs orders." He looked down briefly, eyes fixed on the table. "We can only assume that his fleet has been destroyed and the planet taken."

Everyone present already knew that much, yet hearing it said out loud emphasized the terrible importance of the development. "The one planet that we could not afford to lose," Stark said bitterly, "appears to have been lost. Every advantage we have gained in the war could be moot if we are unable to retrieve the situation."

Stark had not raised his voice, but everyone here knew the intensity of his displeasure, and no one would speak until he had directly asked a question. No one except Dutton. "Number One, I believe that we can recover the planet if we act quickly enough. We must mount a major operation to retake the system as soon as possible." This was a bit of playacting; he and Stark had already devised a plan.

Stark played along. "You are correct, Number Two, but first there is another development we must discuss, another disaster of which I have just now been informed." He paused for a second. "Admiral Liang has apparently ambushed the forces that Fleet Admiral Garret was moving to Eta Cassiopeiae for the resumption of Operation Sherman. As you are all aware, Garret's task force was heavily depleted and scheduled to resupply at Columbia." Every eye in the room was riveted to him. "We do not have many details, but it appears that Cromwell was targeted and destroyed by the attacking fleet. Admiral Garret is missing and presumed KIA."

The quiet in the room was replaced by a series of gasps and other expressions of surprise. Augustus Garret had led a battered and demoralized navy from the brink of defeat to the verge of total victory. And now this? Killed in an ambush? Shock overrode their fear of Number One, and all at once the Directors started speaking in a confused babble.

Stark held up a hand. "Please, please. Let us not lose our composure. If Admiral Garret is indeed lost, none will mourn him more than I. But we must consider next steps." He hesitated, trying not to sound too rehearsed. "The news, tragic though it appears to be, is not all bad. I had unconfirmed reports that the CAC intended something like this, and I arranged for a relief force to be dispatched to meet the admiral and escort him the rest of the way to Columbia. Unfortunately, the task force arrived too late to prevent the attack or save the admiral. They did, however, transit into the system just as Liang's force was breaking off from their attack. Our task force caught the depleted CAC ships on their way back across the system and inflicted a serious defeat. Admiral Liang was apparently captured."

More gasps around the room. Stark paused a few seconds

to allow the news to sink in. "While our forces were able to defeat the CAC fleet, they suffered considerable damage. The entire fleet has been ordered back to 12 Ophiuchi for repairs. I'm afraid it will be six months before we can mount a counter-invasion to retake Carson's World." His voice was somber, verging on defeated. "I trust you all know what this means?"

The reactions ranged from stunned silence to shocked nods of acknowledgement. Finally, Number 10 spoke, her voice high-pitched with stress. "Perhaps we can assemble another force? What about the units still at Gliese 250?"

Stark looked at her. He could see the desperate grasping for a solution in her expression. "I'm afraid not, Number Ten." He panned his glance around the table as he spoke. "We stripped everything bare to assemble the Gliese force in the first place. The units remaining there are all undergoing substantial repairs; few, if any, of them are capable of mounting an offensive. At least not for six months." He exhaled hard then continued. "With the effective loss of operational status for both Admiral Garret's fleet and our rescue force, I'm afraid we have few ships available for anything at this time."

"What about the new construction program?" Number Nine was generally very quiet at these meetings, focusing primarily on her internal security portfolio. Her job was keeping the Cogs and the terrified middle class in line, not plotting war strategy. "This isn't my area of coverage, of course, but we've had reports that work has accelerated and is ahead of schedule. Any possibility of getting these ships online early?"

Very good, Stark thought. She's smarter than I thought. I wonder if that is a good thing or something I will have to deal with later. "Number Nine, I had the same thought, however it appears that there are substantial issues yet to be addressed." Think, Stark, think. Give a good answer. "There has been some rapid progress made on overall structural work, however they apparently had to redesign several of the internal systems. It seems that the missile launchers have a design flaw, which causes an unacceptable failure rate during high velocity launches." That sounds good, he thought. "The latest word is that we'll be lucky to hit the original schedule, but early deployment is out of the question."

She nodded glumly. Good, he thought. She bought it. He looked around the table. They all bought it. "Since there is no point in crying over what we cannot change, let's move on to what we can do." He moved his hands to the 'pad lying on the table in front of him. "I am going to securely transmit the proposed orders being sent to Fleetcom. You can all review this, but essentially, we will be deploying packs of fast attack ships to prevent the CAC from shipping anything from Epsilon Eridani. They've only got one exit warp gate, and we're going to mine the other side and cover it with hunter-killer groups."

He looked up from the 'pad. "We cannot allow the enemy to ship anything from our operation on Carson's World. This is an all-costs directive. If they have taken Number Six's operation intact or close to it, they are probably less than three months from beginning shipments. We must not allow this. We cannot allow them to get past the blockade, but if they mount a strong enough operation we're going to have a hard time stopping them." He paused for a long moment. "If they do get anything through we cannot lose contact with them. We must recover the cargo at all costs. All costs. Even if that means attacking them in the Alpha Centauri or Sol systems."

The room burst into a cacophony. "But that would violate the Treaty of Paris!" Number Ten had managed to yell louder than the others, but they were all saying the same thing.

Stark leaned back in his chair. "I am aware of that." His spoke slowly and deliberately. "But nothing is more important than preventing the CAC from shipping the cargo in question to Earth or one of their core worlds. Allies or not, Li An will never trust the Caliphate with this. So there are only a few places they can go, and Earth is the closest and most direct. I suggest you all utilize every intelligence asset you have to insure things do not come to this pass. We must have better intel from inside CAC C1. That bitch managed to get a leg up on us, but she isn't going to win this." His voice was grim, dark. "We are going to do whatever it takes."

He panned his head slowly around the table, staring briefly at each of the Directors, all of whom sat in stunned silence. "Very well," he finally said. "I suggest we adjourn so that all of you can consider any options for improving our flow of information. Leave no stone unturned." He leaned back in his chair. "That will be all." Then, after a brief pause, "Number Two, please remain. Number Four, please stay online as well; I want to discuss the training programs with you briefly."

"Yes, Number One." The hologram nodded as the others rose and started toward the door.

Stark sat quietly until the door slid shut. "I suspect our friend is on his way to contact Li An even now." His glum expression gave way to a wicked grin. "Do you think he took the bait?"

Number Two laughed. He'd enjoyed Stark's performance. "Yes, I think he bought it. I watched him through the entire meeting. The first time I'd ever considered sitting opposite him to be a good thing." He smiled. "How long have you know that Carillon was working for Li An?"

"To tell you the truth, it was our sweet, sexy little Alex who first suspected." His smile gave way to a look of concern. "If she ends up dead on Carson's World I'm going to miss her. I don't know where I will find another one quite like her."

"No, Alex Linden is one of a kind." Dutton let out a little snort. "Even if she is after my job. Maybe one day I will even accommodate her and retire. Or die. I doubt she cares which."

Stark snickered. "My friend, I'm not sure you are capable of either. Imagining you retired is amusing; what would you do, play golf? And you are too mean to die." The two of them laughed again then Stark turned to the hologram. "Number Four, have the orders been issued as we discussed?"

The laser-generated image was almost perfect, and a casual observer might think it was a human being in the chair, though there was still an occasional flicker when it moved abruptly. "Yes, Number One. As you know, other than Cromwell, our fleet units in the recent battle received only light damage. The enemy apparently targeted almost all of their fire on the admiral's flagship. The combined force is en route to Columbia and will be 100% combat-ready as soon as it resupplies there."

The hologram's arms moved - on the other end, General Samuels was punching up numbers on his 'pad, and the computer was transmitting his motions to the image. "General Holm has been ordered to prepare his forces to embark immediately."

"Excellent." Stark smiled. "I can also add that our four new Yorktown class ships are, in fact, ready to launch." He laughed sarcastically. "The missile launcher problem was miraculously solved in the last ten minutes."

Dutton chuckled softly, and the hologram wiggled oddly and made a strange sound - the system did not reproduce laughter well.

Stark pushed his chair from the table and leaned backward. "Hopefully we have just sent Li An some misinformation. The miserable old bitch put one over on us when she grabbed Carson's World." His face hardened in anger. "But she isn't going to keep it, and she isn't going to get so much as one shipment off of there. I don't know how she scraped up the forces she did, but it must have been just about every available unit in CAC space. When we destroy them...that is going to be the end of the war. The Caliphate is prostrate after Gliese, and we've cut off 80% of their vital resources. When we finish off the CAC fleet and ground forces, we will be the dominant power in space. We will dictate the peace terms."

The three of them sat silently and smiled. "And then we will deal with these colonists and teach them the new order of things out there." His expression was almost feral.

Chapter 12

I Corps HQ
Columbia - Eta Cassiopeiae II

The great plain between I Corps bivouac area and the city of Weston was covered with ground-to-orbit shuttles. The corps was loading up, preparing for its journey to Epsilon Eridani, and everywhere there were armored Marines marching up ramps and into the bellies of neatly aligned shuttlecraft.

Along the western edge of the assembly area, a neat row of larger ships awaited their cargo. I Corps had a tank battalion, and the massively armed and armored monsters tore up the grassy meadow and threw huge clods of dirt behind them as they rumbled toward the waiting transports.

There were palettes of supplies too, being moved on large open trucks, though most of the logistical items were already onboard the orbiting troopships and transport vessels, having been shipped in from other Alliance bases.

Colonel Erik Cain stood in the quad outside the almost-deserted former home of 1st Brigade, watching shuttles ascending, carrying the troops under his command to their waiting ships. He was wearing his armor, but his visor was open. It was a beautiful autumn day on Columbia, and Erik wanted to enjoy a last few minutes of fresh air before the weeks of recycled atmosphere he faced during the trip to Epsilon Eridani. Plus, he'd managed to convince Captain Warren he should embark early and help get the troops settled, so he'd shaken his unwelcome shadow for a few hours. He intended to enjoy the relative solitude.

"Colonel Cain, the 2nd Battalion of the 1st Regiment has completed loading and is awaiting clearance for liftoff. With their departure, all 1st Brigade personnel will have embarked except for the special action battalion." Hector was the name Cain had given the artificial intelligence unit downloaded into his armor. Designed as a virtual assistant, Hector could perform anything from simple tasks, such as saving Cain the trouble of hitting a button to bring up a display, to complex operations, like tracking the incoming data on every trooper in the brigade. "You may want to consider cutting short your contemplative activities and begin to move toward the embarkation area. You wouldn't want to miss your shuttle." The Marine AIs were designed with distinct and developable personalities as a way of enhancing interactivity and reducing stress on officers in the field. Hector, however, was a bit of a nag.

"Shut up, Hector," Cain snapped. "I am perfectly aware of the departure schedules, and I don't need some smartass computer reminding me every five minutes."

"I reminded you one time, Colonel, which is consistent with my purpose." Hector's temperament was always moderate and relaxed-sounding, even when he (it?) was being a pain in the ass. It really pissed Cain off sometimes. "I understand your human need for exaggeration when attempting to make a point, however."

Cain was going to respond, but he'd long ago decided it was a losing fight. He'd been ready to start walking over toward the shuttle, but now he found himself waiting another ten minutes just to make his point. It didn't make him proud to stand there just to spite his computer, but he did it anyway.

He was anxious to be heading back to battle. Cain was no glory hound, seeking combat for its own sake. He'd seen too much fighting, too much death to think of war as anything but a horror. But he'd come to learn that some things were worth fighting for, worth the terror and suffering and bloodshed. The worlds out here on the frontier, so different from the decadent and authoritarian society on Earth, represented to him the best in man...the hope for a better tomorrow, for a fit place to live and grow old. For that - for the brave colonists who dared to build a new civilization among the stars - he would brave the death and hardship of war.

He wasn't happy about the mission, however. Operation Sherman had been a campaign designed to liberate the occupied colony worlds, mostly lost during the difficult early years of the war. To Erik, and to General Holm and the rest of the Marines, this was a sacred task, and it had been a bitter blow when they were compelled to suspend the campaign halfway through. The months in Columbia spent waiting for the resumption of the operation were put to good use training and integrating replacement troops, but after almost a year of inactivity, Cain and his brethren were ready to get back to the task of freeing their people.

But now they were being sent to Epsilon Eridani, a relatively unimportant system that wasn't even populated anymore. The three worlds remaining in Operation Sherman were home to over 2,000,000 people, and Cain could not understand why a deserted mining planet was more important than them. It gnawed at his gut that whatever resource Carson's World had - there was obviously something of value there - the high command thought it was more important than the colonists waiting for liberation. Nevertheless, the sooner they got back to the war in any capacity, the sooner it would end.

He decided he'd stayed put long enough to spite Hector, so he began walking down toward the shuttles. He could have called for a ride, but he wanted to walk and enjoy just a few more minutes of relative peace and quiet. Erik enjoyed time alone, even if he did spend a significant portion of it wrestling with the guilt he felt for all the men and women who had died under his command. That group of ghosts had another member, though mercifully for once it wasn't one that Cain had led to death. Erik still couldn't believe that Admiral Garret was gone. He hadn't known him well, but the admiral had been one of the great heroes of the war. He and General Holm had directed the stunning resurgence of the Alliance, and the loss was almost too painful to bear. Augustus Garret had deserved a better end.

"Colonel Cain?" It was Anne Delacorte's voice on the comlink. Captain Delacorte was Cain's orderly, and she'd proven to be a tremendous asset. Smart and resourceful, she'd also turned out to be a first-class scrounger...an informal skill greatly valued in any military organization. Erik had personally arranged her promotion to captain when they'd returned to Columbia from

Operation Sherman.

"Yes, Anne. What is it?"

"Sir, the special action teams are all embarked and we have received launch clearance." Her voice was cheerful, but fatigued. Getting 3,600 troops loaded onto shuttles and into orbit was a significant task. It had been a stressful day all around. "General Holm has requested that you ride up with him, sir. Do you want us to lift, or should we wait for you?"

"No, you might as well get going." He changed his direction - General Holm's shuttle was on the other side of the field, a couple klicks beyond where his own people were loaded up. "When you dock, tell Colonel Jax I don't know how long I will be, and he should make sure the brigade is settled in."

"Yes, sir." She paused. "What should I tell Captain Warren, sir?" Her voice sounded like she'd bitten into something sour.

"Tell him I finally cracked and spaced myself."

"Yes, sir." She tried to stifle a laugh. "Perhaps I will edit that just a bit. With your permission, of course."

"Whatever you think best, Captain." He enjoyed teasing her a little. "I trust your judgment." He smiled, at least as much as he ever did when discussing his political officer.

"Yes, sir. Have a good trip up, sir."

"Thanks, Anne. You too. Cain out."

Ok, he thought, Jax is handling the troops, and Anne is baby-sitting my babysitter. He let himself relax ever so slightly; there was nothing requiring his immediate attention, so he resolved to enjoy the walk over to the general's embarkation area.

"Well isn't this plush?" Cain walked up the gleaming metal ramp into General Holm's shuttle. A variation on one of the larger craft used to ferry armored vehicles to and from the surface, it was a mobile command center sporting twenty workstations, allowing the general's staff be fully functional even when landing or launching into orbit.

Holm was leaning over the shoulder of one of his aides, staring at figures on a screen. He turned and smiled when he heard Cain's voice. "Only the best." He motioned to the workstations. "I've come to the reluctant conclusion that keeping a corps-sized operation functioning takes altogether too much work."

Cain laughed and stood bolt upright, snapping a reasonably decent salute at the general, at least the closest facsimile of one that could be managed in armor. "I can't even imagine, sir. The brigade is more than enough work by itself."

Holm returned the salute with a smile. "Not bad, Erik. You're getting pretty decent at that."

"Well, you've promoted me so many times I feel compelled to salute myself every morning in the mirror." He grinned. "Practice makes perfect."

Holm laughed and moved toward Cain, extending his gloved hand. Powered armor gloves were made from an artificial thermoplastic material reinforced with fine iridium cable mesh. The result was highly damage-resistant, while still allowing for considerable range of movement. A trained Marine has a surprising amount of tactile dexterity, allowing him utilize his weapons, operate a range of controls and equipment, and even shake hands. "Let's not jump right to perfect, Erik. I said decent." He laughed as Cain took his hand and they shook. "But at least I won't have to cover for you when we have visiting officers."

Holm motioned deeper in the shuttle. "Let's get bolted in. We're launching in five minutes." They walked into the ship, through a hatch that led to the general's private office. There was a desk with the chair retracted and a locking bolt extended to receive the general's armor. There were three brackets along the side wall, and Cain walked over and backed into one.

"Very nice." You don't even need to leave your office to get locked down for takeoff. He leaned back. "Hector, bolt us in." The AI didn't reply, but Erik felt himself pulled up to the wall as his armor locked into place.

Holm was going through the same motions. "Saves time. I land in this thing too, don't forget. It's usually a little more hectic then."

"Liftoff in two minutes." The shipwide com interrupted their exchange. "All personnel switch to internal life support systems." Standard procedure. Everyone was supposed to be on their suit's air and temperature control. That way, if the ship took damage and lost its atmospheric integrity, the occupants would all be protected. It made a lot of sense during an assault; it was less necessary on an unopposed liftoff, where a catastrophic failure was far less likely. But there was no reason not to take the extra precaution.

Cain told Hector to close the visor and activate the internal support systems. He could see that the general was doing the same. He was just about to toggle the comlink on to continue speaking to Holm when his laser-link communicator received a tight beam and Hector piped the incoming message into his headset.

"Erik, let's make sure this talk is just between us." The laser-link system allowed for direct point to point communication between Marines with line of sight to each other. Unlike the comlink, which used encryption to insure the security of broadcasts, the laser communication was impossible to breach without intercepting the tight beam. Between two armored Marines facing each other five meters apart it was absolutely secure.

"Of course, sir. What do you..."

Cain was interrupted by the shuttlewide announcement. "Liftoff in 10 seconds." He paused and waited for the launch. "...3, 2, 1." The ship rattled violently as the thrusters kicked in, and the heavy shuttlecraft left the ground. He could hear and feel the rumbling of the massive engines through his armor as they powered the ship rapidly into the Columbian sky.

"What do you want to discuss, sir." Cain finished his statement once the ship was airborne and the initial commotion of launch had subsided.

"I wanted to talk about this campaign." He paused. Erik could tell he was troubled...more so than he had already been about this whole business. "I got orders from General Samuels."

"Sir?" Cain would probably have just nodded or looked intently at the general in a normal conversation, but you get used to the fact that buttoned up in armor there is no such thing as a facial gesture or expression. It becomes second nature to verbalize everything.

"I am ordered to land the entire corps as quickly as possible and to search out and destroy any enemy forces in occupation."

"But sir, we've never landed a force that large on any planet. Carson's World? It just doesn't make sense." Cain sounded confused. "Plus, it seems like bad tactics to me. Wouldn't it make sense to keep a tactical reserve in orbit? Especially when we have what has to be a surplus of force."

"It gets stranger." Cain could tell that Holm was really uncertain about the mission, the first time he heard the general sound less than 100% confident. "We are ordered not to take prisoners. All enemy personnel, military or civilian, are to be terminated on sight."

Cain was taken aback. War is war, and he'd been in more than one fight where his troops hadn't accepted surrenders, usually when the battle had been particularly costly or difficult. You can discuss morality and ethics all you want, but the battlefield isn't a classroom, and soldiers will repay savagery with savagery. But to be expressly ordered not to take prisoners was something new. As far as he could tell, an Alliance military force had never had such a directive. This mission was getting stranger and stranger.

"I can see by the uncharacteristic silence that you think it is odd as well." Holm's voice was soft, as if he were whispering even though their conversation was totally secure. "There is something very wrong about all of this. I can't even begin to guess at what it is, but I know in my gut we're going to encounter some real surprises in this campaign." He paused. "And I want us to be ready for them." Another pause. "I want you to help me be ready."

"What can I do, sir?" Cain often second-guessed himself, but that was all in his head. He, like the general, was always decisive and confident in action, but for once, Erik Cain had no idea what to do.

"We need to be ready to deal with whatever happens." Holm hesitated, trying to decide how to say what he was thinking. "We have no idea what enemy forces we're going to be facing. So first we need to take care of business and win the battle."

"I don't like landing everyone immediately." Cain was thinking out loud. "A planet's a big place, and we lose the ability to react to enemy force concentrations if we don't have a significant reserve in orbit." He hesitated. "Do you think we can, ah, slow down the landing? Maybe take a little longer to get everyone planetside?"

"We're going to try, Erik. But don't forget the political officers. They know the orders too, and if we drag our feet too much they're going to figure it out." He paused. "I have a few tricks I'm going to use, but we're going to have to figure out what's going on pretty quickly if we're going to have time to react."

"I can vouch for 1st Brigade, sir. Land us first, and I will tear the place apart and find out what the deal is with all of this urgency."

Holm smiled, though in armor, of course, it lost any communication value. "I was thinking just that, Erik." He paused for a beat. "And more."

"More, sir? What do you want me to do?"

"You trust all the officers in your special action teams, don't you? I mean really trust them?"

"With my life, sir." Cain's reply was immediate and firm... just what Holm was hoping for. "Whatever you need, the teams will be ready."

"Erik, most of 1st Corps is going to land and defeat the enemy occupying Carson's World." He took a deep breath. "The special action teams are going to have a different mission, a very discrete one. I want you to deploy them to scout around and find out what is happening on the planet. You will need to be careful and not attract any suspicion. It won't seem all that strange for small teams of our elite troops to be out on scouting missions."

"I'll handle it, sir." Cain had a lot of questions and doubts about this mission too, and he was thrilled to have the general's permission to snoop around. He had a much more pessimistic view of things than Holm did; he wasn't suspicious like the general was - he was positive there was something wrong, and equally certain Alliance Gov was behind it somehow.

"You'll have to deal directly with the company commanders. Major Jensen has his own political officer, and you'll have enough trouble keeping Captain Warren in the dark without having to worry about another one." Holm's voice was a little sad. He hated feeling like he couldn't communicate freely with his own officers. "We're also going to have to be careful how we relay information on this. We're not going to be able to do this through Sarah like we could here. Pass the word, anything to do with this is to be discussed one to one on laser-link only."

"Yes, sir." Cain was already thinking about how to deploy his teams. "You can count on me, general."

Holm laughed. "I know that, Erik. I hope there's no doubt on that score." The ship vibrated as the engines shut down. They could feel the weightlessness as the shuttle achieved its orbit. An instant later the small positioning thrusters fired, moving the craft slowly toward the waiting transport. "We'll be docked in a couple minutes, so let's wrap up now. Your brigade will land first, so you're going to have your hands full. As soon as you can, go over what we discussed with Jax and get him to help you with the teams." Short pause. "And Erik?"

"Yes, sir?"

"Don't forget we're probably going to have a nasty fight on our hands. I'm sure we're not getting the full intel, and we don't know what has made EE-4 so important, but they aren't sending the entire corps for no reason. This operation is costing more than the entire Second Frontier War, so we have to assume there is a good reason to use so much force. So be careful down there."

"You know me, sir. Caution is my middle name."

Holm snorted a laugh. "Only if 'lack of'" is your first name. No more medals, Erik. Be careful. I can't afford to lose you, ok?"

"Yes, sir. I promise."

The ship com blared again. "Docking in four minutes, thirty seconds."

"Why don't you stay for dinner. We can discuss some strategy for the drop, and you can shuttle back to your ship after."

"Yes, sir. I'd like that."

"And I don't think an impromptu inspection stop at the hospital ship would disrupt operations too badly."

"Yes, general. I'd like that too."

Chapter 13

Alliance-PRC Combined Fleet
Epsilon Eridani System
Inbound from the YZ Ceti warp gate

A wave of fast attack ships burst into the Epsilon Eridani system. They came in slow and immediately broke their formation, each ship heading out on a pre-set course, scanning for enemy detection buoys. The CAC had not held Epsilon Eridani long enough to construct a proper detection grid at the warp gate, and the screen of scanners they had emplaced was much easier to interdict. The attack ships carried robot probes on external racks and launched them as soon as they'd positioned themselves after transit.

Immediately after the attack ships, a squadron of cruisers emerged from the gravitational vortex, taking up a defensive position to protect the scouts in case the enemy had stationed forces near the warp gate. The cruisers were PRC vessels attached to the Alliance fleet. The Tokyo-based PRC and the CAC had been mortal enemies during the Unification Wars, and they had taken their enmity into space. The Alliance and the PRC were frequently allied, and almost always when fighting the CAC.

The warp gate was undefended, however, so the cruiser squadron moved in-system and launched its own probes, extending their scanning range. With no pressing enemy threat, the attack ships completed their search and destroy mission, eliminating all CAC scanner buoys positioned around the warp gate. Their task concluded, they launched two robot drones back to the waiting fleet, giving the all clear to advance into the system.

Twenty minutes after the drones entered the gate, ships began to transit into the system. The Cambrai was the first to emerge, closely followed by her escorts. The oldest serving capital ship in the Alliance fleet, she'd been damaged at Gliese 250 and barely completed repairs in time to depart with Admiral

Garret. Elizabeth Arlington was the captain of the Cambrai, a posting she'd assumed just three days before the Second Battle of Gliese 250. She had only served under Augustus Garret for a short time, and he'd spent most of that harassing her to speed up her repair operation. Nevertheless, she still felt his loss keenly. Her junior officers and crew, who'd been under Garret for longer, were almost catatonic.

Cambrai had been positioned at the rear of the formation as the fleet made its dash to the TZ Arietis warp gate. When Cromwell's engines were knocked offline, the rest of the fleet, still accelerating, quickly passed it by. Cambrai had been closest when the third barrage of missiles detonated. The rest of the ships had moved well past point defense range, but Cambrai was still close enough to fire at the incoming missiles, though her sole efforts were only sufficient to stop a tithe of them. Cromwell itself had been gutted by the second wave, and there was no fire at all coming from her. Cambrai was still in scanning range when the explosions began. At least five warheads detonated within a kilometer of Cromwell, and when the massive fireballs subsided there was nothing left of the great battleship. Nothing at all.

She doubted there could have been any survivors, but her people were denied even the futile effort of conducting rescue operations - they were moving away at high velocity and accelerating, and within a few minutes they were beyond even scanning range. She knew intellectually that no one could have lived through the inferno that surrounded Cromwell, but she couldn't shake the feeling that they had abandoned their comrades. A rescue attempt would almost certainly have been fruitless, but it would also have given her people closure.

Cambrai was the lead battleship on this operation, and Arlington had duties beyond indulging her guilt and uncertainties about the loss of Admiral Garret. She forced back the emotions and doubts and focused on matters at hand. "Carmen, tie the probes into our scanning net and send me a continuous information feed." Arlington had bucked the tiresome trend of naming AIs after naval heroes. As far as she knew, she had the only Carmen in the service.

"Yes, Captain Arlington. I am processing all incoming data. There are no contacts to report at present." The AI's had user-programmable voice patterns, but Arlington had kept the default setting which, for female officers, was a non-descript, moderately feminine sounding tone.

"Keep me advised of our fleet status as well." Some commanders relied heavily on their communications officers, choosing to receive information from them rather than directly from the AI. Arlington had a very analytical mind, and she preferred to work through the computer, which gave her somewhat of a reputation as a cold fish among her staff.

"Yes, Captain Arlington. Saratoga is transiting now." The Saratoga was one of the big new Yorktown class battleships. Admiral Compton had been stationed aboard her, so when Cromwell was lost, and Garret with her, Saratoga became the new flagship. She had been slated to come through later in the progression, but Arlington figured that Compton had wanted to take a look at things for himself.

They'd expected at least a delaying action at the warp gate, but there was nothing. No enemy presence at all beyond a thin picket of scanner buoys. If the attack ships had gotten all the scanners, the defenders wouldn't even have a good idea of the force composition they'd be facing. It was all a bit odd. But that was Compton's problem; hers was making sure Cambrai was ready for whatever the admiral needed from her. "Carmen, I want a full diagnostic run while the rest of the fleet is transiting. We've got some tape and chewing gum repairs holding things together; let's use the time we've got to make sure everything is 100%." Cambrai would be ready, she would see to that.

Admiral Terrance Compton sat on the flag bridge of the AS Saratoga, scanning status reports as fleet units transited to the system and maneuvered into position. It was still surreal to him to be in command. Compton had served with Augustus Garret since they'd both graduated from the Academy. They had raised hell together as junior officers, and they became two of the most notorious fast attack ship commanders in the Second Frontier War, racking up a list of kills that still stood as a record.

Compton was no stranger to the pressure of command, but this time it was different. He could feel his insides twisted into knots; part of him wanted to run to some desolate place and mourn his friend. But he didn't have the luxury to weep for a fallen brother. The fleet had lost its leader, its hero, its very heart and soul, but despite their pain and loss, the war went on. His memorial to his friend would be simple and expedient. He would give Garret's people what they needed; he would pull them through this terrible loss, single-handedly if he must, and lead them to victory. He could think of no more fitting way to honor the great man.

He shoved his grief down into the deep recesses of his mind and then obsessed over every detail of the fleet's operation, as if he would fail Garret if a blown lighting track in a cargo hold went unreplaced. He'd been running the crew ragged to make sure things were perfect; the last thing any of them needed was time to think anyway.

But now he was worried. Not because of the data streaming into his control center or any new intel, but in his gut. Things didn't feel right. The enemy had hit this place, apparently with enough force to take out an entire battlegroup as well as the orbital forts, but they didn't contest his entry at all. It smelled like a trap to him, but he couldn't figure it out. His orders left him little latitude, either to halt or even delay the mission, so if it was a trap he had no choice but to advance into it. But he was going to proceed cautiously, orders or no.

He waited until the battle fleet was assembled before proceeding deeper into the system. If there was a hidden enemy waiting, he wanted to be ready. He had a powerful fleet - four battlegroups plus the PRC cruisers. The Saratoga and the Cambrai along with their escorts had left Gliese 250 with Cromwell and Admiral Garret. The Hastings and the Greene had been part of the force sent to forestall the attack on Garret. Having arrived too late to save Cromwell and the admiral, but early enough to catch the depleted CAC ships as they retired, the relief force exacted a terrible revenge, wrecking Liang Chang's fleet and taking the admiral himself prisoner. The bulk of the task force then reinforced Compton, more than replacing the firepower lost with Cromwell.

The combined fleet continued to Columbia, where they were met by the resupply convoy and brought up to strength with missiles and bombers. They linked up with General Holm's I Corps and their array of transports and set out for Epsilon Eridani.

That massive force of transports and assault ships now waited on the other side of the warp gate. Compton was going to be absolutely sure things were clear before he allowed them to transit. This was no smash and grab raid. Waiting on the other side of the gate was the biggest land force the Alliance had ever assembled for war on the frontier. If this was a trap - if Compton's misgivings were borne out - there was no need to compound the loss of warships by having 45,000 veteran ground troops killed on their largely defenseless transports.

The fleet took a day to maneuver into formation and, once formed up, they accelerated toward planet four. Compton ordered scoutships off in all directions, and they sent probes even further out, seeking to insure that they left no hidden enemy force behind them. But for all Compton's meticulous efforts, there were no contacts at all by the time the fleet's probes had reach scanning range of Epsilon Eridani IV.

The probes' data continued along the same unexpected line. There was no enemy fleet anywhere within detection range; the planet was entirely undefended. Compton studied every piece of incoming information, trying to understand what was happening, and his AI fed him probe data as soon as it was received and decrypted.

"Commander Simmons, order Captain Johan to take her squadron to the planet. I want her to scout the entire area and report back. Have her make her best time; I want this information five minutes ago." Compton snapped out the order even while his AI was still sending him reports from the probes.

"Yes, sir." William Simmons was Compton's tactical officer. Garret's entire staff had been lost with him, so Compton's people inherited their roles, just as the admiral himself had been compelled to step into Garret's big shoes. "Estimated best time to arrival, one day, seven hours, ten minutes."

"Joker, send a flash message to the transport fleet. They are to remain in position until the attack squadron has scouted the planet." Joker was Compton's AI, a concession to the admiral's fondness for playing cards, something he'd done with tremendous success until increasing rank made the whole enterprise a bit unseemly.

"Yes, sir. Sending flash message to Hudson now." The AS Hudson was one of two light cruisers deployed near the warp gate to relay messages through by drone. No doubt General Garret's men and women would grumble at another day and a half of delay, but Compton was going to be sure before he put them at risk. They'd just have to wait.

The Pendragon had been decelerating at 4g for almost a day when the ship went into freefall along with the rest of the first wave of transports. They'd been cleared for orbital insertion, and were on their final approach to Carson's World.

They had been compelled to wait several days longer than expected before transiting into Epsilon Eridani. Admiral Compton had been suspicious when he had found no enemy force waiting to engage him, and he'd repeatedly postponed the transports' entry while he scanned the entire area between the warp gate and the planet.

Compton had found debris from the battle that had been fought here several months before. The fortresses, which had been substantial defensive works, were gutted wrecks...dead hulks still orbiting the planet. It was clear that a major fight had occurred here; there were ruined, lifeless ships and debris scattered over a wide area.

The admiral had half a dozen ships out collecting and analyzing the debris. In the absence of any friendly or enemy forces, the wreckage was his best hope of reconstructing what had happened here. Meanwhile, though his gut was still flashing him a dire warning, he could think of no further reasons to delay the landings without violating his orders outright.

The Pendragon, carrying Erik Cain and his special action battalion, slid into orbit alongside her brethren, and launched a spread of planetary probes. The entire transport fleet was doing the same, sending small drones into the atmosphere of Carson's World, scanning for enemy positions and troop concentrations.

The battle computers would analyze the data from a thousand probes and create a projection of enemy strength on the ground. As Erik knew from long and often bitter experience, it would be a relatively unreliable guide to what they would face. There were just too many places to hide troops on an entire planet, too many ways to interfere with scans. The heavy elements present on a mining world like Epsilon Eridani IV interfered with detection devices, making it even more difficult to create accurate estimates. Then-Colonel Holm had used this fact to devastating effect during the last ditch defense of Columbia a few years back, and Erik himself had been with the hidden forces that had surprised the CAC invaders.

Carson's World no longer had a civilian population, so the Pendragon and other assault ships were able to conduct a heavy orbital bombardment, targeting troop concentrations identified by the probes. The enemy had built some hasty strongpoints, and the fleet blasted them hard, dropping small nuclear warheads on the toughest positions. Job one for the orbital assault was to clear out as much of the enemy's air interdiction capability as possible so the landing craft and atmospheric fighters weren't overwhelmed by fire from the ground. If ground units were also depleted or disordered, that was a bonus.

The bombardment lasted only a few hours, and then the guns and launchers of the assault ships fell silent. It was time for men and woman to take ground the old fashioned way, meter by meter.

A tight beam laser communication link connected the Saratoga, positioned 100,000 kilometers from the planet with the heavy assault ship Tinian, currently in orbit. On an encrypted line, two men were having a final discussion before the landing craft were launched.

"Something is off, Elias. I'm sure of it." Compton was uneasy, and it came through in his tone. It took just under a second for the transmission to reach Holm's ship and the same for his response to get back to Saratoga. Compton was used to the hitch in these types of communications, but he still found it irritating, especially when he was already tense. He'd have preferred to meet face to face with Holm, but they both had jobs to do and no time for the indulgence of shuttling back and forth.

"I've had misgivings since I got these orders on Columbia." Holm paused briefly, exacerbating the delay on Compton's end. "There is a lot about this mission we just don't know, but I don't see any options. Our orders are crystal clear."

Holm sat at his desk, alone for the moment, though he'd found it increasingly difficult to shake his political officer. Colonel Killian was a cut above the other liaison officers, and Holm kept reminding himself not to underestimate the man. Most of the others seemed to be Political Academy graduates of relative obscurity, but Killian's family was very well placed; he even had an uncle in the Senate. Clearly, I Corps commander had been considered worthy of a true watchdog.

"You're right. We don't have a choice. I delayed on my end as long as I could. We've got to start your landings, but I can't believe there isn't more down there than a reinforced CAC brigade. If we're not missing something, Alliance Intelligence really screwed the pooch by sending so much force here."

"I'm sure they have some surprises for us down there," Holm replied. "Whatever is hiding planetside, my people will dig it out; I'm sure of that." He let out a deep breath. "I've got to get to work, Terrance. I'm commencing my landing in 90 minutes."

"Very well." Compton's voice was tense. He'd been as careful as possible, taken every precaution he could think of...but still he couldn't shake the feeling that something was terribly wrong. "The fleet is in position, and I have scoutships conducting a deeper probe of the system." He hesitated then added, "And Elias?"

"Yes, Terrance?"

"Be careful."

"You too, my friend."

Chapter 14

Launch Bay Alpha
AS Pendragon
In orbit around Epsilon Eridani IV

The launch bay felt a little surreal to Cain as he stood bolted into the lander awaiting the final launch countdown. A lifetime ago, another Erik Cain stood in a lander waiting to launch out into this very airspace. My god, he thought, has it really been fourteen years? Was I ever that young?

He'd come full circle. Carson's World had been the site of his first mission, and he'd walked into the launch bay back then as a junior private, sweating with fear and desperately trying to remember everything he'd learned in training. The fear was still there; anyone sane would be afraid, though he'd learned to temper it and push it out of his mind. But the training had become second nature and the years of experience had transformed him forever.

Will Thompson had been the senior private in the squad on that first raid, and he'd looked out for Cain, then and later on too. More than anyone, Thompson had helped turn that raw recruit into a competent Marine. He was Cain's first real friend in the Corps, and he'd guided Erik not just on the battlefield, but also about many small things, like how to make life on a spaceship tolerable. They'd served together for three years until Thompson was wounded during the disastrous Operation Achilles, an event that left Cain in command of the squad.

Thompson had gone to the Academy after his recovery, but he was badly injured again, this time in a training accident, and he did another year in the hospital. He retired out of the service shortly after that, and though he had never finished his Academy training, he was mustered out as a lieutenant. Erik had heard he'd settled down on Arcadia, but he wasn't certain.

The support Erik had gotten from the more experienced men and women of the squad made an enormous impression on the young soldier. It was the first time in his life he'd seen people working selflessly together, and he was determined to pay his debt to his old comrades by helping those who came after him. As Cain advanced through the ranks he had never forgotten the way he'd been welcomed into the squad, and he committed himself to watching over the troops under his command, using all his experience and training to help them survive on the battlefield. And the ones that didn't make it, the ones Cain felt he'd failed - they lived with him, tugging at his conscience in the night.

The first time he had bolted himself into a lander to assault Carson's World he had been blissfully without command responsibility. He didn't question why he was there, didn't even worry about what they were doing. All he had to think about was following orders from his team and squad leaders.

This time his burdens were far greater. An entire brigade was dropping with him - 3,600 - troops, and he was responsible for every one of them. They were the vanguard, the spearpoint of the 45,000-strong I Corps, and they were about to launch on a mission that had Cain very worried.

He felt the Pendragon shake; it was the atmospheric fighters launching from their bay in the belly of the great ship. Pendragon carried a squadron of six, and they were going down to strafe and bomb the landing area before his troops hit the ground. It was another testament to the escalation of battles in this war. The last time he was on Carson's World the Marines had no such supporting arms - not even a tank or an artillery piece, and certainly no aircraft. Other than their expended Gordon landers providing limited supporting fire, it was just the Marines on foot. Cain hadn't even seen an atmospheric fighter until Operation Achilles, though the pilots earned their pay in that debacle, saving the invasion force from being overrun more than once. In doing it, they'd actually managed to suffer a higher casualty rate than the ground-pounders, who had lost over 80% killed and wounded. No Marine who fought in Achilles ever said a negative word about pilots after that battle, and anyone who did in their presence was likely to buy a world of hurt.

The Pendragon's launch bays were a scene of meticulous efficiency. Cain had led some excellent troops before, but never anything quite like the battalion billeted with him on Pendragon. There wasn't a soldier onboard who had not made at least five assaults. The special action teams had started as an elite company, trained by Erik Cain as a reaction force. When they'd contributed to humiliating the 2nd Brigade in a series of wargames, the general had asked Erik to expand the force to battalion strength. He'd swept every formation in I Corps, armed with Holm's authority to appropriate any personnel he felt he needed. He suspected a few of the other unit commanders had made some disparaging and anatomically improbable remarks as he absconded with their veterans, but in fact he was very restrained and only took a few from each formation.

Now his elite force was going to get its true test, not just in battle, but executing the special mission General Holm had given Erik. There was some reason I Corps had been sent to retake Carson's World, something that was being hidden from them. They were going to find out what it was, and they were going to do it without calling attention to themselves.

"Initiating final launch countdown." The tinny voice of the battle computer roused Cain out of his introspection. "Depressurizing launch bay."

Cain's blast shield snapped shut, blocking his view of the landing bay. He couldn't see or feel it, of course, but he knew that they were being pressure-coated with heat resistant foam. A few seconds later the outer doors opened.

"Good luck, Marines!" Cain had heard a ship captain give that sendoff more times than he could remember. It was a tradition almost as old as man fighting in space, and one that was universally loved. He couldn't explain it, but it was inspiring. Even after all his battles, it still worked its magic on him; the effect on the less experienced troops was enormous.

Cain gritted his teeth just before the catapult blasted the lander out of the ship and into the upper atmosphere of Carson's World. Even in armor, every bone in his body felt the jarring as the magnetic launch catapult rapidly accelerated the

Gordon down the guiding track and out of the Pendragon's bay.

Enemy fire was very light; the orbital bombardment had been extremely effective, and the atmospheric fighters were flying sorties against any missile launcher or weapons platform that gave away its location. The enemy took some potshots, but nothing that seriously threatened the landing.

The lander zigzagged its way to the surface, executing the wild evasive maneuvers designed to thwart enemy fire. The heat resistant foam began to blacken and break away as the atmospheric density increased. Cain had been through this dozens of times, but he still felt a small thrill when the blast shield snapped back and he could see again.

Sixteen minutes after launch the Gordon fired its breaking thrusters, and they set down gently in the middle of a large, open plain. The locking bolts retracted, and the Marines onboard snapped right out of their harnesses, moving out and taking a position around the lander, ready for action. They were pretty sure there were no enemy troops within range, but carelessness is how Marines end up dead, and these were veterans.

Cain looked out over the terrain. All around the lander, the greenish-yellow fungus that covered the ground was burned and blackened from the heat of the thrusters. Looking up he could see Gordons coming down all over the field, with an LZ every quarter klick. It looked like the landing was going perfectly, and Erik let himself imagine that all his people got down to the surface safely for once...an illusion he was only able to maintain for a few minutes before he got the report of the first fatality. Fire had been very light, but one of the Gordon's had taken a hit coming in. The computer tried to land the ship but lost it on the final approach, and it crashed, killing six of the ten Marines onboard.

His people were the first wave, and their primary mission was to secure the LZs for the rest of I Corps. General Holm and the battle computer had put together an operations plan, which Cain's troops were now executing. Flawlessly executing, he thought proudly, looking out over the plain. His troops were very well trained, and his officers and non-coms were experienced professionals who didn't need him hovering over their every move. He could see his teams deploying in every direction, staking out the LZs, and taking up defensive positions in case the enemy made any moves against the landing. For the moment, Cain found he had little to do.

"I must commend you on the efficiency and professionalism of your landing, Colonel." Kind words, but an unwelcome voice. Captain Warren.

"Thank you, Captain. My men and women deserve the credit." He hoped he hadn't spat out the words with the contempt he felt for the man. In truth, he didn't really care, but he knew it would make life easier if he treated the officious prick with some superficial respect. Not that he found it easy.

"They have indeed been well-trained. No military force in history has ever received a level of support comparable to that provided by Alliance Gov to the Corps."

Somehow Cain knew the little bureaucrat would turn things around and give the government the credit. Most of the troops now deploying so efficiently had been lost souls crushed under the jackboot of that same Alliance Gov, and they were saved from a life of deprivation and despair only because they had the good fortune to be flagged as likely Marine recruits. But Cain held his tongue. No good could come from debating politics with Warren.

"Captain, I am pleased that you are impressed with the performance of our troops, but I'm afraid I am very busy with the landing, so if you will excuse me for the moment?" He was lying; he actually had very little to do. But he could only take so much of the political officer at one time.

"Of course, Colonel. Please do not let me interfere with your duties."

Cain nodded, a gesture that lost something in powered armor and trotted off. He started out just walking in any direction to get away from Warren, but he found himself heading toward Jax's LZ. His people were coming down now, and they should be on the ground by the time Erik reached their assigned position.

Colonel Darius Jax jogged up to the location his scouts had reported. He wanted to have a look around for himself. Jogging in armor was actually a fairly complicated activity that looked a little like ice skating. A normal running motion would result in huge bounding jumps, courtesy of the amplified servo-mechanical systems of the powered armor. The jogger had to move side to side to keep low, and on the battlefield, you usually wanted to keep low.

He could see as he neared the designated coordinates that there had indeed been fighting here. The ground was torn up, and the scrubby yellow fungus was blackened and burnt. There was the debris of war everywhere...weapons, shattered pieces of armor, and as he got closer to the designated coordinates, bodies.

"See, sir?" Lieutenant Clark commed Jax as he approached the cluster of scouts standing on a low hill. "I thought the garrison had been withdrawn."

"They were withdrawn." Jax pulled up next to the scouts and stopped. He was half a head taller than any of them.

"Then who fought here, sir?" That was Sergeant Lunden. Technically, he shouldn't be reporting directly to Jax with the lieutenant there, but scouts were by nature less formal with the chain of command. And Jax didn't give a shit for protocol; if one of his troopers had something to say he wanted to hear it.

"That's an excellent question, Sergeant." He took a few steps, looking around for himself. "Lieutenant, I want your people to take a closer look around. Get me any data you can on whatever happened here."

"Yes, Colonel Jax." Clark motioned to his team. "Let's go. Spread out and look around. I want to know what happened here." He took a few steps, then added, "Let's get video of this while area."

Jax watched them move down the hillside then told his AI to get Cain on the comlink.

"Right here, you big ox."

Jax turned to see Cain walking up the hill toward him. "Erik, we've got something interesting over here." He motioned over the crest of the hill. "Come take a look at this."

Cain walked up next to Jax and looked out over the field below the hill. "There must be a hundred bodies down there." He stared for a few more seconds. "No, more than a hundred."

"This planet was supposed to be deserted when the CAC took it, right?" Jax's deep voice boomed loudly in Cain's helmet. "So who were they fighting?"

Cain frowned then realized Jax couldn't see his face. One of the harder things to get used to about fighting in powered armor is effectively losing the entire lexicon of facial expressions as modes of communication. It's easy to forget how often a smile or a stare gets a point across. "That's a good question." Short pause. "Here's another one. Why aren't they making any effort at all to oppose our landing?"

"This gets stranger and stranger, Erik." Jax sometimes called Cain colonel and others Erik. It was moderately insubordinate, but they were like brothers, and neither one gave a shit for military formality. At least not when it was just the two of them talking. "We need to report this to the general."

Cain sighed. "He's probably on the way down now. I might not be able to reach him until he lands." His tone changed slightly. "Hector, see if you can reach General Holm."

"General Holm is in the launch bay of the Tinian. He is scheduled to depart in seven minutes."

"How about General Gilson?" Erik was looking out over the battlefield as he waited for Hector's response.

"Negative, Colonel Cain. Major General Gilson is currently en route to the surface. Estimated time to landing, eleven minutes."

"Ok, Hector, let me know when General Holm lands."

"Of course, Colonel Cain."

Cain took a deep breath and held it in for a few seconds before exhaling. "Alright, Jax. Let's worry about our day job. We need to keep these LZs secure, so focus on that for now." He looked out over the plain, watching the scouts prowling around, shooting video and collecting debris samples. "Send another search team over here to scour all of this, and dispatch some scouts to look around to see if there was fighting anywhere else." He turned to look back at Jax. "Then I want you to set up some defensive positions covering any approaches to the LZs from the north. If the enemy is planning anything I want us to be ready for it."

"Yes, sir." He pointed north and east. "I already sent three heavy weapons teams to stake out strong positions. "I was planning to send one of the battalions to deploy north and set up a defensive line."

"Perfect." He looked back over the debris-strewn field below them. "And if your people find anything out there - anything at all - report it to me immediately."

"You got it, Erik." Jax gave a rough armored salute and turned to walk down the hill. He was going to personally see to the setup of that defensive line.

"And Jax?"

He looked back at Cain. "Yes, Erik?"

"Be careful, brother. There's a lot of weird shit going on here."

Jax pointed at Cain. "You too, Erik." He paused a second, facing Cain along the crest before turning and trotting down the hillside.

Chapter 15

1st Brigade HQ
Base of the Lysandra Plateau
Epsilon Eridani IV

"Colonel, 2nd Battalion is running into heavy resistance outside the abandoned mineworks." No one but Cain would have caught the stress in Jax's voice. "They are reporting major enemy troop concentrations to the north and east." After a brief pause: "Damn it, Erik, they must have had reinforcements hidden in those old tunnels."

"Ok, Jax. I have 4th battalion in reserve. I'm sending up a company and one of the battalion heavy weapons to support the 2nd." Cain appeared totally calm to any outside observer. He knew trouble was coming - he'd been expecting it all along - and he was sure this was just the beginning. "Jax, you run over there and direct the deployment of the reinforcements. Make sure they are used to maximum effect, because it's all they're getting; I've got to keep some reserves uncommitted."

"Yes, sir." Jax was worried too; Cain could tell. "On my way now."

"Hector, advise Colonel Kendall that she is to dispatch a company from the brigade reserve along with one of the heavy weapons teams. I want them at 2nd Battalion's position in fifteen minutes. Understood?"

"Of course, I understand." God, Hector is a pain in the ass, Cain thought. "Relaying your orders now, Colonel."

Cain comlinked Anne Delacorte. "Captain, I need you to report to me at once."

"Yes, Colonel Cain." Her reply was immediate and firm. "Be there in two minutes, max."

"Colonel Kendall confirms receipt of your orders," said Hector. "ETA to arrival at designated coordinates, ten minutes."

"Thank you, Hector." It really wasn't necessary to thank the AI, but it was easy to forget he (it?) was a machine. Maybe there was something to the annoying personality after all.

Cain's troops had been on the ground a week, which is a long time to be living in powered armor. He'd ordered each battalion to rotate one company at a time out of the line to get some rest, but it was difficult to sleep in armor, so most of the troops just sat around and tried to relax. Everyone was getting brittle and strung out on stimulants. Normally, on an Earthlike world, the troops could pop their suits and get some real rest, but General Holm wasn't taking any chances after the plague that had wiped out the population. Supposedly, the virus had died out once there were no more humans to host it, but he wasn't in the mood to take chances, and when he'd asked Sarah Linden her opinion, she'd agreed completely. Everyone was to remain suited up whenever possible.

The whole campaign had so far been a confused affair, with no real front lines or rational axes of advance. There were no population centers remaining or other landmarks of any importance, so the fight was just a confused melee, with each side trying to wipe out the other, wherever they were. The defenders were dispersed all over the place, taking advantage of strong positions and natural cover and daring the attackers to come dig them out.

There was only one major continent on Carson's World, and the mines and settlements had all been well to the south. In the north, the geology was relatively unstable, with several mountain ranges and considerable volcanic activity. After Cain's brigade had secured the initial landing area, they were sent to cover the northern flank in case any enemy formations had deployed in the rugged terrain.

They'd met considerable resistance as they headed north, and it soon became clear there were far more enemy troops concealed on Carson's World than had been initially apparent. Cain didn't like it one bit. They're bleeding us, he thought grimly. Just putting out enough force to make us launch costly attacks.

"Captain Warren?" The political officer was standing a few meters away.

"Yes, Colonel Cain? How may I help you?"

Cain flashed a message to Warren's armor over the laser-link. "I want to get this update to General Holm immediately, but I don't want to send it over the comlink. It draws some conclusions of mine about enemy intentions and, if I am right, I don't want to risk the enemy hearing it." When Warren hesitated he added, "With the tactical situation at present, I don't have an officer available to send right now. I called Captain Delacorte, but I was going to dispatch her to the abandoned mine to scout near the enemy positions."

"I'd be happy to assist, Colonel." Cain would have given two month's pay to see Warren's expression when he thought about Cain asking him to scout up at the front line instead of Delacorte. At least his hinting at the alternative task erased Warren's objections to being a messenger.

"Thank you, Captain. Please transmit only on line of sight to the general over the laser-link communicator." Good, Cain thought, that gets rid of him for a while.

"Captain Delacorte, reporting as ordered, sir." Erik had been watching Warren make his way back toward corps HQ when Anne walked up behind him.

"Prompt as always, Captain." Cain smiled - again, a wasted gesture in armor - as he turned to face her. "I have a mission for you." Cain switched to direct laser communication. He didn't want anyone else hearing this. "Anne, I want you to make contact with Captains Clarke, Teller and Hamilton. They're all out with the teams scouting to the northwest. I need to know if they've found anything yet. They're under orders not to transmit in the open."

"Yes, sir. I'll find them and bring you a report."

"Thank you, captain. Remember, line of sight communication only on this." He hesitated slightly. "Anne...be careful. We have no idea what is out there, but I have a bad feeling. Take one of the reserve teams with you."

"Yes, colonel." She gave the best imitation of a salute she could manage in armor and trotted off.

He was just about to check in with Jax when his comlink went crazy. Every battalion commander was reporting massive enemy activity. They were being attacked in force.

First Division headquarters was a beehive of activity. Reports had been coming in non-stop for the last hour. Enemy forces were counter-attacking all along the lines, with the heaviest blows coming in the northern sector of the Lysandra Plateau.

Catherine Gilson stood in the middle of her command post, snapping orders into her comlink. Colonel Cain had reported a massive attack on 1st Brigade's positions on the plateau. His data suggested two enemy division strength formations were assaulting his hastily-formed lines. It seemed impossible that the enemy had that kind of strength here, but Cain was the last person she'd suspect of panicking or exaggerating. She'd been about to send most of the divisional reserve to reinforce 1st Brigade when she started getting reports of 2nd Brigade falling back under sustained attack. She decided to hold the reserve until she had a better idea of the overall situation.

She reported the incomplete data she had to General Holm, who also took Erik Cain's report very seriously. He released two air assault wings to her, and she sent them on a series of sorties in support of First Brigade. That's when she got the real surprise - the enemy had air assets too, and they'd engaged her own.

Above the plateau, and over the rocky foothills to the south, a great air battle raged, while on the ground her division was hammered by repeated attacks. "General Holm, Gilson reporting."

"Yes, General Gilson?" Holm sounded stressed. Clearly she wasn't the only one calling him with problems. "What is your status?"

"Sir, Colonel Cain's people are under massive attack. The air assets I sent to aid him have been intercepted by enemy fighters. They are heavily engaged and are unable to provide close ground support at this time."

"Yes, I am getting multiple reports of enemy air wings. Our pilots are facing a considerable battle for air supremacy. What other aid do you have available to dispatch to Colonel Cain's position?"

"Sir, any meaningful reinforcements sent to Colonel Cain

will leave me with almost no divisional reserves." She paused. "And 2nd Brigade is falling back and will likely need support as well."

Holm grimaced as he thought to himself. Erik Cain is not overreacting, he knew that much, so he figured he really needed the reinforcements. "Dispatch your reserves to reinforce 1st Brigade. I am sending you the Oceanian Regiment to give you a divisional reserve. They are currently unengaged and at full strength."

"Yes, sir."

"And Catherine?"

"Yes, sir?"

"I'm authorizing your division to deploy specials if you need them. With the size and intensity of this attack, I'm sure the enemy is going to go nuclear anyway. For once, let's escalate first. Pick your moment...when it will have the biggest impact.

"Yes, General Holm." He could tell she was already thinking of her tactical deployments. "Thank you, sir."

"Just make it count, Cate. And hold that line. Holm out."

Cain stood in a hastily-dug trench, peering carefully over the edge, his visor amplification cranked up. The enemy had tried to take the position three times, and the ground in front was littered with the dead and dying. His troops were heavily outnumbered, and it was getting worse. The attackers seemed to have endless reinforcements, while Cain had just deployed the last of his reserves. He'd moved up to the trench himself after the second assault. The general would probably yell at him, but his troopers needed him close right now. When the enemy had come at them the third time, Cain was on the line firing with his troopers.

It turned out to be a great way to get rid of Captain Warren. The political officer expressed concern about Cain exposing himself up on the front lines, but he declined to come along himself. Yes, that is what soldiers do, Cain had thought. We fight, you useless fucking peacock. He thought it, but he'd managed not to say it. Barely.

The enemy forces his troops were facing were mostly South American Imperial Guard, front line troops, but not the equal of Cain's veterans. Still, I Corps had been caught flat-footed. Alliance Intelligence had been sure it would be several months before the empire could deploy in force. *I've got some news for you guys*, Erik thought. *They're here in force.* Of course, Cain and General Holm - and Admiral Compton as well - had all been worried about this operation from the beginning. But they'd been given no choice. They were ordered here, and they went in.

Cain had to admit that even he was surprised by the scale of the enemy attack. He'd expected trouble here, but even his worst estimates fell well short of the reality he now faced. There were Imperial troops here with the CAC forces, and some of his units had run into Janissaries as well. Even worse, he was hearing chatter on the comlink about Europan units as well. If true, there were forces here from four of the Superpowers, which meant they almost certainly outnumbered I Corps. By how much he could only guess.

He'd moved half his troops back to a second line a klick away from the first. It would weaken his forward defense, but he was worried about enemy nukes, and he didn't want his forces concentrated enough to be vulnerable to catastrophic damage from a couple warheads. Left to themselves, troops tended to bunch together, especially in tough fights.

Now he'd gotten the clearance to use his own nuclear weapons, and he had a surprise planned. *For once we get to act rather than react*, he thought. Alliance doctrine tended to shy away from taking the initiative in the escalation of battles. "And they know that too," Cain muttered to himself, thinking of the enemy commanders.

"Jax, three minutes." He'd sent Jax back to command the second line and to supervise the nuclear barrage he was launching in 180 seconds. "Everything ready?"

"Everything is good, Colonel." Cain couldn't remember anything he'd ever asked Jax to do that the big man didn't get done. "Bombardment impact in one-six-five seconds. Second wave will advance three minutes later."

"Excellent." Cain was attacking with the first line ninety seconds after his nukes hit, just long enough for the shockwaves to subside. His entire brigade had been pushed back with heavy casualties by clearly superior forces; the last thing the enemy would expect was an attack. Erik didn't exactly have clearance to go on the offensive, but he hadn't been ordered to stand fast either, so he managed to justify his actions. To himself, at least. Whether he'd be able to make that case to others would largely depend on what transpired in the next hour or so.

"Colonel, nuclear barrage in sixty seconds. I suggest that you move deeper into the trench." Hector's advice was sound. The warheads would be hitting the enemy position close to Cain's own - he needed to keep his head down.

"Hector, put me on comlink with the regiment."

"Com active, Colonel."

"First Regiment, this is Colonel Cain. I want everyone to grab some dirt and stay hidden until the shockwaves have subsided. Anybody pokes his head up and gets it blown off is going to have to deal with me...and trust me, you don't want that." He paused. "When you get the alert we are going up and over immediately and take the enemy position. This is a limited offensive, so don't get carried away. We're going to tear up their lines and disrupt their logistics, and then we are coming back."

"Fifteen seconds, Colonel."

"Broadcast countdown to the regiment, Hector."

"Ten, nine, eight..."

Jax's mortar crews are firing now, he thought.

"Five, four..."

Cain slid down the side of the trench and crouched, lowering his blast shield.

"Two, one..."

In his suit with his visor covered, Cain couldn't see the blinding flashes as eight 20kt warheads detonated along the enemy front line, but he heard the explosions and the sounds of dirt and rocks bouncing off his armored back. He counted silently to himself - Hector could have easily kept a countdown, but it gave Erik something to do.

"Ok, 1st Regiment, let's go." He jumped out of the trench and moved quickly toward the enemy position, waddling side to side in the motion that allowed an armored soldier to run without bounding into the air. All along the trench lines, at 20 meter intervals, the men and women of the 1st Regiment followed their brigade commander into the residual atomic maelstrom.

The scene was surreal. Silhouetted against the patchy dawn light were eight mushroom clouds in a nearly perfect line. Cain knew better than most what was happening along that enemy position. A nuclear explosion had come close to killing him, and it took a year in the hospital before he could return to duty. The death and misery he had just inflicted on the Imperial troops was almost unimaginable. Welcome to the war, he thought grimly.

He knew the enemy would retaliate with their own atomic weapons, so he was determined to do the maximum amount of damage and get his troops back to cover before they were targeted. It only took a few minutes to get to the enemy lines. He was near a hotspot, and his radiation monitor was reading in the lethal range. He'd be fine in his armor, but even a minor wound would breach his suit and expose him.

The enemy trench had been obliterated, and there was a large crater just off to his right. All around there were bodies, armor black from the heat and twisted and torn apart. There were no live enemies he could detect and no nearby fire.

His scanners showed firefights to the east and west, in between warhead impact points, where some enemy troops had survived. The defenders were dazed and disoriented, though, and Cain's troops quickly wiped out most of them, sending the rest fleeing to the rear.

"Colonel, we are receiving multiple reports of enemy supply convoys." One of Hector's jobs was to monitor all the incoming messages - there was no way a human could listen to them all - and alert Cain to the ones requiring his attention.

"Show me."

Hector put up a schematic on Erik's visor. "It appears that there are two primary locations. Reports are similar. Enemy anti-gravs carrying palettes of weaponry and supplies. Types and quantities not yet available."

"We caught them resupplying." Cain's voice was dark, almost sinister.

"It appears so, Colonel." Cain hadn't really been speaking to Hector; he'd just been talking out loud. This is an opportunity, he thought. Let's not waste it. "Hector, get me Colonel Jax."

"He did what?" General Holm didn't think Cain could still surprise him, but he was usually wrong on that score.

"He launched an attack, sir." Lieutenant Raynor couldn't hide the admiration in his voice. "He hit the enemy line with a nuclear barrage and advanced right through it."

The young officers loved Cain. Holm wanted to disagree, but he really couldn't. Despite his age, experience, and caution, he too loved to watch his moderately crazy colonel in action. "Status?"

"He reports light casualties, sir. His forces have advanced 5 kilometers and established a new line. He has possession of the heights, and his position is anchored on the western mountain range." Raynor paused - he was still listening to reports coming in as he was updating the general. "Sir, he has taken two enemy convoys." He looked over at Holm. "It appears he attacked as they were moving up supplies...including specials, sir. Colonel Cain has captured twenty enemy warheads."

"Nice work, Erik." Holm whispered softly to himself. That should slow them down a little, he thought.

"Sir, Colonel Cain advises that his advance has placed him on the flank of the enemy forces engaged with 2nd Brigade. He requests permission to attack."

"Get him on the line, lieutenant." Holm paused. "I want to speak with him."

Barely a second passed before Cain's voice was coming through the general's headset. "Yes, sir?"

"Erik, you're a crazy son of a bitch, do you know that?"

"So I've been told." Cain tried to suppress a laugh with only partial success. "By you, in fact."

"Your attack was a bold move. Brilliant. You surprised the hell out of them, and that will set their timetable back." He exhaled slowly. "But they won't be surprised if you attack again. You've got a good position there, but I don't want you to take too many casualties trying to push farther. We still don't have an accurate assessment of enemy strength, and until we do, we have to assume we're heavily outnumbered." Holm took another deep breath. "You can launch a few spoiling attacks to take some pressure off of 2nd Brigade...they could use the support. But do not launch a major attack. We just don't have the resources to sustain it right now."

"Yes, sir." Cain paused. "I'll shoot 'em up a little and scare them on the flanks. That should get them to ease up on their own attacks for a while. Maybe they'll shift some of their strength over to me."

"That's good. But nothing more." He waited a few seconds. "Understood, Erik?"

"Yes, sir. Understood." After a few seconds: "Sir, I never intended to advance this far, but we've occupied an excellent position. Our right flank is against the mountains, and we've got the highest ground for kilometers. I was going to pull back to my old position after raising some hell, but I think I should fortify this location instead. I'm really a thorn in their side."

Holm had the map up inside his visor. "It is a good position, Erik, but if 2nd Brigade gets forced back you'll be cut off."

"I think we can hold here, sir." He paused. "Even if we're cut off for a while." Another brief silence, then: "General, I really think we can do more to damage the enemy by holding this advanced position."

Holm closed his eyes. Cain was right. His 3,000 troops could inflict more harm on the enemy's operations were they were. But it felt like a forlorn hope, a suicide mission. How many of those 3,000 would come back? Holm knew the enemy would throw everything they had at that position. Cain knew it too, of course. But he was still requesting permission to hold there. It took everything Elias Holm had inside him to force the words out. "Do it."

Chapter 16

Northern Face of the Lysandra Plateau
Epsilon Eridani IV

Lieutenant John Marek crouched behind a jagged rock out-cropping, shattered chips of stone bouncing off his armored back. His platoon had been pinned down for at least an hour. They'd beaten back five enemy assaults, but half his troops were down, and they were running low on ammunition. They were under fire from at least three heavy auto-cannons, and he'd just received word that the enemy had broken through Third Company on his right flank. He'd sent one of his snipers to cover the approaches from the now-exposed right, but that wasn't going to be enough.

He didn't know how much longer he could hold this position. His troops were situated in good cover, and their fields of fire had savaged the attackers and sent them reeling back with heavy casualties. But if the enemy wanted his little patch of ground badly enough, they could take it. They knew it, and Marek knew it too.

"Sergeant Anton, take the reserve squad and form a line on the right, perpendicular to our current position." Marek kicked up the magnification level of his visor and scanned the terrain along the flank. "There's a low ridge about 200 meters north. It's not great cover, but it's better than nothing." He paused. "Make sure you take one of the SAWs with you, and goddammit, find a good spot for it, because you're going to need all the firepower you can get."

"Yes, sir." Anton offered a cumbersome armored salute then crouched further down and slipped behind a low rocky ridge running south from Marek's position. A few seconds later he was out of sight.

A loud, deep voice blared in his headset. "Lieutenant Marek, Colonel Jax here. I need a status report." Marek almost jumped up, not a good idea with the fire coming in just above his head.

He hadn't expected to hear from the colonel directly.

"Yes, sir. My squad is in cover behind a long rocky ridge. We are under heavy sustained fire from at least three heavy weapons. I have 23 casualties...8 dead. I have reports that Third Company has retreated, so I sent a squad to cover my flank. That was my last reserve."

"Third Company was overrun, but I have reinforced them and they are regrouping to counterattack." His voice was steady and commanding, but Marek could hear the fatigue too. "I need you to hold until they can get back in position."

"I will try, sir, but I don't know if we can beat back another major push. We're low on ammunition, and my line is getting very thin." Marek wanted to tell Colonel Jax he'd hold no matter what, but he just wasn't sure he could. And Jax needed reliable information, not bravado and empty promises.

"I'm sending you some scratch fire teams we put together from broken units." Jax was doing a mental calculation on how many he thought he could spare to send to Marek. He started at four, but ended up at two. Marek's position was far from his only trouble spot. "I'm sending you two teams; use them to plug your line." He paused. "They're full strength, but remember these are not fresh reserves; they're bits and pieces of other units that have been thrown together to make something useful. They've been through the ringer already, and they're at least as tired as your people. Use them to plug your line or create a small reserve." He could hear Jax exhale heavily. "I'm sending them up with some extra ammo, but go easy, because we're light on supplies everywhere."

"Yes, sir." He hesitated for a few seconds. He would be glad for the extra ten troops, but he seriously doubted it would be enough if the enemy came in force again. "We'll hold, sir." He hoped he sounded more confident than he felt.

"I know you will, lieutenant." And if through some miracle you do hold, it will be Captain Marek, Jax thought. "Good luck." A long pause. "And lieutenant, it's only a matter of time before the enemy hits us with specials, so keep your men on Code Orange protocols. We captured their forward cache on our initial attack, but they've had time to bring more up by now... not to mention anything that had already been deployed to field units."

"Yes, sir." Nuclear defense tactics called for him to adopt an extended formation, spreading his troops out as much as possible. Unfortunately, that was somewhat counterproductive to putting up a strong defense.

"Report any enemy activity immediately. Directly to me, lieutenant. Understood?"

Marek's response was sharp and clear. "Understood, sir."

"Jax out."

Marek had his AI bring up a schematic of his platoon, though it was barely a section now. The squad he'd sent with Sergeant Anton had seven of its normal complement of ten. It was his strongest unit; everything along his front line was in worse shape. One squad was down to two, but at least they'd salvaged a SAW.

He needed to stretch out his line more. Right now one or two nukes could take them all out. The terrain was good, at least. They were in between two long, spiny ridges, which offered decent cover against a detonation either in front or behind. Unless the enemy dropped a hot nuke right in the 20 meters or so between the outcroppings, at least some of his people would survive an attack. Whether they'd be in any shape to repel an assault was another matter, of course.

He ordered one of the squads to extend the line south, and he directed all units to pull one-third of their strength out of the forward position and into deeper cover below the rock wall. He rolled his eyes up to study the slightly shimmering image of the tactical display projected inside his visor. Good, he thought... Anton had his people in place already. The veteran sergeant was a real professional. Marek had been grateful more than once over the past few days to have the seasoned non-com in his platoon.

The enemy fire still hadn't let up. Whatever ammunition shortages his own troops were dealing with, the enemy seemed to have plenty to spare. He reminded his troops several times to be careful and stay low when redeploying, but two of them got hit anyway. One dead, another seriously wounded, but with no chance for evac to a field hospital - 1st Brigade had been cut off for 12 hours now - there was a pretty good chance it would two dead. The suit could keep a wounded Marine alive for a while but not forever.

"Lieutenant Marek. Sergeant Anton here, sir. We have multiple sightings of enemy troops advancing south from Third Company's previous position. It is likely I will be engaged shortly."

"Thank you, Sergeant. Keep me posted." Marek tried to sound confident to Anton, but he wasn't at all sure that any eight men and women ever made could hold that northern line.

"Enemy bombardment incoming, Lieutenant Marek." His AI reported first, but only beat the first squad leaders by a second or two...and the first grenade by five. Explosions erupted along the entire line, showering his troops with dirt and blasted rock. They were in good cover, and it took pretty close to a direct hit with a grenade to cause a serious injury to an armored Marine. He wanted to return the fire, and he knew his troops did too, but they just didn't have the ammunition to spare. "All troops, hold fire. I repeat, do not return fire." Popping off grenades ineffectually at long range would make them feel better for a minute, but they needed to conserve what they had and use it where it would matter.

"I want everyone on alert for another assault. Eyes open, people." He knew they would come again. The grenades were just to rattle his troops and force them down from their vantage points before the attack. He wasn't going to let it work. "Croppen, Wilitz, I want you guys focused." He had two snipers situated higher on the rear rock formation; they had a clear view of the entire field, and he needed them to do some serious damage when the enemy came.

"Enemy attack!" The voice was a loud and little high-pitched. His people were mostly veterans, but they were also getting worn down. "Looks like they're coming in force." It was Corporal Rask, and she calmed down a little after her first outburst.

Marek's AI automatically organized the feeds from the rest of the platoon, updating the tactical schematic as more information became available. "Lieutenant, it appears that we are facing a company strength attack. Initial data indicates intact formations, which strongly suggests this is a fresh reserve unit at or close to full strength"

Well that's it, he thought. No way we're beating back a company. Worse, Imperial companies were half again the size of Alliance ones. He had 200 troops coming in against his beleaguered crew. Making things worse, Anton reported his squad along the northern flank was under attack as well.

"Alright 2nd Platoon, everybody ready. Pick your shots until they hit 500 meters, then let loose with everything you've got. Remember who we are, Marines. And make sure they remember too!" He switched the com to just the two snipers. "Croppen, Wilitz, I need you guys to take a bite out of this advance. Whatever it takes, you need to rack up a body count if we're going to have a chance here." He knew what it would take, and so did the two sharpshooters. Normally, they'd move after every couple shots. It kept them safer, but it took time too. If they fired more times from one spot they could hit more targets... at least until some enemy sniper nailed their location and took them out.

Marek climbed up to the top of the outcropping he was using for cover and found a good vantage point for firing. The auto-cannons were still raking the position, so he hunched behind, waiting. They'd have to stop the supporting fire when their assaulting troops got close enough. He'd kept his com open with the two snipers. They would count off their kills, and he wanted to track how they were doing. They were both already at three, having dropped targets that were 2,000 meters away, partially obscured on broken ground.

The Imperial troops advanced across the field, using gullies and low spots for cover. They were well-trained, but not combat veterans, and they were more careless than experienced troops would have been. Marek's Marines made them pay for every

sloppy step. The attackers had about 30 casualties when they hit
the 500 meter mark, but they'd drawn blood as well, and four of
the defenders were down. Marek was about to give his troops
the order to fire full, but just as he swung over the top of the
ridge to take aim, he saw something in the distance. Just a dot at
first, but moving rapidly toward them, growing larger as it did.

The fighter was sleek and aerodynamic, designed for flight
in an atmosphere rather than space. To the ground pounders it
seemed to be moving at a tremendous velocity, but it was actually traveling at less than a fifth of its maximum speed. It had
slowed and dived to provide close support to Marek's Marines,
and it streaked across the field, parallel to their position, strafing
the attacking troops. It was taking a terrible risk, exposing itself
to close range ground fire, but its heavy auto-cannons ripped
into the Imperial forces. The huge hyper-velocity rounds tore
right through powered armor, obliterating at least thirty of the
advancing troops.

Even as it finished its run, half a dozen missiles were fired
from the enemy lines. The fighter banked and angled high,
climbing with the maximum thrust its atomic engines could generate. It streaked quickly into the sky, faster than the eye could
follow, but it wasn't fast enough; two of the missiles exploded
right next to it, shredding the wings and blowing holes in the
fuselage. It tumbled down, spinning wildly out of control and
crashed north of the battlefield in a massive fireball.

Still, it had done its damage, and the attacking force was
staggered. Marek closed his eyes for an instant in empathy and
appreciation for the pilot's sacrifice. Then he ordered his troops
to open up, and they poured fire into the disordered enemy; the
shaken attackers hesitated, broke and ran. The Marines were
cheering wildly over the comlink, shooting indiscriminately at
the fleeing enemy. As much as Marek shared their desire to
shoot down the routers, he ordered them to stop. They just
didn't have the ammunition to waste on enemies who were no
longer a pressing threat.

"Everybody get back down!" He knew the enemy would
resume firing with their heavy weapons now that their own

troops were out of the field of fire. His people had their blood up, and he didn't want to lose anyone for being too excited to remember to get his head down.

He felt his own adrenalin start to drain away, as the immediate threat faded. Of course, they were so strung out on stimulants by now it was hard to tell what was a natural reaction and what was artificial. Ok, he thought, that's six attacks we beat back. He felt a rush of elation, quickly tempered by his next duty. Counting the cost.

"Squad leaders. Casualty reports." He listened quietly as his four squad commanders, only one of whom had held that position three days before, rattled off their counts. Another ten casualties; he was down to thirteen fit for duty, and along the northern flank only Sergeant Anton and one trooper were still standing. Both snipers made it, though, for which he was grateful.

Things improved slightly when the two fire teams sent by Colonel Jax arrived. Marek sent one team north to Sergeant Anton, deploying the other right into his own line. He would have loved to have something in reserve, but he just didn't have the force to spare.

The enemy hadn't resumed the auto-cannon fire. Maybe they're running low on ordnance too, he thought doubtfully. He took advantage of the lull to get the wounded moved down into the gully between the two ridges. It was the safest place for them until he could get them evac'd...and it didn't seem like that was going to be anytime soon.

Marek used the time to review his positions, and he shifted his squads around. He wasn't sure if he was really improving things or just making himself feel useful. He was just about to order one on of his snipers to readjust his position when the comlink came to life. "All personnel...Code Orange. Repeat Code Orange."

Marek dove low behind the rock. "Platoon, take cover. Everyone down, now. Repeat, every..." Marek's visor shut down to protect his eyes from the blinding flash. An instant later, the shockwave smashed into the rocky outcropping, shattering the top half of it and covering him under a landslide of obliterated rock. The nuke had detonated in front of the line, south of Marek's position. The squad on the southern flank, less than 200 meters from ground zero, was wiped out. To the north there were survivors, though most of them were wounded and buried under the debris from the collapsed rock wall.

Anton's people came through it better. Farther north, they were outside the immediate blast zone. Anton's armor suffered some minor damage, but nothing serious. He looked south, seeing the mushroom cloud rising behind the blasted position occupied by the rest of the platoon. And behind that he saw enemy troops advancing.

"Lieutenant Marek, they're coming again." He called into the comlink, not knowing what to expect. No response. "Lieutenant? Are you there, sir?" If Marek was down, Anton was in command of the whole platoon. Or whatever was left of it. "Lieutenant?"

Marek lay pinned under a pile of smashed rock. He was wounded, badly he thought hazily, though there was no pain. That much he owed to the suit, to the cocktail of drugs it had injected into his battered body. His reactor had shut down, and his heavily damaged armor was operating on battery power. He couldn't move, though whether that was due to his injuries or simply the loss of reactor power he didn't know. His vision was blurry; he could feel himself slipping further away, into unconsciousness. He thought he heard a voice calling to him, but it was faint and far away...and then it was gone.

Chapter 17

Alliance-PRC Combined Fleet
Epsilon Eridani System
Deployed around Epsilon Eridani IV

"Admiral Compton!" Commander Simmons' voice was uncharacteristically high pitched. "I am receiving a laser transmission relay from Cambrai. Priority Alpha One." That was Alliance code for an extreme emergency. "Coming through now, sir." He paused while the computer decrypted and fed him the message. "Admiral, Captain Arlington is reporting that Captain Johan's attack ships have detected large enemy forces in the outer system."

Compton sat in his command chair, outwardly calm though he could feel his stomach clench. "Relay me any information immediately as it comes in." After a short pause: "Put the fleet on yellow alert."

"Yes, sir. Fleet alert status yellow." Simmons looked down at his board. "New transmission, sir. Captain Johan has identified at least six battlegroups." He hesitated, staring at the screen. "Enemy formation includes Imperial South American and Europan units, sir." He turned his head and looked at the admiral, a shocked expression on his face. Most of the rest of the flag bridge crew were doing the same. The compartment was almost silent.

Compton wasn't all that surprised at the South Americans. Not really. It was no secret they were coming into the war. Alliance Intelligence had assured him the empire wouldn't be ready to mount any offensive operations for several months, but they'd screwed up before. They'd lied before too. But Europa Federalis was a shock. The CAC had two new allies? Both with forces already deployed? His thoughts were grim...this was not good. Not good at all.

Simmons looked back to his screen. "Sir, Captain Johan reports that the enemy was sitting dark in the outer system, beyond the orbit of planet seven." The seventh planet was the system's outermost; beyond that there was a relatively dense belt of sub-planetary objects - perfect for hiding a fleet. "She detected them when they fired their thrusters." Another pause. "Their present plotting suggests they are now moving to intercept us."

"Commander, order Captain Arlington to make a course back to the fleet at once." Cambrai had been detached to support Johan's squadron, but Compton was outnumbered enough without leaving a battleship exposed to being picked off. "I want a conference with the battlegroup commanders in twenty minutes." Arlington would still be too far out to participate in real time, but he'd catch up with her later. "Joker?"

"Yes, Admiral Compton?"

"Please put together a proposed thrust plan to intercept the projected enemy course at..." He slid his fingers along the touchscreen, scrolling through the map of local space as he did. "Here." He'd stopped right at the orbit of planet five, which was on the same side of the primary as Carson's World, not too distant from where he proposed to meet the enemy. He didn't want to get too far away from Carson's World, but he wanted some velocity too. Plus, there was an asteroid belt just beyond planet five, and he thought he might find that useful tactically, especially if he got the worst of the initial exchange.

"Yes, Admiral Compton. Working now. I will have proposed thrust instructions for all ships in approximately three minutes."

"Commander Simmons, get me a link to General Holm. I've got to warn the ground forces."

"Yes, sir." His hands danced over the control boards. A few seconds later he looked up. "Sir, General Holm is in the field. His aide is trying to reach him now." The Marine comlinks could transmit to ships in orbit, but Saratoga was 400,000 kilometers out, just beyond the planet's second moon. Holm would have to use the communications setup in his HQ to reach Compton.

"Sir, Captain Arlington confirms receipt of your orders, sir."

Simmons paused, still listening to his earpiece. He looked back at Compton. "She requests permission to remain on station until Captain Johan's ships are able to reverse course and build velocity back toward the fleet."

"Denied." Compton didn't like deserting the scouts either, but he simply could not risk one of his capital ships. "Tell her to get back here as quickly as possible." He took a deep breath. "I'm afraid we may have to ask a great deal from Captain Johan and her people before this engagement is decided. But difficult choices are the province of war."

"Joker, where's that thrust plan?" Compton could feel the adrenalin. He hoped it would last, because he wasn't going to get much sleep for the next week or so.

"Downloading now, Admiral Compton." The AI's voice was calm and unflappable. "Projected time for the fleet to adopt the target formation, six hours, eighteen minutes."

"Estimated time to enemy fleet arrival?" Compton knew he was asking the computer for a wild guess.

"Too many variables to create a meaningful estimate. Based on maximum documented thrust potential for known vessels, the minimum time is two days, three hours, and twenty minutes. However, that would require sustained full thrust with no periods for maintenance or crew recovery." No fleet could blast full for two days straight without stopping. Not if they wanted their crews functional afterwards. Not to mention the risks inherent in running their propulsion systems and reactors all out with no breaks or maintenance checks.

"Your best guess, Joker." Compton tended toward being a little impatient, and the present circumstances did nothing to temper it.

"Factoring known Imperial and CAC naval doctrine and my assessment of the tactical situation, a reasonable estimate would be three and one-half to four and one-half days." The quasi-sentient machine paused, obviously for effect, since it didn't need the time to think. "Any greater specificity would require almost random assignment of variables, rendering the resulting projection tactically useless." Even the straitlaced naval AIs came off as a bit obnoxious at times.

"Sir, I have General Holm on the line."

"Pipe it to my headset, commander." Compton closed his visor. He thought he might want some privacy with the general. "Elias?" It took about two seconds for his message to reach Carson's World, and the same for the general's reply to make it back to Saratoga. It was an annoying way to communicate, but both he and Holm were used to it.

"Yes, Terrance...what is it?" Holm sounded tired and distracted.

"I've got an enemy fleet up here." Right to the point.

"I assume we wouldn't be having this discussion if it wasn't a substantial force. Am I right? Did they follow us through the warp gate? Why didn't the pickets warn you?"

"Bigger than my fleet, to answer your first question." Compton sighed. "No, they didn't come through the gate; they were here already. Lying dark in the outer system." There was growing anger in the admiral's voice. "If those damned orders hadn't pushed us to move so quickly, I'd have never let your people transit before I'd scoured this system. I knew there was something going on. I could feel it. I wish the politicians would leave tactics to the professionals."

"You know I agree, but we should probably stay on more productive subject matter for now." Holm sounded more disgusted than angry...and more fatigued than either. "I'm in a shitstorm down here too. I'm getting reports and requests for reinforcements from everywhere. I don't know how the enemy managed to get this big a force here, but they've got units pouring out everywhere."

Compton swore under his breath. "This whole fucking thing has been one giant ambush. And our vaunted intelligence service not only failed to warn us, they pushed us right into the trap." He took a deep breath and exhaled. "We have to figure we're both heavily outnumbered. The enemy wouldn't have planned this if they didn't think they had the force to pull it off."

"Agreed. It certainly feels like I'm outnumbered down here, though I can't seem to get a reliable count on enemy strength.

We're just going to have to deal with the hands we've been dealt...both of us."

"Our orders don't give any latitude for pulling your people out of there." Compton was speaking more or less rhetorically. He knew they didn't have enough time to upload I Corps and accelerate quickly enough to escape the enemy battlefleet, even if they'd had the authority to withdraw. Holm knew it just as well.

"I couldn't break off now without it turning into a rout, anyway. My line runs 300 klicks east to west, and it's under attack at every point. And one of my brigades is totally cut off." He hesitated then said, "Maybe you should think about withdrawing the fleet. Especially if the enemy has too big an edge. You could come back when the odds are more even."

Compton snorted. "When will that be? We took everything in Gliese that wasn't streaming atmosphere or running on half-power." He paused for a second. "Besides, there's no way I'm leaving your people stranded here. Even if my orders allowed it, which you know perfectly well they don't."

Holm let out a half-hearted laugh. "Well, thank you for that show of support, but the truth is there isn't much you can do for us down here anyway. So if getting the hell out of here is the right choice, do it. Either way, if we both live through this I'll buy you dinner. Anywhere in occupied space. Your choice." He paused, then said with a soft chuckle, "The Basilone Club at the Academy is good. I think they'll let a navy officer in." He paused again. "As long as we don't make a habit of it."

Compton returned the laugh. "Sounds good. I suppose Marine food won't kill a navy man. As long as he doesn't make a habit of it." After a few seconds he added, "I need to get your transport fleet out of there, though. They're sitting ducks if any warships get past me. If there's anything you need in those supply ships, we need to get it to the surface now."

"That may be a problem." Holm let out a labored breath. "We've got a considerable fight for airspace down here. My people don't have air superiority yet. I'm not even sure they will. Anything trying to land now could take it hard."

"Damn, this just keeps getting worse." Compton thought for a few seconds. "What do you need most?"

"Ammunition. And medical supplies. I'd also evac some wounded and non-essential personnel if I could get them safely into orbit."

"Ok, can you hold on for a few minutes?" Compton didn't wait for an answer; he switched off the line with Holm. He was back about three minutes later. "Ok, Elias. I spoke with Admiral Wells." Wells was the commander of the transport and supply fleet. "He's pretty sure he has enough volunteers to bring down whatever you need. His pilots know the risks they'll be running. Contact him directly - he's under instructions to follow your orders. Get whatever you need, but get it done in twelve hours, because that's all I can give you. In twelve hours and one minute, that fleet has to be thrusting out of orbit." He paused for a second. "Good enough?"

"Good enough." Holm was distracted, already thinking of the bare minimum he needed to transport down. "I'll try to finish in eight. And, Terrance...thanks." After a brief hesitation he added, "Good luck up there."

Compton smiled weakly. "Yeah, you too."

Admiral Wells had said he could get volunteers, but he didn't mention they'd all be crazy sons of bitches. Holm stared in disbelief as he watched the scanners. Shuttles weren't supposed to fly like that - especially not when they were full of weapons and ammo. He'd ordered every atmospheric fighter he had left in the air to run interference for the transport craft landing the supplies. That was going to leave his troops exposed for a while, but it was better than having them run out of ammunition.

He'd never seen shuttles descend so quickly, zigzagging wildly and diving right through the atmosphere. They were wrecking their heat shields...and condemning themselves to a one-way trip. There was no way these ships were making it back to orbit, at least not without major repair jobs. So the volunteer pilots threw in their lot with the ground forces; none of them were leaving Carson's World unless the planetside battle was won. Almost a quarter of them never even made it to the surface alive, their shuttles hit by SAMs or shot down by enemy fighters.

Holm's biggest disappointment was the inability to get any of the wounded evacuated to the hospital ships. There was no way he could justify the risk of sending pilots or injured soldiers back up through that maelstrom, even if any of the shuttles had been fit to fly. One of the ships did bring some volunteer medical staff down to the surface to reinforce I Corps exhausted personnel. Sarah would be glad to see them; she needed every bit of help she could get, and it looked like things were just going to get worse. She'd set up a makeshift hospital in one of the mines, but low on supplies, overwhelmed with shattered men and women, and unable to evacuated any wounded, it was fast becoming a house of horrors.

He was worried about her too. Sarah Linden was one of the most beautiful women he'd ever seen, but when he last saw her on the com she looked like death. He doubted she'd slept in a week, and the stimulants were taking their toll. She'd looked at him with eyes sunken deep in her exhausted, blood-streaked face, her long hair tangled and sloppily tied back. He was sure he looked just as bad, but it was his command prerogative to worry about his people, not the other way around. He would have ordered her to get some sleep if he thought there was a chance she'd obey. Maybe it was better for her to stay busy; it would give her less time to worry about Erik who, as usual, had managed to find his way into the hottest spot on the field.

The battle was raging, and both sides had gone nuclear, making the surface of the planet a very dangerous place. I Corps HQ was also located in one of the underground mines, which had been hurriedly braced and fortified. Holm ordered the supplies stored deep in several other abandoned mines, as far as possible from the reach of enemy bombardments. It was the only option he could think of that gave him a chance of keeping it secure, though it also complicated distribution and made the supply net to his front line units even more tenuous.

They didn't quite make Holm's boast of eight hours to complete the resupply operation, but they did finish in less than ten. The supply situation still wasn't ideal, but it was a lot less dire than it had been, and that gave them a better chance to win the fight. And the transport fleet had an extra two hours to build velocity and get away before the enemy battle fleet was in range.

Holm hated sitting underground in the headquarters watching monitors while his troops were fighting for their lives. He wanted to get up to the surface and into the front lines along with his people. But that's not what they needed from him. Doing that would make him feel better, but it would also make it more likely they'd lose this fight...which meant they would all die. He hoped a certain colonel remembered that.

The men and women of 1st Brigade had been cut off. They held a strong position behind enemy lines, which they had seized in a daring attack, and their presence was severely disrupting the enemy advance, albeit at a terrible cost. The brigade needed their brilliant colonel alive and in command, not gloriously dead in some mud-filled trench. They were in serious danger of being totally overrun, and if anyone could pull them through the next few days, Holm knew it was Erik Cain.

Chapter 18

Foothills of the Tarsus Mountains
North of the Lysandra Plateau
Epsilon Eridani IV

"There is definitely an identifiable energy signature." Captain James Teller had named his AI Zack. Special action team commanders had enhanced AIs, and Teller's had been coordinating input from the extensive scanning grid his troops had deployed. "The source is heavily shielded, but I have confirmed it from three different detectors."

Teller sighed. He was still skeptical. They were deep in the mountainous wasteland north and east of the formerly inhabited areas of the planet. To the southwest, the rest of 1st Brigade was fighting for its life, as the enemy poured more units into trying to drive them from their commanding position. Teller was pissed to be off chasing shadows while his brothers and sisters were struggling and dying against overwhelming numbers. But orders were orders. Colonel Cain sent them here to look for something, and wherever Cain commanded, James Teller would go.

Zack was silent, awaiting input from Teller. When none was forthcoming, the AI continued its report. "The signature is very faint, which suggests state of the art shielding and stealth technology." Teller still said nothing. "I infer from your lack of communication that you remain unconvinced that there is some type of hidden facility in this area." The AI's voice didn't change, at least not significantly, but it sounded almost petulant to Teller. "I assure you that my determination is reliable, whatever your initial expectations may have been."

"Don't take it personally, Zack." Teller was both amused and annoyed at his sometimes overzealous virtual assistant. "I just don't see what the hell would be up here." He'd never doubt Cain, but he just couldn't figure out what his brilliant and eccentric commander was up to this time. It wasn't like Erik Cain to let his men and women die on the battle lines while he sent badly needed strength off on wild goose chases. "Alright, Zack, put together a search grid based on your energy readings. If there's something out here, we need to find it."

"Now projecting schematic of suggested search zones." A map of the area shimmered slightly in front of Teller's eyes. Three blue ovals marked locations the AI had denoted as high probability search targets.

"Ok, Zack, number those three search zones and transmit to all team members." Teller's voice was matter-of-fact. He was still skeptical, but he was here to search, so he was going to make sure it got done right.

"Transmitted."

"Sawyer and Harmon, check out zone number one." Teller was cautious; if there was something out here he had no idea if it was defended or what they might run into, so he was keeping most of the team together and sending out two man crews to scout. "Kissock, Mallow, check out zone two. Smith, Harrison, search zone three. All of you, report anything to me. Anything at all, even a feeling."

He waited as the three search parties acknowledged. "I want the rest of the team on me, ready to respond to any threat. We don't know what we're looking for, but there is an energy source out here somewhere, and it may or may not be hostile." Yeah, right, he thought. What the hell have we run into lately that wasn't hostile. "I want the search teams to use extreme caution. Colonel Cain sent us up here, so he thinks there is something important hidden someplace. I don't intent to let the colonel down. Do any of you?"

He got a chorus of "no sirs." Ok, he thought, now we'll see if there is something up here. He kept his com open to the search teams and monitored their position on the schematic Zack was projecting inside his visor. The ground was very rough, mountainous with a series of jagged ridges flanking small canyons. Moving around safely was slow business, and it was an hour before Teller got anything other than a normal status check.

"Captain Teller." The voice on the comlink was calm, businesslike. These troops were hardcore veterans. They'd report calmly and completely if they'd rounded the corner and ended up face to face with a CAC armored division. "Sergeant Sawyer, sir. We may have found something."

"Report, Sawyer." Sawyer had served in Achilles and half a dozen other hotspots. If he thought he saw something out of the ordinary, Teller was going to listen.

"Sir, we crossed over a high ridge and worked our way down into the canyon. It's wider than the other ravines, more open. We're looking at the rock wall across the valley. There's a lot of loose rubble all along the slope." He paused, as if he were still observing and analyzing as he spoke. "I'm on mag 10, and I'd swear that a lot of that loose stone is newly blasted. There's a lot of jagged, broken rock all along that hillside." Another pause. "Sir, I'd swear some sort of ordnance detonated on that ridge. That looks like a manmade landslide to me."

Teller had been unconvinced about this whole expedition, but Sawyer had his interest now. "Sergeant, hold your position. Do not approach until I bring up support. Understood?"

"Acknowledged, sir. Holding our position until further instructions."

Maybe it's nothing, Teller thought. Could be just an off-target missile that impacted there. But he wasn't going to take any chances. "Squads one, two, and three…on my mark. Deploy along the ridgeline in support of search team one."

He paused while the three squad leaders acknowledged. Before moving out himself, he switched his comlink to connect to the search parties. "Search teams two and three, scout around the flanks of the position identified by team one. I want to know if there is anything on the far side. I don't care if you see a pebble that looks out of place – you tell me about it."

"Understood, sir."

"Acknowledged."

Teller scaled the rocky slope in front of him. It is relatively easy to climb in armor – strength, at least, isn't an issue – but it is tricky to maintain footing on loose stone and gravel. He took it slowly, making sure he had a strong foothold before continuing.

He was about two kilometers from Sawyer, and it took him almost thirty minutes to reach the sergeant's position. He peered over the rocky spine atop the ridge and looked across at the debris strewn hillside. *He's right*, Teller thought, *that rock was definitely blasted by something. That's not a natural formation.*

He could see on his tactical display that the squads were almost in position. "Squad one, deploy to my right. Squad two, deploy to my left. Observe and cover the hillside." He stared out over the piles of broken stone. "Squad three, advance to the slope and search those rock piles. One and two are covering you – if there is any trouble, hit the deck. Don't forget, you've got backup in place."

"Yes, sir. Third squad advancing now." Sergeant Drake was a real veteran. He'd been admitted to the Academy a year before, but he didn't want to leave his men until after the campaign. He was the best squad commander Teller had, which was why it was third squad out there on point.

Teller stood behind a large rock, peering around as Drake's troops made their way down the slope and across the broken ground of the ravine bottom. Drake moved forward alone, climbing partway up the loose rock of the opposite slope, leaning over and examining the chunks of blasted stone.

"Third squad, advance and start clearing away some of this stone." He stood straight up. "Captain Teller, this rock was definitely blasted, and I see no signs of a missile or other ordnance. It looks like some kind of charges were detonated."

There really is something manmade up here, Teller thought. "Sergeant Drake, have third squad clear way some of that debris." He took a deep breath. "First and second squads on alert. I want every centimeter of that hillside under observation."

The troopers of third squad began clearing away stone and debris. An armored Marine could move tons of rock in just a few minutes, but they were having difficulty on the hillside. Whenever they cleared an area, more rubble slid down the slope from higher up. They'd been at it for about 30 minutes when they found something.

"Sergeant, I think I've got something here." Private Jerrold was highest up on the slope, and he'd managed to clear a small section of loose rock to reveal what appeared to be smooth metal.

Sawyer climbed up to take a closer look, and he and Jerrold moved some more rocks, increasing the cleared area to roughly a square meter. Underneath was a sheet of plasti-steel, only lightly weathered. "This is new," Sawyer said to himself. Then, on the comlink to Teller: "Captain, we've got some type of steel construction hidden under these rocks." Short pause. "It appears to be fairly new."

"Let's clear some more of it and get a good look." Teller climbed up over the ridge in front of him. "I'm coming down for a look." He slid down the slope to the base of the valley. "First and second squads, look lively. We have no idea what this is. For all we know it is some type of CAC installation." Teller charged his rifle as he walked over.

By the time he got there, Sawyer's and Drake's troops had cleared away a large amount of stone to uncover what appeared to be a large hatch or door, about 4 meters by 3. It was totally smooth except for 3 columns of reinforcing bolts evenly spaced across its width. The hatch was built into the slope at a 30 degree angle.

"This thing looks solid." Teller was speaking to himself as much as anyone else. "Larson, Captain Teller here. Report your location." Larson was an engineer attached to Teller's team. He'd been posted back with the other specialists, but now they needed him."

"I'm four klicks from your location, Captain." Larson had a very low voice, which was sometimes difficult to hear clearly on a comlink.

"Report to me at once. I have something I want you to look at." Teller kneeled down and tapped the hatch with his gloved hand. The thing is definitely solid, he thought. But what the hell is it?

By the time Larson arrived, Sawyer's troops had completely cleared the area, exposing a 4x3 meter reinforced plasti-steel hatch build right into the surrounding rocky slope. The edges of the door disappeared into the solid rock on all sides.

Larson came trotting up, two assistants in tow. "Lieutenant Larson reporting, sir." He gave the clumsy salute a suited Marine could handle and stood at attention, though his head turned to look at the strange steel hatch build into the mountainside.

"We need to know what's on the other side of this thing. Colonel Cain needs solid information, and we can't just knock on the door now, can we?" Teller had reported directly to Cain as he'd been ordered. The colonel had been right in the middle of what sounded like a hellish battle. He told Teller to find out what this thing was, and not to worry about being gentle about it. "I want you to blow the thing, Larson."

Larson's head moved slowly as he scanned the door. "We might be able to get through pretty quickly with the plasma torch." He was staring intently at the hatch as he spoke. "It would be less damaging to whatever's on the other side – it would take a significant charge to blast this thing."

Teller thought for a minute. "I'm not too worried about what's on the other side. The garrison had been completely withdrawn, so whatever is in there, it can't be ours." He paused, inhaling deeply, then exhaling. "What will be faster?"

"I think we can get a decent sized hole cut through there as quickly as we can blow through." He looked up from the door to Teller. "And if there's something hostile in there, we haven't ripped the whole hillside open and we just have a small egress point to defend."

"Do it." Teller was decisive by nature, and he preferred the controlled approach. They could always blow the thing wide open later.

The nuclear-powered plasma torch is an extremely effective cutting tool. One of Larson's assistants had it attached to his armor in lieu of weaponry, though it required two people to actually operate it properly. Larson's first guess was about ten minutes to get through, but the door was thicker and more heavily reinforced than he'd expected, and they'd had to crank the torch up to full power for more than twenty minutes.

Teller left first squad deployed along the opposite hillside, in cover and ready to provide supporting fire if necessary, but he brought the second down into the ravine. While Larson's crew finished cutting their hole in the hatch, Sawyer and two of his troopers stood ready to head in.

The engineers pushed hard, shoving the cut away section of the door inside where it landed with a loud thud. Sawyer peered through the opening then, with a quick command to his companions, he swung around and through, closely followed by the two troopers.

Teller waited for Sawyer's report, standing just back from the now-breached hatch. There was a short period of total silence, maybe ten seconds, then Sawyer was on the comlink. The sergeant was a hardcore veteran, and Teller had seen him unflappable in desperate circumstances. But now his voice was high-pitched and excited.

"Captain, you have to see this, sir!"

Teller walked forward, stooping slightly to pass through the opening. He saw Sawyer and his troops standing in the open staring out over a vast underground chamber. He turned and looked out past Sawyer. "Oh my god..."

Then the shooting started.

Chapter 19

Field Hospital One
Epsilon Eridani IV

Sarah Linden stood under glaring bright lights, leaning over a blood soaked table that held a shattered human body. Her scrubs had once been light blue, but now they were mostly crimson. The makeshift medical ward was a nightmare, her beleaguered staff like Aztec priests in the middle of horrific blood rituals.

They'd had to set up the hospital in an old mining complex - there was no secure place for it on the surface. The battle raged everywhere, and both sides had gone nuclear. Moving underground had meant abandoning the prefab hospital units - they were much too large to get into the tunnels - but it was the only way to keep the wounded safe. Reasonably safe, at least.

She knew Erik was right in the center of the storm, but she tried to put it out of her mind - she had a job to do. She focused on the men and women who needed her attention, but a lot of them were from 1st Brigade, and the more of Cain's broken and battered troops she saw, the harder it was to push back the fear. Worse, 1st Brigade had been completely cut off for more than a day now, and their wounded weren't even getting to the hospital anymore. If Erik was hurt, he was lying on some rocky plateau where she couldn't even help him. The thought made her nauseous.

She couldn't imagine losing Erik. Her past was dark and painful, and while the Marines had saved her from destitution and despair, she had still been alone. The past was still there, always, clawing at her from inside. She had focused on her career with unshakeable determination, and she became one of the most capable surgeons in the Corps. But there was nothing else in her life, not until Erik Cain came to her hospital. The two of them were broken toys, but they fit together somehow and healed each other. She loved him desperately, and she wasn't sure she could face the loneliness again if she lost him.

Sarah had spent most of her medical career serving in the big hospital on Armstrong. She'd certainly seen her share of horribly wounded men and women; Erik himself had come to her with both his legs gone and so poisoned by radiation he was too weak to move. But even he'd been stabilized before he got to her. The raw brutality of the field hospital had been quite a shock. She'd adapted to it during Operation Sherman, but none of those battles had approached the savagery or scale of this one.

Wounded were brought to the hospital stuck in the twisted wreckage of their armor. Before a doctor could even deal with their injuries, they had to be extricated from a suit that was designed to withstand direct hits from modern weapons. If the damage was bad enough to scrag the armor, they had to cut the trooper out with plasma torches. It was slow and dangerous, and many of the patients died while the techs were still struggling to get them free of mangled heaps of osmium-iridium alloy.

The sheer number of casualties coming through overwhelmed her exhausted med staff. They weren't even trying to treat the wounds anymore; they were just working to stabilize their patients and keep them alive until they could get back to them and finish the job. They had some portable med units with integral AIs, but they'd used all of them long ago. The partially treated men and women were now being lined up on the cold stone floor of the mine, stretching almost out of sight down the long tunnel.

"Damn it," she muttered under her breath as she struggled to close a gaping chest wound. Not being able to evacuate anyone is killing us, she thought. How many more are going to die in this forsaken mine who would have lived with proper care? She had three medships with the transport fleet, each capable of handling over 1,000 wounded...2,000 in an emergency. But they'd withdrawn with the rest of the support ships now that an enemy battlefleet was bearing down on the planet. She couldn't even send the wounded up before the transports left, because the skies of Carson's World were swarming with enemy aircraft.

Admiral Compton had his hands full dealing with the incoming warships, but even if he won the fight that was coming, it was going to take days, maybe even weeks. So dealing with the wounded was going to remain Sarah's problem for the foreseeable future, and this bleak mine was going to have to suffice. General Holm's frantic resupply operation had eased her logistical situation; she had enough medicines and other expendables, at least for the moment. And the volunteer medical staff from the hospital ships had been invaluable. She'd supplemented them by conscripting the walking wounded to assist in the hospital, freeing anyone with even a shred of medical training to treat incoming cases.

She'd originally had five aid stations set up on the surface as well, closer to the fighting, but the intensity of the battle had forced her to scale back to one secondary location. The general had assigned every transport and anti-grav sled he could spare to collect the wounded, but it was still taking way too long for most of them to get help.

The patient sprawled on the table before her had been dead for five minutes before she stopped her frantic efforts. Finally she jerked her hands from the chest cavity and turned away. This man could have lived, she thought, if I had the equipment I need. His heart and lungs had been severely damaged, but she could have kept him alive if she could have gotten him into a critical care med unit. Then she could have grown him a new heart and lung once they were back at Armstrong. But the crit care units she had were all in use, and he wasn't the first soldier to die today because of that. With good nutrition and a few rejuv treatments he could have lived to 120 years or older. Instead, he died at 25, bleeding and broken on a miserable, dusty planet far from home.

She walked away from the table, struggling to hold back the tears. The frustration was welling up inside her. She wanted to be alone, to scream and cry and throw things. But there was nowhere she could be by herself...nowhere at all. Privacy was an unreal fantasy in the bustling field hospital. And she was in command, which meant she couldn't lose it, not in front of these people. She could feel it every second, the constant burden, the unyielding pressure. She could feel the glances, the stares, as they looked to her for the strength and support they needed to go on.

She'd seen the stress of command and how it affected people. She'd watched what it did to Erik. How many times had she lain next to him at night, feeling him thrash around and listening to his nightmares? How many nights did she wake up to see him gone, up walking around or working at his desk because the sleep wouldn't come? She knew she'd always have to share him with his ghosts. She'd watched General Holm too, and even Jax. It affected each of them in his own way, but it was always there. Command wasn't a privilege or a reward to them; it was a responsibility, one they accepted with grave solemnity.

Now she had joined that club, and she finally understood what the pressure felt like. She thought of Erik and all the difficult situations he had led his troops through. *How do you do this, love? How do you stay strong for them when all you want to do is run and hide?*

Her introspection was interrupted. "Major Linden?" She noticed they called her major more often now that she was in command; before it had always been doctor, though she'd been just as much a captain then as she was a major now.

She turned around to find Lieutenant Bailey, one of the medical assistants, standing there. He was trying hard to look sharp and alert, but she could see the exhaustion in his eyes. She wondered what he could see in hers. "Yes, lieutenant?"

"Major, I think you should come." He paused. "We have a high-ranking casualty, and she is being…ah…difficult."

She motioned for him to lead her there. "Who is it?" She had let out a breath when he'd said "she." For a second she thought it might be Erik.

"Major General Gilson."

Gilson, she thought. Commander of 1st Division. Erik's immediate superior. "Give me a status report." Then, when he didn't answer in an instant: "Now!"

"Yes Major." She'd flustered him a bit, and he was trying to regain his focus. "She was hit in the chest and the left leg. She was very fortunate with the chest wound; it shattered two ribs, but didn't cause any other major damage." He motioned for her to walk around the corner toward one of the triage areas. "The leg wound is worse. It hit the artery, but her suit stopped the bleeding. Still, there is massive damage. Dr. Hollis isn't sure if we can save the leg or should just amputate and regenerate."

She was about to respond when they turned another corner and she saw the general laying on a table trying to sit up. Sarah ran the rest of the way and put her hands on Gilson's shoulders. "General, please lie down. You won't help anything if you rip open the dressings and bleed to death." She slid around so Gilson could see her. "I'm Doctor Linden, sir. Chief of Medical Services. We're going to take good care of you."

"I remember you, major." Gilson's voice was strong and commanding, but she was clearly struggling with the pain. "As I was telling your doctor here, I need you to patch me up as quickly as possible so I can get back into the field."

The rest of the staff looked shocked that this badly wounded woman was talking about going back to the battle, but Sarah had seen this type of personality before. In fact, when war and other circumstances allowed, she lived with one of them. Truth be told, if she would have admitted it to herself, she was one of them too.

"General, I understand that you do not wish to be away from your troops, but you are seriously wounded and…"

Gilson cut her off. "Major I am perfectly aware that I am wounded." She shifted to face Sarah more directly, wincing in spite of her best efforts to suppress it. "But I have to get back, regardless of my condition. Even if I am dragged around in a cart." She took another breath, gritting her teeth against the pain of her broken ribs. "General Slavin is dead."

That puts Erik in command of the division, Sarah thought. He must be overwhelmed. "Colonel Cain is next in the chain of command, isn't he? I'm sure he will take care of your people."

"1ˢᵗ Brigade is cut off and surrounded. The enemy is throwing two divisions at them. They're com is being jammed, and the enemy have hit them with a nuclear barrage. That plateau is a nightmare. I don't even know if Colonel Cain is still alive or how many of his people are still standing."

Sarah willed herself to stand there, but her legs got weak, and her mind was reeling. She felt the breath sucked from her lungs as she listened to Gilson's words, and she couldn't force anything intelligible out of her mouth.

"Cain's people are breaking up the entire enemy attack, forcing them divert more and more force to assault his position. I was leading an attempt to reestablish contact with him, but I got hit by a mortar round. My aide was killed, but I got lucky. We need to break through to 1st Brigade before they're wiped out. I don't even know the status of the attack right now."

Sarah had to fight back the urge to help the general get up and back to the battle. Anything that would help break through and rescue Erik and his people. But it was just an irrational impulse that she quickly suppressed. Gilson would end up bleeding to death if she tried to do too much more than stay where she was.

"I'm sure General Holm will see that 1st Division is ably led." Sarah had regained her focus, but her voice was tentative. "I'm afraid it is impossible for you to return to the battle, but I can arrange a comlink to the general so you can make sure the division is in good hands." Sarah turned and yelled to one of her assistants. "I need a secure comlink to General Holm over here. Now!" She couldn't get Gilson back to the front, but she could do her best to make sure the drive toward 1st Brigade was not interrupted.

A technician brought over a small com unit. Sarah put the headset on and spoke softly into the microphone. "Major Linden requesting immediate communication with General Holm."

"General Holm is actively directing combat operations, major." The voice was harried, tired. "This is Colonel Clark. Can I assist you? Is there a problem at the med facility?"

"Colonel, I have General Gilson here, seriously wounded." Sarah's voice was polite, but insistent. "She is very concerned about the status of 1st Division since she was hit."

"I'm glad to hear she is there, Major." Clark sounded relieved. "The general has had her people searching everywhere for her. We've had her listed as MIA."

"Are you able to give her a status update on her division." Sarah paused. "It would help us here. I need to get her settled down so I can treat her."

"Yes, Major Linden, I am certain I can give the general a satisfac…" His voice grew faint; he was speaking to someone away from the microphone. Sarah could barely hear him saying, "Yes, sir," when there was a rustling sound in her headset, and a new speaker came on."

"Sarah? How are you holding up over there?" It was Holm. His voice was hoarse from overuse, and he sounded exhausted.

"We're keeping it together, sir." She took a quick breath. "Sir, General Gilson is very concerned about 1st Division's operation to rescue 1st Brigade. She's wounded, but she'll be fine if she lets me treat her and stops trying to break out of here."

"Everything is fine with 1st Division, Sarah. I'll tell her myself, but first I want to tell you. Her attack hit the enemy forces assaulting 1st Brigade hard, forcing the enemy to divert more troops to the sector. It's opened up a gap in their lines. I'm about to lead the British division myself straight through, then around to relieve 1st Brigade." He paused, taking a short breath. "I'll get him out of there, Sarah. Things are bad where he is - I won't lie to you, but we both know he's a survivor. And there's no way I'm abandoning him. No way."

Sarah felt the tears welling up again, and she struggled to force them back, with only partial success. "Thank you, sir. I know you won't."

"Now try to focus on your job. Getting Erik and his people off that plateau is mine." He took another breath, deeper this time. "Now put General Gilson on, and I will assure her that her people are in good hands."

"Yes, sir. Thank you again, general." She pulled the headset off, twisting it to extricate a clump of her long hair that had gotten stuck. "General Gilson, General Holm wants to speak with you." She helped Gilson get the headset on, then she walked slowly away.

"Please, general," she whispered softly under her breath, sniffling and brushing away a tear. "Please bring him back to me."

Chapter 20

Alliance-PRC Combined Fleet
Epsilon Eridani System
Approaching the orbit of Epsilon Eridani V

The enemy fleet had accelerated cautiously, far more slowly than Compton had expected. He'd delayed implementing the fleet deployment order then he had to modify it twice. He had no intention of letting the enemy pull him too far from planet four.

He was outnumbered. He'd known that much since Johan's scoutships had flashed back their initial readings on the hostile fleet that had been hiding in the empty vastness of the outer system. Then things got worse, though that didn't surprise him; things usually got worse in situations like this. More enemy squadrons fired their thrusters, joining those already detected as they moved ponderously into battle formation. His four battle-groups faced eight, which meant he was in serious trouble.

He'd match his ships one for one against any task force in the CAC navy, and more so against the less experienced Imperial and Europan crews. But two to one was a different story. Skill, experience, and tactics were paramount in an even battle, but all space combat was at least somewhat attritional in nature, and there was an inescapable mathematics that took over when one side had twice the hulls, twice the weaponry.

The Alliance forces had been outnumbered at Gliese 250, but not as badly as they were here. And at Gliese they'd had minefields and the massive space station bolstering the defense, advantages they lacked in Epsilon Eridani. They'd had one other weapon at Gliese…Fleet Admiral Augustus Garret. Compton was a gifted tactician and an experienced veteran. But he knew he couldn't fill Garret's shoes; no one could. Garret had been the greatest genius ever to lead a battlefleet in space. He was irreplaceable.

The enemy's slow advance had at least allowed Captain

Johan's squadron to make good its escape. They'd been moving almost directly toward the enemy fleet when they detected it. They braked full, but even at 18g deceleration it took them some time to significantly change their vector. If the enemy had accelerated more aggressively, Johan's people would have been caught in missile range of the enemy, which means they would have died. Now they were blasting off in a seemingly random direction, their vector taking them clear of the massive enemy fleet.

But that course was not random at all. Compton had flashed orders to Johan, relayed by laser communication through Cambrai. They were to flee, moving at maximum velocity until they cleared detection range of the enemy fleet. Then they were to loop around behind and scout the outer system more intensively. *They fooled me once,* Compton thought grimly. *Never again. If there is anything else out there, we're going to find it.*

"Commander Simmons, all bomber crews are to man their ships." Compton spoke the command matter-of-factly, but the order was an unexpected one.

"Sir? You want the bombers launching now?" Simmons usual composure momentarily failed. The admiral's order was unorthodox and unexpected.

"I am not accustomed to repeating orders, commander." It was a reprimand, but not a severe one. Simmons was an excellent officer. *Besides,* he thought, *I surprised the hell out of him with that order.*

"Yes, Admiral Compton." Simmons switched to the fleet-com. "All ships are to bring bomber squadrons to full alert. Report launch readiness." Simmons could not figure out what Compton intended. The fleet was moving slowly, and the launch platforms wouldn't impart much intrinsic velocity to the bombers. And they were still way too far from the enemy to launch a strike.

"Joker, transmit operational order Straight Flush to Commander Simmons' board. Encryption code Mustang." Compton had prepared the orders himself. No one else in the fleet, except of course Joker, knew the contents.

"Orders transmitted, admiral."

"Commander, the orders Joker just sent to you are to be relayed to the bomber squadrons once they are ready to launch. The coding program will decrypt the orders once the squadrons are away." Compton knew he was taking a big chance, but he had to gamble if he was going to have any chance to win this fight. But he didn't need his crews worrying about it – and he didn't want to take a security risk if there were CAC or Imperial spies onboard.

"Yes, sir." Simmons was silent for a few seconds as his hands moved over his boards. "Orders downloaded to all squadrons, sir." He snapped his report sharply, subconsciously compensating for his earlier unintentional insubordination.

"Very well." Compton acknowledged, just as crisply. He was going to launch his bomber wings in twenty minutes. The plan was unconventional to say the least, but it might give him an edge. *You'd be proud of me, Augustus,* he thought. *This is right out of your playbook. I hope you're with me, old friend. I need you now more than ever.*

Twenty-seven lightyears from Compton's flagship, a small vessel accelerated toward a warp gate. Twenty-seven lightyears is an almost unimaginable distance by conventional reckoning, though of course such distances had become largely irrelevant since the discovery of warp gates.

The ship was scorched and pockmarked with battle damage, but it was basically intact. Inside, Jennifer Simon sat in the pilot's acceleration couch, flying the ship with considerable help from the AI. Simon was a communications officer, not a pilot. But right now she needed to be a pilot.

Her arm throbbed. She knew it was broken – in two places, she thought. She'd wrapped it the best she could, but there was nothing else for her to do now. The small ship only had one med unit, and that was occupied.

She locked in the final course through the gate, and the AI cut the acceleration down to just over 0.5g. Simon let out a deep breath; the ship had been thrusting at 3g, and the lower pressure was a relief on her arm. She unhooked herself from the couch and walked slowly back toward the med unit to check on her patient.

God, I look like hell, she thought, as she caught her reflection in the mirrored surface of the metal door. The burns on her face had begun to heal; at least the pain had subsided considerably, though she thought she was still likely to frighten small children…at least until she could get some proper reconstructive surgery. She'd gotten a pretty good dose of radiation, but she'd taken the injections to counteract the worst of it. She wasn't vomiting anymore, at least, though she was still weak.

She walked back to the enclosed med unit and looked down through the protective glass at the unconscious figure. "Status report."

The medical AI's voice was female, its tone soft and soothing. "Admiral Garret remains in a coma, though his body has responded well to treatment for his other injuries. His head trauma has also been treated, however I continue to recommend that no effort be made to awaken him from his coma until he is in a full medical facility. My ability to treat potential complications is severely limited."

Simon stood, silent for a moment, staring down at Garret's peaceful face. I can't believe we've made it this far, she thought. She turned slowly, willing away the fatigue, and walked back to the pilot's station to get ready for the transit. Once through the gate they should be able to contact some Alliance vessel or outpost.

She owed her life to Captain Charles. It had been his will and his unrelenting determination to save the admiral that had gotten them through the maelstrom of the dying Cromwell and on to Garret's cutter. The admiral had refused to abandon the ship, and Simon had served him long enough to know that changing his mind was an impossibility. But then the ship took a hit and Garret was knocked unconscious by falling structural debris. That injury saved the admiral's life.

Charles stormed onto the flag bridge with four of his Marines and ordered them to take Garret to his cutter. He told Simon and the rest of the admiral's staff to go as well, but halfway to the bay the ship took another hit, breaching the rear section of the compartment. A blast door slammed shut behind Simon, and on the other side, trapped in the stricken compartment, the rest of the staff died, blown out into space and bathed with lethal radiation.

Simon was hurt too, but she could still walk. She followed the Marines to the cutter bay and got Garret into the med unit. She called to the Marines to stay, but they refused to abandon Cromwell while Captain Charles was still aboard. She was still arguing with them when they shut the hatch, leaving her alone in the small craft with the admiral.

The ship lurched hard, slamming her into the bulkhead as the cutter cleared the debris strewn launch bay and blasted free of Cromwell. She landed on her already broken arm and shrieked with pain. Captain Charles had triggered the automatic launch sequence remotely. She just barely managed crawl to the command chair and engage the viewscreen in time to see Cromwell vaporized by a spread of thermonuclear explosions. The cutter was buffeted by the shockwaves, and it hull was burned and blackened, but it was already clear of the lethal zone.

She'd had a hard time reconciling with the loss. Captain Charles, Commander Barton, the rest of the staff…all gone. But there had been no time to mourn, and no room for the self-indulgence of grief. There was only one thing that was important…saving the life of Fleet Admiral Augustus Garret.

The cutter had the same intrinsic velocity Cromwell did, and the battleship had been moving quickly, fleeing toward the exit warp gate. Simon knew that if she'd applied any thrust now the enemy might detect the small craft. In fact, since it was apparent that this entire attack was nothing more than a massive assassination attempt, it was likely they'd be on the lookout for any escaping vessels or lifeboats. So she ordered the AI to run silent, and the cutter zipped past the warp gate and into the outer reaches of the system.

Once they'd cleared detection range, Simon ordered the ship's AI to begin decelerating, though with both Garret and her both wounded, they could only tolerate limited pressure. She'd instructed the AI to keep maximum thrust to 3g, which significantly slowed their vector change. Finally, after days of maneuver they were positioned back at the warp gate and ready to transit.

She leaned back in the couch and closed her eyes as the ship slid into the transit horizon of the gate and out into the TZ Arietis system. One step closer.

Lieutenant Commander Peter Wheaton sat in the command seat of his fighter-bomber, methodically running through the pre-launch systems diagnostic with the craft's AI. Bombers didn't have official names like warships did, but it was customary for the crews to assign one anyway. Wheaton called his Darkwind, after the main character from a book he'd loved as a child. Since he'd never bothered to name the ship's AI, it went by the same designation.

"All systems are cleared for launch, Commander Wheaton." The computer had a human-sounding voice, but it spoke very evenly, with no emotion – imitated or otherwise. The naval AIs lacked the personality development algorithms of the Marine versions. "All units reporting fully operational status."

Wheaton was the commander of bomber squadron 3. His six craft were ready to launch, though he had no idea why they were going so early. He hadn't expected the order for 18 hours or so, and he was shocked when the klaxon sounded. At first he assumed some hidden enemy force had surprised the fleet, but it quickly became clear that wasn't the case at all. He'd just have to wait and see what the admiral was planning. His crews had been debating the orders, and he'd told them all to cut the shit and focus on getting their craft ready. He had to remind himself to take his own advice; speculating on what Compton was planning was a waste of time. Terrance Compton was an extremely skilled commander, even if he wasn't the equal of Admiral Garret. He knew what he was doing.

Bomber crews were heavily cross-trained. It didn't make sense to have a craft become combat ineffective if one crew member was lost, and the AI could fill a lot of roles too, when necessary. In addition to a commander/pilot, each bomber carried a weapons specialist, an engineer, and a plotting/targeting technician. His people could fill in for each other on an ad hoc basis, but they were veterans and extremely proficient in their primary roles.

The bomber wings attracted a certain breed of recruit. Wheaton thought of his brethren as adventurous, though many characterized it differently. He'd heard crazy, psychotic, and deathwish just to name a few. The wings were the highest risk jobs in the navy, with casualty rates that usually exceeded those of front line Marine assault units. He didn't consider himself suicidal, but he had to admit that taking a 60 ton vessel measuring less than 28 meters down the throat of a half-million ton battleship took a certain bravado.

He'd run the diagnostic twice – and ordered the other five ships of the squadron to do the same, eliciting poorly muffled groans from the crews. Tough, he thought. I may not know what we have to do, but I'm sure we're going to need everything we've got, so these ships need to be 100%.

He'd just gone through the report from his last bomber when the launch alert sounded. His squadron was going out second, behind the 4th, so they sat in place for two minutes before the ship began to move toward the launch track. He had very little to do; the Cambrai's battle computer would manage the entire operation. He wouldn't take over until they were in space and received their mysterious orders.

The magnetic catapult was capable of imparting significant incremental acceleration to a launching bomber. Wheaton and his crew wore their pressure suits and strapped into their couches, and he gritted his teeth against the bone-rattling acceleration of launch.

It didn't come. The bomber slid slowly down the catapult's track and gently out into space. That wasn't the only surprise. Cambrai and the other motherships had positioned themselves to launch the craft to the rear, and what minimal force the catapults did apply served to reduce the intrinsic velocity of the bombers. The squadrons were launched away from the enemy, and they were falling slowly behind the fleet.

The main com screen activated, displaying Admiral Compton, his neatly trimmed hair still mostly blonde, despite the deep ridges in his careworn face. His voice was soft and conversational. "By now you have all launched, and your AIs are executing minor course changes to place your squadrons in formation. I have chosen to broadcast the recording of these orders to all bomber crews, and not just squadron or ship commanders."

He paused very briefly. "As you all know, we are facing an enemy with significantly greater strength than us. We're looking at an uphill fight, and we're just not going to win it unless we surprise them somehow." Compton didn't really believe they could win anyway, but there was no reason to share that with the crews.

"Once positioned, your squadrons will follow the fleet. At your present velocity, you will be positioned approximately 200,000 kilometers behind the main body when the fleets engage at close range. You will be running dark, with no thrust and only minimal systems active. You will be on total radio silence, with communication only on direct line of sight laser transmissions…and that only if absolutely necessary. You will be a hole in space, undetectable until you fire up your thrusters."

Compton's eyes bored out from the viewscreen, his intensity building as he spoke. "We will not be launching a conventional bomber attack against the enemy fleet. I have kept four squadrons in reserve, configured as interceptors to face the enemy bombers. The rest of our bomber wings…all of you…" He gestured toward the screen. "…will remain hidden in reserve until we are engaged with the enemy fleet at energy weapons range."

The crews watching the tape began to understand. A bomber attack on the enemy fleet at close range while it was heavily engaged with the Alliance forces would almost certainly achieve total surprise. If they could get in quickly enough, and make their runs count, they could inflict enormous damage.

"It is my hope the enemy will assume that we do not have

a full complement of bomber squadrons, and that the combat space patrol is our full strength. As you all know, we suffered very heavy bomber losses at Gliese 250, and it is just possible that the enemy will deduce that we were unable to replace those in time for this operation." He paused, his eyes glancing down momentarily as he spoke of the bomber crews in the fight at Gliese. He knew how much those losses had stung Garret, and they had affected him just as badly. He'd seen few such displays of selfless valor and he, like Garret, credited the victory to those pilots and crews.

"I don't need to remind you that the fleet will be facing an enormous missile barrage before we even get into close range. We are almost certainly going to suffer major losses before you are given the signal to attack, and we are all counting on you, on your skills and determination, to help even the odds. When you attack you must make every shot count. I want all of you to focus on the Imperial and Europan capital ships. They are new to the conflict and their point defense and damage control are likely less efficient than that of the CAC and Caliphate forces. You are to target only capital ships. I know the escorts will be shooting at you, but I need you to ignore that take out enemy battleships."

Compton hesitated again, for a bit longer this time. "You were all assigned to this fleet after the Battle of Gliese 250, but you are aware of what happened there. Your comrades redefined the word courage in that fight, and they paid for our victory with their sacrifice. Here, you fight not only for them, not only for this fleet and the thousands of naval personnel it carries. There are also 45,000 veteran Marines on the surface of planet four, even now fighting for their lives. Our orders are to hold at all costs, but even if they weren't, even if they allowed for us to fall back and run for the warp gate, I would never leave this system and abandon General Holm and his troops to certain destruction. This fleet will win here, or it will die here. Before this story is written I will ask every man and woman in this command for every shred of devotion and valor they possess. As I am asking all of you now. I am counting on you; we are all counting on you. Godspeed and good luck to you."

Wheaton stared intently as the now-blank screen, his jaw clenched, his eyes moist. He couldn't speak for anyone else, but he was ready. He didn't have to speak for anyone else...192 crew on 48 bombers felt as one. They would not fail.

Chapter 21

Near 1st Brigade HQ
Northern Spur of the Lysandra Plateau
Epsilon Eridani IV

"Give me another stim, Hector." Erik Cain hadn't slept for a week; the drugs were the only thing keeping him standing.

"Colonel, there is a limit to the dosages your body can endure." The AI actually managed to sound genuinely concerned. Cain could never quite decide if he thought the quasi-sentient computer's emotions were real or a carefully constructed illusion.

"Just give me the shot." Cain was irritable, and he snapped his response, then sighed and softened his tone. "There is no alternative, Hector. I can't exactly go take a nap right now, can I?"

Cain felt the injection, and within a few seconds the cloudiness began to clear from his head. He was grateful the AI didn't feel the need to respond to his rhetorical question.

He hadn't exceeded his orders when he attacked the enemy and seized this position, at least not technically, though he wondered if a board of inquiry would see it the same way. He knew in his gut they were in trouble on Carson's World, and when he saw the chance to grab the northern heights of the Lysandra Plateau he took it. His attack went better than he could have expected, and 1st Brigade advanced deep into enemy territory.

His initiative had created an opportunity. His position was a knife thrust into the side of the enemy, and he was a threat to the flank of any advance they might make. They had to take him out before they could move south and overrun the rest of I Corps. But the position was highly defensible, and 1st Brigade's men and women were veterans...and totally devoted to their brash, stubborn, and unconventional commander. They would fight to the last if he asked them to, and they knew if it came to that, Erik Cain would be in the line with them.

The enemy had been attacking non-stop for days, and slowly and at great cost 1st Brigade was being pushed back. Cain had no idea how many casualties his people had inflicted; he'd stopped trying to keep track when he hit 10,000. But 1st Brigade had bled too, and well under half its 3,600 troops were still in the field. Companies were holding lines where a battalion would have stood a week before, and squads were covering frontages a platoon would be hard-pressed to handle.

They'd been cut off for four days, and supplies were running low. Cain had been everywhere, rallying the troops and person-ally checking every position, sometimes moving an auto-cannon or other weapon a few meters to improve the field of fire. Out-wardly he was determined and optimistic; everywhere his troops saw him he was the avatar of victory, utterly certain they would prevail. In his own head, he was wracked with doubt and not at all sure they could hold. He'd even developed a contingency plan to withdraw his survivors into the mountains to the east and turn them into a guerilla raiding force if they could no lon-ger hold a conventional position.

He knew this battle would add mightily to his pantheon of ghostly companions, the shades of troopers who'd died under his command. Cain had never managed to stop blaming him-self for the Marines he lost, and this was probably going to be the worst of all. It had been his choice to seize the plateau, and while it was tactically a brilliant move in terms of the battle as a whole, it also placed 1st Brigade squarely in the line of fire. He had made that choice; his soldiers just obeyed his orders. The fact that, almost to a man, 1st Brigade would have volunteered to follow him into the deepest ring of hell, didn't occur to him or ease his guilt. But Cain never let any of that interfere with his command decisions. In the field his purpose was to win the battle, whatever the cost. His guilt and self-loathing would wait until the fight was won.

He knew General Holm would be trying to break through to them, but there had been no communication for days. He'd never seen jamming this intense or covering such a wide area. He assumed they were facing something new developed by their enemies, though in fact it was more of a massive application of existing technology rather than any high tech breakthroughs. Even without confirmation, Cain was as sure that the general was coming as he was of his name. He just hoped the relief came in time.

At least his political officer was leaving him alone. Captain Warren had not been prepared to follow Erik Cain into the types of places he routinely went, and he'd spent most of the last week in the cave 1st Brigade was using as a combination HQ and aid station. The few times he'd come along to the front lines, Erik suspected he'd tested the limits on how much urine a fighting suit could reprocess.

Now he had Captain Teller on the line. The general had asked him to deploy his special action teams to try and find out why this planet was so important to both the CAC and the Alliance. Cain also agreed that there was some secret, though he hated detaching his best troops to track it down when he needed them on the battle line. Now, it seemed, they had found something extraordinary, so much so that Teller wouldn't discuss it over the com.

Cain wanted to go; he wanted to see the secret of Epsilon Eridani IV. But there was no way he could leave the brigade... not now. Especially not now when he'd just lost his right arm. Jax had been hit by a sniper a few hours before when he'd gone up to the front to scout the enemy movements. The big ox would pull through, but he wasn't taking command of the brigade anytime soon, nor was he heading 20 klicks over the mountains to check out whatever Teller found. Right now Cain's soldiers needed him, and they came first. Whatever was in that cave would just have to wait.

Angus Frasier was crouched in a deep foxhole, counting down the seconds from sixty. The colonel of the Scottish Regiment of the Royal Marine Division, he was positioned dead center in the six kilometer position occupied by his waiting troops. To a man they were in heavy cover; in just a few seconds the enemy lines would be rocked by six nuclear explosions, and the

Black Watch, as they unofficially called themselves, would drive right through the chaos to link up with Erik Cain's Americans on the beleaguered northern end of the Lysandra Plateau.

Frasier had come to know Cain fairly well since both of their units had been selected as part of I Corps OB. He'd found somewhat of a kindred spirit in the gritty Yank, as he'd taken to calling him. Yank was a term that had fallen largely into disuse since the formation of the Alliance, but the Scots in the service clung fiercely to any shred of tradition, and the Black Watch even more so.

Frasier had a similar history, having found his way from the worst of the Edinburgh slums to a highly placed military command, and the two were similarly devoted to their soldiers. The stubborn Scot had no intention of letting Cain's troops be overrun, not while there was breath in his body. The rest of the Royal Marines had driven this far, and suffered heavy casualties in doing so. Now it was up to Frasier's Scots, along with James Prescott's Canadian Regiment deployed 12 kilometers south, to cut through the final enemy line and relieve 1st Brigade.

When he got to ten in his countdown, Mack, his AI, gave him an automated warning, and he crouched lower – they were deployed very close to the blast radius, and anyone caught unprotected was likely to end up a casualty.

In armor you don't feel the wind from the shockwave or the heat from the blast, but you can hear the rocks and debris bouncing off your suit. Visors automatically deactivated and blast shields slammed shut, protecting the eyes of the Scots from damage. Their suits measured the outside temperature and monitored radiation levels, but their tactical plan was based on timing, not analysis of data. Sixty seconds after the blasts, the soldiers of the Black Watch leapt out of their covered positions and attacked.

Across the field, largely unheard by the armored enemy, the sound of bagpipes filled the air. The music was recorded, of course, blaring at deafening levels from a number of small bots that accompanied the advancing troops. More tradition, and while largely ineffectual at intimidating the enemy, it did have a morale effect on the Scots themselves, who heard the music on their suit coms. Frasier imagined what it must have been like, centuries before, when troops marched to the fight to the sound of live pipes.

Frasier's troops swarmed quickly across the open field, largely ignoring cover in order to maximize the effects of shock from the nuclear attack. They took sporadic fire from a few surviving enemy strongpoints and suffered light casualties as they moved quickly through the devastated zone, splitting into columns and avoiding the worst of the hotspots.

The enemy was bringing up reserves to backstop the stricken position, mostly second line Europan troops – no match for the veterans of the Black Watch, who tore into them savagely and sent them fleeing to the rear. But modern war is messy, and the Scots were starting to take heavier losses as they drove the last stretch toward 1st Brigade's position.

Frasier looked at the schematic on his visor. One last attack and they would break through to Cain's position on the plateau. One last group of enemies to face. If these are more reservists, Frasier thought, we should reach the Americans in less than an hour.

But they weren't reservists; they were frontline Janissaries, and there were a lot of them. "There's no going back, Angus," he muttered to himself. He set his comlink to address the entire regiment. "Listen to me, Black Watch!" He was worried about this attack, but his blood was up, and it came through in his speech. "The American 1st Brigade has been cut off for days now, attacked relentlessly from all sides. We are going to relieve them, and we are going to do it now! In front of us is the last group of enemy between us and our comrades."

He paused, allowing his words to hover briefly in the air. "Scots, are you with me? For I'll not come back from this battle unless our brothers and sisters come back with us." He reloaded his mag rifle, and held it at the ready. "Let's go, Scots! Our friends are waiting for us, and we cannot abandon them."

He lunged forward, disregarding all tactical directives on the proper place for a colonel in his unit, another trait he shared with Erik Cain. The entire regiment advanced, but they were bogged down almost immediately by heavy fire. The Janissaries were veterans just like them, and the two formations savaged each other. All along the line, heavy weapons teams grabbed any vantage point and poured fire into the enemy line. Troops crawled forward, desperately struggling to gain a few meters, and paying dearly for it.

Frasier was in the thick of the fight, and he picked up a minor wound on his arm. He wasn't at all sure they'd be able to break through. The Janissaries wouldn't surrender, and they wouldn't retreat either, not until they were shattered. And the Black Watch was running out of soldiers and ammunition.

The savagery of the fight increased, with neither side willing to back down, and it looked as if the two units would annihilate each other. Suddenly, Mack alerted Frasier to another body of troops moving up behind the enemy force. His heart sank – if the enemy was getting reinforcements the battle was as good as over. But a second later the transponders identified the new arrivals as friendlies. Whoever they were, they slammed into the rear and flank of the Janissaries, while Frasier and the Black Watch redoubled their effort from the front. In a few minutes the Caliphate troops were broken, most of them dead, the rest in flight.

The two Alliance forces had fought their way toward each other, and alarms went off in headsets warning against firing on friendly targets. Their comlink encryption protocols made it difficult for the Scots to contact the new force without knowing who they were. But Frasier only had to wait a few seconds.

"Colonel Frasier?" The voice coming through Frasier's comlink was rock solid, though the speaker was clearly fatigued. "This is Brevet-Lieutenant Anton, sir. Colonel Cain sends his regards." He paused for an instant. "And the thanks of the entire 1st Brigade."

Chapter 22

AS Saratoga.
Epsilon Eridani System
In the asteroid belt past the orbit of Epsilon Eridani V

Compton's head ached. A rough bandage was tied around his temple, crusted with blood and hanging loosely on one side. The crude dressing was less than an admiral rated, certainly, but he'd flatly refused to allow one of the surgeons to take the time to treat him. There were over 400 casualties on Saratoga, and many of them needed attention far more than Compton did.

The helmet that had saved his life sat next to his command chair, nearly split in two. He'd barely managed to get a replacement before the stricken flag bridge lost its pressurization and life support. The hull integrity had since been restored, but the debris was still strewn around, including the heavy conduit that had come close to depriving the fleet of its commander.

Compton was proud of his staff. They worked diligently at their posts, seemingly oblivious to the mayhem and destruction surrounding them. Damage control bots wheeled around, making whatever repairs were feasible under the current, difficult conditions. Saratoga remained at battlestations, and the Battle of Epsilon Eridani, though in a brief lull, was still raging.

The fleets had exchanged devastating missile barrages. The Imperial and Europan forces had far less combat experience than either their CAC/Caliphate allies or their Alliance enemies, and it showed. With forces from four different powers, the enemy fleet had a hard time syncing data systems and coordinating their attacks, while Compton's strike was precisely targeted and flawlessly executed. But the Alliance volley was only half the size of the one they faced, and even with the enemy's poor targeting and data synchronization, Compton's ships took as much damage as they inflicted. He'd done about as well as he could have hoped, but he also knew he couldn't win a battle of attrition.

The enemy bombers came in right behind their missiles, but they were mostly South American wings with no recent combat experience. Compton had held back a force of his veterans as a combat space patrol, their ships configured as interceptors. They obliterated the inexperienced enemy attack force, which managed to inflict only a few hits, none causing serious damage.

When the forces entered close range of each other, the energy weapons duel began. Laser batteries opened fire, ripping into armor plating and slicing through compartments and vital systems. Compton's fire control was superior, and his ships were scoring a higher percentage of hits than their opponents. But they were also outnumbered two to one in hulls, and they were losing the overall contest. Cambrai was especially hard hit; she was an older design, with fewer angel dust launchers and an outdated ECM suite – and she was still suffering from some of the damage she'd taken at Gliese. Captain Arlington had worked wonders keeping her in the fight.

Compton had waited. He sat on his flag bridge, silent and impassive, as the laser battle raged, an unshakeable block of granite. He'd waited until the enemy ships had closed to knife-fighting distance of his own, decelerating to a crawl to remain in close firing range and finish off his outgunned force.

Only then did he utter a word. "Joker, execute Straight Flush."

The bomber crews had been following the fleet at a constant velocity, back just far enough to remain undetectable as long as they kept their power output to a minimum. Now they received the words they had been waiting for…Straight Flush.

Reactors fired up to maximum power output, and engines came to life. The crews were strapped into their couches, the only way they could endure the 18g acceleration they would experience as their squadrons thrusted hard toward the fleet.

The enemy detected the massive power outputs almost immediately, but they were already heavily engaged with the Alliance fleet, and there was little they could do to react in time. Compton's bomber squadrons ripped through the enemy forces virtually unopposed. The pilots knew the situation, and they could see on their scanners the damage their comrades had taken. They closed to point blank range and ravaged the enemy capital ships with plasma torpedoes, then decelerated and returned for a second pass before the two fleets had completely disengaged.

The bombing runs had saved Compton's fleet, inflicting enormous damage on the surprised enemy ships and disrupting their laser barrages. The Bolivar, already severely damaged by Saratoga's heavy laser cannons, was destroyed outright, and the rest of the enemy battleships were hard hit. The bombers took few casualties on their first attack, but the enemy ships were ready for the second, and the squadrons suffered heavy losses as they sliced back through.

After the engagement, Compton ordered his fleet to decelerate and regroup in the asteroid belt, and damage control parties worked feverishly to get weapons and ship's systems back online for the second round of battle...which they all knew would be soon. The roughly fifty percent of the bombers that survived had a more circuitous route to change their vector and rejoin the fleet, and they were landed and rearmed as quickly as possible.

The enemy fleet also needed time to regroup. Compton had ordered the bombers to focus on the engines of the targeted vessels, and many of the enemy ships were suffering from seriously degraded thrust capacity. The strategy had given the enemy commander a choice. He had clear firepower superiority, but not all his ships were able to exert the required thrust levels to quickly regroup. If he chose to force the engagement immediately, many of his ships would be unable to revector and join the formation, and he would surrender the numerical advantage. Conversely, if he decided to attack with the assembled fleet it would take time to make repairs and position all his ships, giving Compton a respite to get his own battlegroups back in fighting shape.

Compton knew what he would do – he would attack with whatever he could as soon as he could, pressing hard no matter what the cost. They could still hit him on better than even terms, and that would leave them with reinforcements to send in later, while all of his strength would be committed. But he was banking on the enemy admiral making the other choice. CAC commanders tended to be conservative and to value numerical superiority, and the allied Imperial forces were green and likely to feel better if they had overwhelming strength, especially after the shock his bombers had inflicted and the loss of one of their battleships.

He didn't know what he would do with the extra time. Work the damage control teams to death, of course. In the end he was playing for time, but he didn't see how time could really help him. There was no cavalry on the way, none that he could think of. Certainly, the high command would try to scrape something up, but it could be months before they got here, and he definitely didn't have that kind of time. Neither did General Holm. His strategy was ultimately futile, but it was all he had. Why die today, he thought, when you can die tomorrow instead?

In the end, he had more time than he'd expected. The bombers' attack has severely disordered the enemy, and several of their battleships required considerable field repairs to get engines back online. The CAC commander was indeed hesitant to reengage without all of his strength, and it was almost a week before the reformed enemy force was bearing down on Compton's waiting ships.

He planned to utilize the asteroid belt defensively to blunt the expected missile attack. The enemy had cleared its external racks and expended much of its ordnance in the first engagement; their volley would be much smaller this time. Compton was in the same position, but he preferred to fight it out at energy weapons range; his primary strategy for the missile exchange was simply to survive it.

He'd deployed ECM probes on a number of the asteroids. Once activated, they broadcasted the scanner image of an Alliance capital ship. His actual ships would fire their own missiles, then shift laterally and deploy directly behind four of the larger asteroids. Hiding behind a 50 kilometer hunk of rock felt a little like a soldier crouching in a foxhole, and the effect was similar. The positioning increased the difficulty for the targeting AIs, in essence giving his ships some cover. Missiles would lack a direct line of sight to effective detonation range, forcing them to decelerate and revector to get close enough to their targets, exposing themselves for an extended time to interdiction from the escort vessels.

When the attack finally started, the regrouped enemy fired their volleys as they entered launch range. Garret's ships responded, sending their own missiles on a lengthy trek toward the enemy. As he watched the plotting of the enemy missiles on his scanner, Compton waited to see how his strategy would pan out.

In the end, he couldn't have been more pleased. His plan worked better than he'd dared to hope. The enemy missile strike, already smaller and more ragged than the previous one, was largely ineffective. Some warheads targeted the asteroids with the ECM generators, wasting megatons of destructive force on massive chunks of barren, unmanned rock. Other missiles hurriedly modified their thrust to attempt to close with the Alliance battleships lurking behind the asteroids, exposing themselves to the devastating point defense of the escort ships.

Saratoga was the worst hit of the capital ships, taking damage from a warhead detonation 6 kilometers distant. The ship shook violently, and one of the reactors was scragged. Another 100 or so of his people became casualties, but the ship was still marginally battle capable, and that was all he was thinking about right now. A few escorts and one of his cruisers were destroyed, targeted by missiles that could not lock on to any capital ships.

Compton's barrage was more effective. He'd concentrated his fire, targeting only two of the enemy capital ships. A wall of missiles bore down on them, and they and their escorts frantically engaged their point defense, savaging the incoming weapons. Still, they could not stop them all, and the target vessels were engulfed in thermonuclear fury. The already-damaged Lu Chow was bracketed by close range detonations less than two kilometers away, and she broke up under the furious impact of the shockwaves, with all hands lost.

The Prince de Conde was also hit hard, and she was streaming atmosphere and reaction mass. Her engines almost destroyed, she was unable to maintain the acceleration rate of the fleet and drifted behind the main force, her decimated crew struggling to save the ship.

Compton had eighteen hours before the fleets reached missile range of each other, which meant his people had less than nineteen hours to live. They spent the time on feverish damage control efforts, focusing on repairing anything that could shoot.

Three hours before the fleets entered laser range, Compton's bomber wings launched. They were going to repeat their unconventional attack, but this time there would be no surprise, which meant that most of them would die. Even if they survived the assault, it wasn't likely there'd be any landing platforms left after the fleets engaged each other. The launch bays were silent as the crews manned their craft. They were grim and determined, and if they were going to die they were going to do it with pride, and they were going to take a lot of their enemies with them.

Well, this is it, Compton thought. We'll make them pay, at least. Enough so this fleet is in no condition to attack anywhere else. The war will go on, and that much we owe to our comrades in arms. He was calm, resigned to the situation. Part of him hoped to win the fight, of course, and he was sure that, one on one, his people were more than a match for their enemies. But it wasn't one on one, and the hard mathematical reality of warfare would assert itself. Twice as many weapons firing at half as many targets; it was simple math. He hoped for victory, of course, but the forty year combat veteran knew he was really fighting to inflict as much damage before his people went down. He wondered what Leonidas thought that last morning at Thermopylae, before the Persian masses launched the final assault.

"Sir, major energy spike at the warp gate." Commander Simmons's voice pulled Compton from his grim contemplations. "Something is transiting into the system."

Compton's mind raced. Who could it be? The warp gate was 120 light minutes away, so whatever transited had actually been in the system for two hours. He couldn't imagine how they could be friendlies; he was sure there was no significant force the high command could have sent here so quickly. He wondered grimly, could the enemy actually have more ships to throw into this fight? Not that they needed them.

Sir, we're getting a message now." Simmons turned to face Compton. His normally calm voice was high-pitched and he spoke quickly, excitedly through the broad smile on his face. "I don't know how, sir. It's Admiral Garret!" He paused, still listening to the incoming transmission. With four Yorktown class battleships."

Chapter 23

East of the Lysandra Plateau
Epsilon Eridani IV

Cain stood outside the blasted entryway to the underground complex. There were shards of blackened plasti-steel and shattered rock strewn around the large opening. He was silent, still digesting Captain Teller's report. Teller was still being vague about the cavern, preferring Cain to see for himself.

Teller's people had cut their way through the large steel door, but when they were fired on they fell back and blew the entire thing. The firefight had been short; the troops inside were some type of security force the Marines had never seen before, but they were no match for Erik Cain's special action teams. Teller had been about to hit them with some heavy ordnance when the troops shooting at his people suddenly ceased fire and a woman contacted him over his comlink.

"This is Christine Cole, project manager of this facility, contacting the Marine commander." She spoke in perfect, unaccented English. "I have instructed our security forces to stand down immediately. This is an Alliance installation. You were fired upon in error. Please cease hostilities."

"All units, condition green 7." Teller's command directed his forces to hold in position and stay on highest alert. It also authorized them to fire if they felt threatened. "Attention, Christine Cole. Your people have attacked Alliance Marines and ignored our orders to cease fire and stand down. You are to surrender this facility at once and your security force is to deactivate weapons and march out immediately. Failure to comply will result in an immediate resumption of hostilities, and we will take the installation by force without further notice."

The voice on his comlink tried to negotiate with him, but he cut her short, giving her one minute to accept his terms. When her continued attempts at persuasion were not only ineffectual, but outright ignored, she finally agreed to surrender.

She ordered the security forces to power down weapons and obey the commands of the Marines. Teller was listening on the com line. *She doesn't speak like an engineer*, he thought. *This woman is used to giving commands, and she did not like being refused. Not one bit.*

"Security force personnel, listen carefully." Teller had waited for Cole to finish transmitting her surrender order then he jumped on the line. "This is Captain James Teller, 1st U.S. Marine Division, Alliance Space Command. You are ordered to deactivate all weapon systems immediately and remove your helmets. You are to march out in single file and follow the instructions of any Marine personnel. Failure to follow instructions or the detection of an activated weapon will result in the immediate resumption of hostilities."

The surrender was completed without incident, and over 200 security troops and 2,500 workers marched out. Teller had called for reinforcements from the search teams in the area, and he detached several newly arrived platoons to administer and guard the prisoners. Christine Cole came out with the last party, which clearly consisted of managers and supervisory personnel. She was wearing a protective suit, not quite armor, but something more than the normal gear worn by the other administrators. As per Teller's command, she had removed her helmet, revealing a tangled mass of golden blonde hair.

"Captain Teller, I am Christine Cole." He was shocked to find a beautiful woman standing there, her blue eyes focused right at him as she spoke, despite the fact that his own were masked by his helmet. Most people found it disconcerting to look right at someone in full armor during a conversation, but not her. "I must insist that your troops remain outside the facility. This is a highly classified project." Her voice was pleasant, but there was something else there. Something commanding, even threatening.

"I am sorry," Teller said, "but that is out of the question. This planet is an active battle zone, and I have to investigate and occupy this facility. I can assure you that any secure information will be safeguarded with appropriate care."

She started to argue with him, but he cut her off again. She is a manipulative one, he thought. Teller was a cold fish, though - a bit of a martinet and immune to her charms and pleas. Finally, he called Sergeant Sawyer over and had him remove her from his presence. Sawyer was the perfect choice, he thought with an amused grin. She might as well try to charm a block of frozen helium.

Teller assembled a team and entered the facility, but they only got about 100 meters before they stopped in their tracks. "God damn," Teller drawled, staring dumbstruck at what he saw. "OK, everybody out." His stern command broke the stunned silence on the com. "Now!"

The search team turned and walked quickly back the way they had come. Teller posted guards at the entry with orders to allow no one to pass; then he called Cain.

The climactic battle for the plateau was in full swing, and Jax had just gone down, so Cain ordered Teller to hold fast and guard the cave until he could get there. Teller wouldn't discuss what he'd seen over the comlink, and Cain accepted the captain's judgment on that and didn't press him.

It was nearly two days before Cain was able to break free and get to the cave. When Angus Frasier's Scots broke through, the enemy was demoralized, and they pulled back all across the line. Reinforced by Frasier's troops and Prescott's Canadians, the plateau was strongly held and resupplied. 1st Brigade's exhausted troops pulled back to a supporting position and, with contact reestablished, Cain was able to see to the evacuation of the wounded.

With the line stabilized and his people resting, he was finally able to take some time to get a look at whatever it was Teller had found. He used a bit of creativity – lying, actually – to give Captain Warren the slip, and he headed up over the mountainous ridge.

Now he stood outside the blasted entrance to the cave, Teller at his side. "Let's take a look, captain." He motioned for Teller to lead.

"Yes, sir." Teller commed his second in command and

ordered that no one else enter the cave, then he began walking forward.

Cain followed, looking all around as he walked. The entry to the cave was wide, the rock walls smooth. Someone had bored through here, either digging the tunnel from scratch or widening whatever was here before. The floor of the cave was covered with sheets of metal grating, providing a solid footing and allowing water to drain away.

The tunnel continued for 100 meters, sloping downward, then opened into a massive underground cavern. To either side there were ramps leading down, large enough for a heavy carryall to traverse. Directly ahead was a catwalk overlooking the massive chamber.

Cain walked to the railing and stared out over the unimaginable sight before him. The floor of the cavern was over 50 meters below and the ceiling at least that far above. Along the far wall he saw massive columns rising from the base nearly to the ceiling. He cranked up his visor's magnification to get a closer look. The huge structures appeared to be constructed of some black substance, totally smooth except for shallow grooves every half-meter or so.

"Hector, I want this all on video."

"Already recording, colonel." Hector didn't always wait for instructions. Cain often thought the AI considered itself more of a partner than an assistant. One of these days, he pondered, I'm going to unplug the arrogant little shit.

At the base of the columns was a cluster of machinery in various shapes and sizes, all constructed from exotic and unfamiliar materials. Cain's first thought was to wonder who built all of this. Except for two brief periods when it was seized by the CAC, Carson's World had been occupied by the Alliance since it was first colonized. Could Alliance Intelligence have built this, he wondered? Or some government controlled megacorp? Why would they have built it here?

An instant later, the staggering truth began to dawn on him. "Hector, can you determine the age of his facility?"

"Any reliable estimate will require considerable analysis of the materials, however a cursory scan suggests an age on the order of 500,000 Earth years." The AI spoke with a calmness and steadiness that was utterly incongruous with the enormous implications of its words. "The projection is rough, however, with a margin of error of plus or minus 150,000 years."

Cain just stood there, silent, stunned, looking out over the amazing construction before him. The conclusion was so incredible, so utterly unexpected, he could feel it forming in his mind, almost in slow motion. Finally he spoke to himself in barely audible tones. "This was not built by man."

Humans had been in interstellar space for more than a century, and in that time they had colonized hundreds of worlds and explored hundreds more. Life, they had found, was abundant, at least plants, bacteria, and simple animals. More evolved life forms were considerably rarer, with perhaps thirty worlds hosting creatures roughly equivalent on the evolutionary scale to rabbits or squirrels. Three examples of animals on par with primitive Earth primates had been found, but no evidence of other intelligent, civilized life had ever been discovered. Man had come to conclude that he was alone. Until now.

Cain stood staring out over the cavern, trying to come to terms with the enormity of this discovery. As he looked more closely he began to notice the more modern constructions, the cranes and ramps and prefab structures clustered around the ancient artifacts. They have been excavating here for years, he thought.

"This is why we were sent here with such urgency." Cain established a line of sight laser link with Teller, who was standing next to him, just as paralyzed in awe.

"It is amazing, sir." Teller spoke slowly, deliberately, as if dragging his attention from the amazing sight before him was an almost insurmountable struggle. "You understand why I didn't report in greater detail over the comlink."

"You were absolutely correct." Cain took a deep breath. "I want no one else in here until further notice. Understood?"

"Yes, sir." I will remain at the entrance myself to supervise security.

Cain fell silent again, as old mysteries bubbled up, called from the recesses of his memory by the sudden presence of answers he had long sought in vain. Fifteen years peeled away, the blood, the death, the sacrifice. He was back in the launch bay on the Guadalcanal, minutes from the first time he'd landed on Carson's World. This is why we were sent here, even then, he thought. Then, more realization. The CAC knows about this; that's why they seized the planet fifteen years ago. That is why they were using gas to chase down the militia. They were here to find this facility.

My God, he thought. Fifteen years of war. Was this the cause? God knows, the powers don't need a lot of reason to fight each other, but the scope and intensity of this conflict had been unprecedented. Was it because of this? Is this why the Alliance took such a gamble with Operation Achilles, desperately trying to end the war quickly and protect their hold on this place?

This amazing, terrifying, astonishing find. Cain's mind raced. Centuries of scientific advancement at our fingertips, an age old question answered, a watershed event for mankind. And the Superpowers turn it into another reason to fight each other. As if they didn't have enough already.

"Colonel Cain." A familiar voice on the comlink. An unwelcome one. "I must speak with you at once."

"Captain Warren, I am occupied at present." The political officer brought Cain quickly back to reality. "I will be with you shortly."

"Colonel, I must speak with you immed…"

"Captain Warren." Cain emphasized the "captain" part. "I will be there shortly. Cain out." He shut the com line and told Hector not to accept any incoming communications from Warren.

He turned to walk back toward the surface, then stopped and turned toward Captain Teller. "No one gets in here without my permission." Cain repeated his earlier order more emphatically.

"Yes, sir. I understand." Teller was one of Cain's toughest veterans, and his troops were the best of the best. Security couldn't have been in better hands.

The two of them walked back slowly, both still deep in thought about what they had seen here. Cain's introspection was short lived; Warren was waiting for him at the entrance to the cavern, his way blocked by three of Teller's troops, armed weapons in their hands.

"Ok, Captain Teller, what can I do for you?" Cain tried to pretend he cared, but he doubted his performance was all that convincing.

"Colonel, you told me you were going to check on a report of an enemy emplacement." The political officer's voice was nasal and a little whiny. Not that Cain needed another reason to dislike Warren. "I should have been informed about this installation immediately."

"Look, captain." Cain had just about had all he was going to take from the officious little prick. "If it has escaped your notice, this entire planet is a battlefield. We have been in the middle of a very serious fight. We still are, in fact; once the enemy regroups they will be back at us, I can assure you of that." Warren started to respond, but Cain cut him off. "This installation could have been a CAC stronghold; it could have been occupied by enemy forces. Do you know how we find out if that is the case?" His voice was caustic now, dripping with derision. He'd been bottling up his thoughts for weeks, and now it was coming out. "We go and check it. Something that's hard to do when you spend most of your time cowering at HQ." Cain's voice had reached a thundering crescendo. Worse, he was castigating the hapless political officer on the open com-link, humiliating him in front of everyone in the area.

Cain turned to face the Marines standing around the entry to the cavern. "Captain Teller, no one is to enter that cavern without my specific permission." He was still on the open com-link. "If Captain Warren causes any problems place him under arrest." Cain's voice was cold as ice. "And if he attempts to enter the cavern, shoot him."

He turned and walked off, leaving everyone standing around in stunned silence.

Chapter 24

Task Force Omaha
YZ Ceti System
En route to the Epsilon Eridani warp gate

The four capital ships of the task force were marvels of man's engineering capability. Each measured 2,012.5 meters in length and massed nearly a million tons – the largest vessels ever constructed. The sides of the ships bristled with missile launchers and laser batteries, and built into the spine of each was a bow-firing x-ray laser cannon capable of inflicting enormous damage at a range greater than any other ship-carried energy weapon. And in the belly of each of these behemoths, firmly secured in massive steel cradles, were 24 heavy fighter-bombers, four complete squadrons.

The Yorktown class was something new in space warfare, a massive escalation of the arms race that had been going on for more than a century. The first three ships produced had been sent to Gliese 250 and, by all accounts, they had been the margin of victory. The class vessel, the Yorktown herself, was still in the Gliese 250 system, her crews working overtime to bring the ship back to operational readiness.

Those first three vessels had been crewed by veterans, the pick of the fleet, carefully selected to steward the navy's new superweapons. But these four ships, which by all accounts had been expected to be another year in the shipyards, were largely manned by green crews, most of them fresh out of training. There simply were no veterans available when the vessels were surprisingly ready so far ahead of schedule.

But the commander of the task force was a veteran...perhaps the greatest naval officer ever to command starships in battle. Admiral Augustus Garret sat in the command chair in the center of Midway's flag bridge. His posture was odd to any onlooker; he leaned awkwardly to one side, his torso strangely twisted. He was in pain, though he would never let that interfere with duty, and it was difficult for him to position himself comfortably.

He reflected on the bizarre sequence of events that had led him to this command center. He'd been sure the assassination attempt against him had succeeded as he lay on the deck of Cromwell's flag bridge, slipping slowly away. His last thoughts had been regret - regret for all the men and women who were dying just because the enemy wanted to kill him.

But he didn't die and, to his surprise, he awoke in Midway's medcenter, surrounded by doctors and medical technicians. How he got there was a mystery to him, one no one shed any light on until Jennifer Simon walked in, tears streaming down her face as she saw him lying in bed, very much awake.

Simon herself looked like she'd been through a bit of hell. Her arm was lightly wrapped; it had been badly broken and poorly tended, but the medical staff on Midway re-broke and refused it. It would be as good as new in a few days. But what Garret really noticed was her face. Her hair had been shaved on one side of her head, and from ear level to her chin she had been badly burned. That too, had been treated, though it was going to take a fairly lengthy skin regen treatment before she looked like her old self.

"I take it I have you to thank for my current warm-blooded status?" Garret was grim and deeply troubled by what had happened, but he managed a weak smile for his communications officer.

Simon stood for a second, speechless, more tears welling up in her eyes. "It was Captain Charles, sir. He tried to evacuate the entire staff, but Cromwell took another hit, and..." She paused, sniffling and trying to continue through the tears beginning to pour down her face. "...and they were all killed, sir." She hesitated again, trying to push away the mental images of her lost friends and comrades. "I was in the front with you. A bulkhead slammed shut behind me; it saved us both but the rest of the staff was trapped on the other side."

Garret's face was impassive. He grieved for his lost staff, just as he did for his old friend, Byron Charles, and the entire crew of Cromwell, but Garret rarely showed his emotion. Long years of command had taught him that; he gave up the right to display his pain when he accepted those first stars on his collar. His job was to be strong for his people, and that is how he conducted himself. Always. Even when wounded or scared. Even when resurrected from certain death.

He was surprised to be alive, but not that Charles had tried to get him off the ship. He'd been insisting Garret leave Cromwell, but it wasn't in the admiral's makeup to abandon his people... even if that's what duty demanded. Garret thought about his old friend and flag captain, with both fondness and sadness - I bet he was on my bridge 30 seconds after I was knocked out. So Charles had managed to save his life after all, shoving him in his cutter and blasting it off just in time to escape the thermo-nuclear fury that claimed Cromwell...and her captain and crew.

He talked with her for a long while, trying to help her deal with all that had happened. She was a young officer, and he was proud of how she had held things together. Terrified, wounded, alone...she had saved his life and gotten them rescued by a naval task force. Now that they were safe it started to back up on her, and seeing him again finally broke her control. The guilt of surviving when your comrades died is difficult to deal with; he'd been through it before, far too many times. But this was new to her. She'll get used to it, Garret thought sadly. She's young and smart and dedicated; one day she'll be sitting in a chair like mine. Then she will really understand. I wonder how much of the young officer I know today will survive.

After he spoke privately with Lieutenant Simon, he surprised everyone. "Help me out of this bed." He was calling to a medical technician standing next to him reading from the bank of monitors over his head.

"Sir?" The medtech stepped back and looked down at Garret, his mouth open with surprise.

"I said help me get up." He twisted his body toward the edge of the bed. "I'm taking command of the task force."

The medtech was a young lieutenant, and he suddenly found himself facing a problem well above his pay grade. In a near panic he tapped his communicator and called for the ship's chief surgeon.

But the chief surgeon, and the ship's captain after him, did no better. Saying no to a fleet admiral was a practical impossibility, and once Garret was told communications with Epsilon Eridani had been cut after the invasion force had gone in, there was no dissuading him.

The best they could do was convince him to wait while they fitted him for a customized medical pressure suit and helmet – a normal one wouldn't have fit over the dressings on his many wounds, and without one he'd have been defenseless if the flag bridge lost pressurization.

Now, to the chagrin of his doctor, he sat on the flag bridge as the task force transited to Epsilon Eridani and whatever awaited them there. Garret didn't have complete battlegroups, just four capital ships and two fast attack squadrons, so he was going to have a hard time scouting and screening the battleships. But the lack of communication from the invasion force meant something was wrong; Terrance Compton would be in command, and if he hadn't reported, something was indeed very wrong.

He sent a single fast attack ship through first. He knew it was a one way mission if there were enemy forces guarding the warp gate, but he sent them anyway. The crew knew it as well, but they went without complaint. Unlike those manning the capital ships, the crews of the attack squadrons were veterans, and they knew what was at stake. If this was an ambush, Garret simply couldn't risk the battleships. The attack ships were called suicide boats for a reason.

This time, however, the scout came through its dangerous mission unscathed. Less than forty minutes after the ship transited, a drone returned, reporting that the area around the warp gate was clear. There were CAC scanner buoys and communications relays deployed, but no ships. Normally, Garret would have had the scouts search for and destroy all detection devices before the main fleet transited, but he didn't have close to enough escorts to do the job, and he wasn't willing to delay when Compton's fleet might be in trouble.

He gave the order to transit, and one by one the massive battlewagons fired their thrusters and disappeared into the warp gate, leaving only a faint blue halo to show they had ever been there. Garret knew the enemy would detect his presence and the composition of his forces, but it was unavoidable if he was going to come to Compton's aid quickly. It might even be advantageous, he thought. He had no idea of the current situation, and it was possible that the enemy's reaction to his arrival could even be beneficial. Certainly, it might take some pressure off of Compton, assuming his forces hadn't already been destroyed.

"The Saint Mihiel has transited, sir." Jennifer Simon was still suffering from the effects of her wounds, but she insisted on joining her boss on the flag bridge, taking her unwillingness to accept no for an answer almost to the point of outright insubordination. "The fleet is fully assembled. The 23rd FAS squadron is positioned in the lead; the 19th is in direct support of the battleships."

It was almost a laughable formation. Four escorts scouting ahead and a single one attached to each battleship. Garret imagined the visual would have been amusing, with the lone 100 meter attack ship flitting alongside his two kilometer flagship.

One thing was certain - Garret was going to make sure it was Lieutenant Commander Simon once this was all over. By rights, she had another three years to serve in her lieutenancy, but she'd earned her circlets early. "Thank you, lieutenant. Please prepare to broadcast a message on wide beam."

"Yes, sir." She'd hesitated for a second and almost responded that the enemy would be able to intercept the transmission. Stupid fool, she said to herself silently, the admiral knows that better than you. A few seconds later: "Ready to transmit, sir."

Garret cleared his throat. "Attention Alliance naval forces. This is Fleet Admiral Garret, commanding Task Force Omaha." He took a deep breath, wincing at the pain from his injuries. "Admiral Compton, you are ordered to report your status. I am inbound with the battleships Midway, Spotsylvania, Hampton Roads, and Saint Mihiel." He gestured across his throat and Simon cut the transmission. Maybe that'll take some pressure off of your people, Terrance, he thought. If any of you are still alive.

"Set a course for Carson's World, 10g thrust." Lieutenant commander Reginald Harrison was filling in as tactical officer. Garret felt the loss each time he instinctively wanted to bark an order to an officer who was no longer there. Even Joker had been a casualty of the CAC assassination attempt. Both the AI's primary system and the backups were destroyed along with Cromwell. Garret had a new command AI available, but nothing like the customized system he'd had for so many years. The quasi-sentient machines weren't human, but bonds of a sort did develop, and users usually felt a sense of loss if an AI was destroyed. Of course, Garret had a lot of loss to deal with, though he'd shoved it all down deep for the duration of the current crisis.

"Course calculated, sir." Harrison was a little overwhelmed to be serving as tactical officer to the admiral, and it was apparent in his tone and mannerisms. Despite his best efforts to ignore the hero worship, Augustus Garret had become a legend, and effectively coming back from the dead was only pouring fuel on that fire. "Ready to lock into fleet AI."

Garret found the awed reverence he was getting from everyone annoying - and it only increased his survivor's guilt - but he didn't have much choice except to ignore it. They were heading into battle, and if serving under the "legendary" Admiral Garret was going to help morale, he'd put up with it. For now.

"Engage in three minutes." Garret shifted painfully in his seat, trying to get comfortable. He had refused any serious pain-killers; he needed 100% of his sharpness and judgment going into an unknown situation. The acceleration is going to hurt like a son of a bitch, he thought somberly. Nothing to be done – I need to find out what is going on here. "Commander Harrison, order Captain Clinton to take her squadron ahead at maximum acceleration, full search pattern dispersal. She may execute when ready. I want to know what is happening in this system." Clinton's four ships weren't close to enough to properly scout, but it was all he had, so it would have to do.

"Yes, sir. Relaying orders now." Harrison paused for a few seconds, listening to his headset. "Captain Clinton acknowledges, sir."

Garret only nodded. Yes, I have to know what is going on here, he thought. Then he gritted his teeth against the pain he knew would come when the engines fired up.

Chapter 25

Field Hospital One
Epsilon Eridani IV

The casualties had been flooding in, taking the already swamped hospital to the breaking point. Patients lay everywhere, in any spot where enough space could be cleared to hold a human being. General Holm had been relentlessly attacking toward 1st Brigade, and by all accounts was making progress. But here, in this series of dank caves that Sarah Linden had turned into a massive medical facility, could be seen the cost of that progress, the bitter price paid in blood and pain for each meter of ground taken.

Sarah felt like the walking dead, grimy with layers of dried sweat, her body aching everywhere, her head feeling like a saw had cut its way through. Her usually beautiful hair was matted and caked together, tangled and crusted with dried blood. She had been busy around the clock, living on stimulants and nutrition bars and trying not to think about Erik and his people on that besieged plateau taking everything the enemy could throw at them. There had been several thousand casualties since General Holm's drive had begun, but still nothing from 1st Brigade, which remained cut off and unable to evacuate any wounded.

General Gilson had calmed down, though she was still a difficult patient. Sarah had made a deal with her and performed surgery with the general's consent, stabilizing the worst of her wounds. Then she kept her part of the bargain, providing Gilson with a comlink so she could communicate with her division. She wasn't officially commanding them, but Sarah didn't think anyone on the other end of that com was going to refuse anything the general "suggested."

She had just finished surgery on a badly wounded private. She stepped away from the operating table, wondering if the patient was going to survive, and hating herself for starting to lose the capacity to care the way she had before. So much death, she thought, what is one more? She was beginning to think none of them were ever going to leave Carson's World anyway.

"Doctor Linden, there are more wounded at the entrance. We need a doctor to supervise triage." The voice was coming from one of the junior medical technicians.

She turned to look. God, she thought, he looks young. For the first time in her life, Sarah Linden felt old. She wasn't yet 40, but she'd seen more than her share of horrors. "I'll do it." She motioned for him to lead the way. She knew all her people by sight when this started, but try as she might, she couldn't remember his name. Another few days of this, and she wouldn't be able to remember her own.

She walked through the long tunnel to the outside. She'd chosen this mine because it was deep in the mountainside where it was well-protected from enemy bombardment. Although it would certainly shake things up, and probably seal them all inside, she figured the hospital itself could survive even a nuclear detonation.

There was sunlight hitting the ground ahead as she walked down the corridor. It must be daylight outside, she thought. It had been some time since she'd kept track of day or night. It was all the same deep inside the mountain. She half-closed her eyes against the dazzling morning sun as she walked outside. It was a beautiful day, clear and cool…a day she would have relished on Armstrong or Columbia, but here, amid the death and suffering, it only mocked her.

There were transports lined up, dozens of them. This is the biggest load of wounded yet, she thought grimly. How can there be so many? "Ok, let's get moving people." The business-like side of her took over, and she found herself barking commands without consciously thinking about it. "Let's get them lined up next to the carryalls. Get them out of their armor. Call for the plasma torches as you need them." She had three crews with the portable cutting tools. Marine armor was made to be tough, so when it was bent and twisted enough, the only way to get a wounded Marine out was with a nuclear-powered plasma torch. It was delicate and dangerous work – one slip could easily kill the patient or the operator. Or both.

She had conscripted all the walking wounded and convalescing patients who were ambulatory, and they worked along the row of transports, helping to get the new arrivals unloaded. It wasn't an easy job; those with operable armor could usually get themselves down, but the others were encased in several tons of high-density metal-polymer hybrid. A medic couldn't just throw a wounded Marine over his shoulder and carry him inside. There were cranes and lifts, but not enough, so frequently the most seriously wounded were the last to get help.

Sarah walked up and down the line of transports, supervising the unloading, and stopping to tend to the worst cases. She had just finished feverishly working on a badly wounded lieutenant – she'd stabilized him but she didn't think his chances were better than 50/50 – when she looked up and saw four techs struggling to unload a large Marine from the next transport. His back was turned to her, but she could see his helmet was off.

"Get Lieutenant Marek first." Her head snapped around; she knew that voice. "He's hurt worse than me." The big Marine had a distinctive voice, deep, rumbling.

"Jax!" Sarah shrieked, far louder than she had intended. "It's you!" She ran over to the edge of the transport, looking up at the hulking colonel.

"Sarah." He winced as he angled his head down to look at her. "It's good to see you." He didn't seem to be critically hurt, though it was obvious he was in considerable pain.

"Let's get him down." She motioned to the techs struggling to help Jax out of the transport. "Now!" She looked back at the hulking colonel. "Jax, is…"

"He's fine, Sarah." Jax managed a weak smile. "He told me to tell you he's dying for one of Aoki's burgers." He winced again as they hauled him out of the carryall and laid him gently on the ground.

Tears welled up in Sarah's eyes. He's ok; he's really ok, she thought. He'd sent her that message so she'd know he wasn't hurt. Aoki Yoshi was a PRC officer who'd served as liaison to the Alliance. He and Erik had become close, and Aoki had frequently talked about his days in Washbalt, when his father had been ambassador to the Alliance. Aoki had told Erik about his favorite burger spot, and when he and Sarah were on Earth they went out and found the place. Now it was his signal to her.

She ran over and knelt next to Jax, trying to examine his wounds. "We need a plasma torch over here." She looked back over her shoulder, shouting out the commands. "Immediately." She turned back toward Jax. "I told both of you to be careful. I see you weren't listening."

"Yeah," he said, managing a pained smile, "you know Erik puts us through the wringer." His expression turned serious. "He saved the entire expedition. You should know that." He took a deep breath, wincing as he did. "The enemy was hitting us in force everywhere, and we weren't prepared for it. By seizing that plateau he forced the enemy to hold up their attack, and we bled them like crazy when they hit us. He bought General Holm the time he needed." He gave her another weak smile. "He'll probably get a new medal, maybe two." He started to laugh, then coughed and groaned in pain.

Sarah smiled. "Erik doesn't need another medal." She put her hand on Jax's armored shoulder. "And you need to rest. Let them get you out of this can, and I'll patch you up myself." She leaned over and kissed him on the cheek. "Don't you forget, colonel…" She emphasized the colonel. "…I'm the boss here." She stood up and started to walk away. "And now I have to get back to work. Unfortunately, you're not the only one here who managed to walk into enemy fire."

She moved up and down the line of transports, driving her exhausted staff to even greater exertions. She had been about to take another stim, but the news that Erik was unhurt filled her with new energy. She was a dedicated doctor and an officer of the Corps – she would give her all to save any of her fellow Marines, anytime. But these were Erik's men and women. She couldn't help him out on that nightmarish plateau, but she could take care of his people.

"Ok, let's pick up the pace." She addressed her entire staff on the com. "These Marines from 1st Brigade have been sit-

ting on that plateau for days. I want them all inside and tended
to, ASAP." Even as she spoke, she heard the rumbling sound
behind her. Turning around, she saw another column of carryalls full of wounded coming up the hill. "Faster, people, faster."

Chapter 26

East of the Lysandra Plateau
Epsilon Eridani IV

Cain looked out over the massive alien creation, understanding but still somehow knowing he could not truly grasp the staggering implications. It is odd, he thought. In some ways life will go on as before. Yet in others, in ways I cannot even imagine, things will never be the same, for me, for all mankind. We will never be alone again.

General Holm stood next to Erik, staring into the depths of the great cavern with similar awe and shock. Cain had called him and insisted he come here, refusing to discuss what he had found.

"I really don't want to speak about it over the com, sir," Erik had said. "If you ever trusted my judgment, do it now, general." Cain's voice had been steady as always, but Holm could tell that something had shaken him up, something other than spending a week under constant enemy attack.

Holm had never before left his post in the middle of a major operation, but he trusted Erik Cain more than anyone else, so he delegated temporary command and left almost immediately. He had wondered while they were en route to the planet, but he could never have guessed the secret of Epsilon Eridani IV, not in a million years. Now he understood why Cain had been so circumspect, and he agreed completely.

The two were silent for some time, looking out over the massive structure that dominated the cavern. "I want constant security on this site." Holm knew he was giving a redundant order; Cain had already posted his special action teams to guard the entire area. "No one is to be allowed in without my authorization."

Cain was relieved; he wanted nothing more than to turn over the responsibility for this site to the general. "Yes, sir." He paused, troubled.

"What is it, Erik?" Holm knew Cain was concerned, and he thought he knew why.

"General, it is apparent that this excavation has been going on for some time. Years in fact." He hesitated again. His mind was going dark places, and he wasn't sure he should burden the general with his speculations.

"Go on, Erik." Holm turned to face Cain, though that was a fairly pointless gesture in armor.

"Sir, it must be Alliance Intelligence who ran this place. They're going to want it back." He paused again. "How many of those people we have detained out there are operatives?"

Holm sighed. "I'm sure you're right, Erik. Alliance Intel was probably trying to keep a wrap on this place. It's an unprecedented find. If it wasn't kept secret, every superpower would have been here trying to get control. The technological implications of researching all of this are staggering. Successful adaptation of this technology would shatter the balance of power."

"That could be a problem too, sir, don't you think?" The laser link between them assured that their conversation was private. "It will take years, possibly decades to adapt any of this into usable form. The CAC obviously knows about this; the other powers will soon as well." He paused, trying to frame what he wanted to say. "They'll never let us get that far. This whole war probably started because the CAC wanted to get this away from us. If they fail, what will they do?" Cain didn't wait for an answer; he provided his own. "They'll tell the other powers. No one will want the Alliance to have sole control over this kind of technology – it would be suicide. Even our allies will turn against us."

Holm let out a deep breath. "It would be the final war." His voice was soft, his tone grim. "And we'd lose before we had the chance to deploy any new technology." He paused. "This could even shatter the Treaty of Paris. There could be war on Earth as well as in space."

They were both quiet for a minute. Finally, Cain broke the silence. "Sir, have you considered the possibility that Alliance Intel wanted this technology to themselves? To deploy any way they wanted…even against us?"

Cain's distrust of the government bordered on paranoia, but what he was saying made sense. "Is that what you think, Erik?"

Cain hesitated again. He tended to keep his more extreme thoughts to himself, but he trusted Holm completely, and if he was right the general had to know. "I do. Doesn't it seem strange to you that the military was hardly involved here? Why isn't there a massive Marine base on this planet? Why isn't this whole area fortified? They had to know the CAC, at least, had intel on this place. Yet they kept us out of it. Why?" He hesitated, but when Holm didn't answer right away, he added, "And who are these security troops? They weren't frontline quality, but they were fully armored and fairly well trained. Where did they come from?"

"We have a lot of questions to address." Holm spoke slowly, groping his way toward answers that didn't come easily. "I'm particularly worried about these troops. They may have some training and experience deficiencies, but that gear is hardcore military. There is apparently another Alliance military organization that we know nothing about."

Cain inhaled, holding his breath for a few seconds as he considered Holm's last comment. "I hadn't taken it that far, sir." He paused again, his mind racing with the implications. "Someone in Alliance Gov is building a secret army. There's no other conclusion."

"Erik, the Charter gives the Corps sole responsibility for providing ground troops for extraterrestrial defense. Whoever is doing this is violating over a century of law and tradition." He had lowered his voice, almost whispering. It was a subconscious reaction – he could have screamed and the communication would still have been 100% secure.

"There was a plague here that killed every civilian on this planet." Cain's voice was hushed too, another instinctive response. "An epidemic that comes out of nowhere and kills everyone almost immediately and conveniently drives the Marine garrison offworld?" He motioned out over the expanse of the cavern. "And doesn't affect the staff deployed here at all?" He turned back toward Holm. "Does that make any sense?"

"My God, someone intentionally wiped out the population." Holm's tone was somewhere between a question and a statement. "Erik, I want you to get a crew in here right away. Draw them from your teams, the ones you trust the most. I want every centimeter of this place on video. Have them search from one end to the other and log everything."

"Yes, sir." Cain was already mentally putting together a roster. "I'll make it clear they are all to exercise extreme discretion."

"Get me a complete report as soon as you can." Holm turned back to look out over the cavern. "I have to get back to HQ. This lull won't last." He paused, then turned back toward Cain. "Erik, you're a reckless lunatic sometimes, but you saved the day here. I wasn't ready for the amount of force the enemy had waiting to ambush us. This crazy, brilliant maneuver of yours broke up their initial attack completely." He hesitated again. "Thank you."

Cain was generally unburdened with concern about what others thought, but Holm was one of the few he did care about. Mentor, second father, friend. He would have followed the general into hell itself. "Thank you, sir." He paused, then added, "That means a lot, sir."

They stood there quietly for a few minutes, looking out over the railing, each deep in his own thoughts. The silence was broken by Captain Teller on Cain's comlink. "Colonel, I'm sorry to disturb you, but the supervisor of this facility is extremely insistent that she speak with my superior."

"Very well, captain. Advise her I will be with her shortly." He switched to his direct link with Holm. "General, the former administrator is giving Captain Teller a hard time. With your permission, I will go out and deal with her."

"Good idea." He turned from looking out at the cavern to face Cain. "Remember, no one gets in here but your hand-picked team. And I want the members of that security force questioned as soon as possible. They are to be kept separate from the civilian staff."

"Yes, sir." He turned and started to walk down the corridor.

"And Erik?" Cain stopped and looked back. "I know you already had an altercation with Captain Warren."

"Ah…yes sir, that was…"

Holm cut him off. "Erik, I don't care about that. I just wanted to say that none of the political officers get in here. I don't care what they say or how much they complain. Until I am able to confer with General Samuels, this area is off limits to them."

"Yes, sir!" Cain would actually enjoy telling the government snoops to get screwed. "My pleasure, sir."

Cain stood outside the blasted entrance to the tunnel, look-ing out at the various groups milling around. Mostly his people, some standing guard, some escorting groups of detainees as they began to march west. He'd ordered the civilian workers separated from the security personnel and for both groups to be evac'd to the plateau for eventual transport to a detainment area, probably near Holm's HQ. But they'd probably have a long wait; Cain would be damned if he was going to divert any trans-ports to moving these people until every one of his wounded had been evac'd to the field hospital.

He was about to com Teller when he saw the captain stand-ing on a hill about twenty meters from the tunnel entrance. He was facing a woman whose back was turned to Cain. She had long blonde hair cascading down her back. For an instant he thought it was Sarah. No, he thought. Not possible. He walked toward them, and when he was about five meters away Teller motioned toward him and she turned around.

He stopped in his tracks. It wasn't Sarah, but the resem-blance was uncanny. She was a couple centimeters shorter, and her hair didn't have the reddish tint Sarah's did in the sun, but the similarities greatly outnumbered the differences.

"Colonel Cain, I need to speak with you." Her voice was different that Sarah's, lower-pitched, and the tone was darker, more intimidating.

Cain hesitated for a moment, still distracted by the resem-blance. Finally he answered, his voice a little tentative. "What can I do for you?"

She stared at him. His visor was set to transparent, so even though he was armored, she could see his face. "Colonel, I must insist that you return control of this facility to my staff at once. The Tarsus Corporation has a Presidential Charter providing exclusive rights to explore this archeological site." She extended her hand. In her open palm was a small data chip.

Cain had an urge to dismiss her abruptly, but she looked so much like Sarah he found it difficult. "I am sorry, Supervisor Cole – it is Cole, right? – but I am not authorized to allow anyone except designated Marine personnel into the cave. I'm afraid that's final."

A master manipulator, Alex could sense that something was holding him back. She'd half expected him to have her escorted forcibly to the detainment area. What is it, she thought? Is he just a sucker for a pretty face? No, it must be more than that. Erik Cain had a reputation for many things, but being a soft touch was definitely not one of them. "Colonel..." – she spoke gently this time, her tone sweeter, less confrontational – "...please call me Christine. I'm afraid you don't understand. This facility is extremely fragile. My personnel are highly skilled. With all due respect, your Marines are not trained to handle this type of artifact."

"Supervi...Christine, I can assure you that no one is going to disturb any artifacts in that cavern. Our interest is maintaining security, nothing more." Teller stood listening, surprised at Cain's tone and his efforts to explain. The captain had been expecting something more akin to a volcanic eruption, but for some reason Cain was restrained.

"But Colonel..."

"I am sorry, but the matter is closed." His voice was sterner, not cold, but he was clearly losing his patience, a commodity he possessed in extremely limited quantities.

Back down, she thought. You're not going to change his mind; don't waste whatever goodwill you seem to have. "Very well, Colonel Cain." Her voice was soft, almost seductive. Don't overdo it, she thought. This man will see through bullshit. "I see that I have no alternative, so I will obey your orders."

"Thank you for your cooperation." He was looser; the tension that was building was gone. "Captain Teller, please have Supervisor Cole escorted to her people, and see that they are all made comfortable until we are able to transport them to a more appropriate place." He turned to face Alex. "Christine, I am afraid that I have many duties. Good bye." He turned and started walking back toward the cave entrance.

"Thank you, colonel." That was odd, she thought. I'll have to do a little research on the good colonel. But how the hell am I going to get control of the facility from these damned Marines?

Chapter 27

AS Midway
Alliance Combined Fleet
In orbit around Epsilon Eridani IV

Garret sat on the bridge of Midway, still uncomfortable, still in pain, but profoundly relieved. There had been some tense moments over the past four days, but now he was master of the Epsilon Eridani system. He'd even allowed himself the indulgence of a moderately powerful painkiller. It wasn't enough to seriously impair his response time, but now he could finally afford to be just a touch below 100%. At least the thundering pain in his head, his constant companion for four days, had become more of a dull ache.

As with most victories, this one didn't come without cost, though the losses had been far less than he'd expected. His broadband communication announcing his arrival had probably saved Admiral Compton and his people. The enemy fleet had been about to close to energy range of his battered ships. Facing overwhelming firepower, Compton's force would have had little chance of survival. They would have bled the enemy as the price of their lives, but in the end, they would have fallen.

Compton had been sitting on his bridge when Garret's broadcast came through. It gave him a shred of hope and, failing salvation, a chance to die for victory rather than defeat. There wasn't a doubt in his mind – if he were in command of the enemy fleet he'd come in full bore and wiped out his smaller armada before Garret's task force could close. Garret would have done the same – Compton was sure of that.

But CAC commanders were conservative. The penalties for failure were severe and did not encourage bold action. And Admiral Dieng was dealing with Imperial and Europan allies who had already suffered greater losses than they'd bargained for on this operation.

Compton played a hunch. His first instinct was to accelerate away from the enemy at maximum thrust. That would buy time, but the incoming fleet already had some velocity, while his ships were virtually stationary, deployed around the asteroids they had used for cover against the missile attack. Running would have delayed the enemy's reaching energy weapons range but not long enough for Garret to arrive. So Compton stood firm, bluffing, signaling that he wanted the laser duel. Prey on the enemy commander's concerns about Garret, he thought.

Compton had waited and watched, the minutes passing like eons. Finally, after what seemed like hours but was actually only a few moments, the reports started coming in – the enemy was decelerating, trying to reverse course before entering laser range. Compton was relived, though he tried to maintain his usual cool, unflappable image for the crew. In the end, the two fleets were briefly in each others' effective ranges and exchanged fire for a few minutes before the incoming ships were able to reverse course and disengage. Saratoga took significant damage, and her heavy laser cannons were knocked offline, but not before they scored another hit on the battered Prince de Conde.

The bridge of Saratoga was filled with the pungent odor of burnt electronics, and repair bots wheeled wildly around, bringing salvageable systems back online and bypassing those that had been chopped up or fried into useless junk. Compton breathed a sigh of relief and leaned back in his command chair, eyes closed thinking how near they'd come to annihilation. The battle wasn't over – far from it. But the enemy commander had made a mistake; he'd chosen the course that seemed more cautious, and with that decision he'd thrown away his best chance at victory.

With the enemy retreating out of range, Compton now ordered his ships to accelerate in the opposite direction, away from the enemy. He didn't want the opposing commander to change his mind – there was still time to engage his force before Garret arrived – so he put a little extra distance between them.

The overall forces in the system were close to even. If Garret's fleet had consisted of full battlegroups instead of just the capital ships, the Alliance would have had the clear edge. But even lacking escorts and support vessels, Garret still had the only ships that were fully armed and equipped. His battleships had full external missile racks and, all together, sixteen squadrons of heavy bombers. All his bomber crews were green as hell, but the enemy didn't know that.

Before committing to another bloody fight, he decided to try an unorthodox strategy. "Attention Europan and South American naval units, this is Fleet Admiral Augustus Garret of the Alliance Navy." Garret was sure the CAC's allies would have been told he had been killed, so he decided to get the maximum impact he could from his sudden return from the dead. He didn't know if they'd believe it was him, but he was sure it would give them something else to think about, and maybe sow some doubt in their minds about what their CAC allies told them. "To my knowledge, there is not yet a declared state of hostilities between our nations."

He paused for several seconds. Let them wonder a little, he thought. "I am prepared to offer a truce. If you agree to follow a pre-agreed course out of the system, I will refrain from any hostilities against your ships." He paused again, but only briefly. He wanted to finish before the CAC commander could intervene. "You will be allowed to depart this system and return by the most direct course to your nearest base." They won't want to abandon their ground forces, he thought as he was speaking. "If you accept these terms, General Holm will offer a similar truce to your forces currently engaged on the surface." He was making big promises for Holm, but he was sure the general would back him up. "If they surrender and lay down their arms they will be repatriated as quickly as transport can be arranged."

Garret was wildly overstepping his authority. He wasn't even technically in command of the four battleships he'd commandeered, though no one was going to challenge the orders of the Navy's senior field officer, even if he was still technically dead. But agreeing to truces and promising to allow enemy warships to retreat unmolested through friendly systems was far more uncertain ground. And unilaterally promising to repatriate tens of thousands of enemy troops was even more of a stretch.

Garret was still 20 light minutes away from the enemy fleet, so it took some time for his message to reach its recipients and more for any response to get back to Saratoga. While he waited, he focused on readying his green crews for the battle they might have to fight and running diagnostics on his new and untested ships, but forty minutes later he was staring at the com, waiting for a reply that might come at any time…or not at all.

The entire flag bridge staff sat tensely, waiting to see if Garret's offer would be accepted. If it wasn't, his people faced a serious fight, one they could very well lose. But if the Imperial and Europan contingents withdrew, they would seriously outnumber and outgun the CAC and Caliphate forces that remained. Soon they would know.

Admiral Jacques Maret sat in his command center, his helmet visor closed so no one could hear his communications. He was conferring with Fleet Admiral de Santos, his French being translated to Spanish by his AI before transmission. "Have you conferred with Admiral Dieng?" He waited while his communication traveled the four light seconds to Emperador and the response made its way back. Maret had agreed that Santos, as leader of the larger task force, should discuss the situation with the CAC commander in chief.

"I have. He is adamant that he will not conduct negotiations." Santos' voice was slightly electronic; the Imperial AIs weren't as sophisticated as the Europan, and the translator didn't replicate Santos' voice as perfectly as Maret's did his. "I believe he is afraid of ending up in one of Li An's little rooms."

The CAC's venerable spymaster had instilled considerable fear in the Coalition's senior officers, and she also knew what was hidden in the mountains of Carson's World. Dieng's orders were clear; they expressly forbade retreat. If he obeyed he might die in battle, but if he withdrew he'd likely face a far more unpleasant death at the hands of C1's interrogators. Worse, if he was branded a traitor his family would join him in Li An's chamber of horrors.

Santos and Maret had agreed that they would counter Garret's truce offer with a proposal that the entire fleet, including CAC and Caliphate units, withdraw from the system. Neither admiral liked the idea of abandoning allies, even tenuous new ones, but neither was prepared to commit their forces to a fight to the death over a planet of no apparent importance. They'd been sent to participate in an ambush, not a battle of attrition, and certainly not against the legendary Admiral Garret commanding a force of superbattleships. They were prepared to try to bluff Garret into letting them all leave, but Dieng's refusal put an end to that option.

"My choice, at least, is clear. Honor is satisfied and Dieng has chosen his own fate. I cannot expose my task force to possible annihilation, especially as Prince de Conde has already been heavily damaged. I will accept Garret's terms." Maret had been under secret orders to conserve his forces; Europa Federalis was already at war with the German-dominated Central European League, and they could not afford serious losses, especially in capital ships.

"Indeed, Admiral Maret, I concur." Santos was a member of the Imperial family and as such he was well aware of the parlous financial condition of the empire. This fight had already cost him a battleship, and he knew the Imperial Navy could not afford further losses, especially not in a fringe system nowhere close to the worlds the empire sought to acquire. "I, too, will accept the admiral's terms. I propose that we send a joint communication." He paused briefly. "Let us extricate our forces from this mess."

Garret shifted uncomfortably in his command chair, unsuccessfully trying to angle his body in some way that didn't hurt. It had been almost 90 minutes since he'd sent his truce offer, and he was about to give up and start preparing for the massive fight to come.

"Sir, incoming message from Admiral Maret." Lieutenant Simon turned to face Garret as she spoke. "Transferring to your headset."

There was a brief delay, then Maret's voice came through in

accented, but extremely passable English. "Admiral Garret. I wish to offer my best wishes and those of Fleet Admiral de Santos." Maret's voice paused. He was probably figuring out how to tell an enemy he's happy he isn't really dead, thought Garret, amused. "I had been shocked to hear of your demise, and I am gratified to see that these reports were in error."

Garret smiled. We may try to kill each other, he thought, but that's no reason not to be polite. Sometimes I think we are under the impression this is all a game and not the deadly business it really is. Yet he knew that he, too, often participated in the same farce.

"If you are prepared to provide adequate assurances that we will be allowed to leave this system and return with all speed to our respective nations' space, both Fleet Admiral de Santos and I are prepared to accept your terms."

Garret let out a deep breath; he was glad they were communicating at long-range and not sitting together at a table where his adversaries would have seen the relief he felt. He usually had a good poker face, but he really preferred to avoid a difficult fight with his green troops and brand new ships, and it showed. He carefully put together his response, providing specific instructions to the Europan and Imperial commanders and transmitted it.

After the allied contingents departed, the outcome of the battle for Epsilon Eridani was never in doubt. The CAC and Caliphate ships put up a hard fight, badly damaging Saratoga again and seriously wounding Compton, but they were outgunned and systematically destroyed. Garret was relentless, pursuing every enemy vessel as it tried to flee. Now there wasn't a CAC or Caliphate ship left in the system. The Alliance owned Epsilon Eridani space. The cost had been high, but not nearly as bad as it might have been.

Now Garret was going to call General Holm. Space was theirs; now it was time to deal with the surface.

Chapter 28

I Corps HQ
Durang Valley
Epsilon Eridani IV

Darius Jax walked painfully toward a large modular structure set in the middle of a cluster of similar but smaller buildings. He was limping and leaning on a cane to take some weight off his right leg, but he was happy to be out of bed – or the pile of rags that had passed for one. He'd expected Sarah to give him a hard time about leaving, but her hospital was so overcrowded, she'd sent him away with a hug and instructions to "go bother Erik instead of me."

He'd checked on some of 1st Brigade's wounded before he left. Most of them seemed to be doing well, despite the difficult conditions in the hospital. Even Lieutenant Marek looked like he was going to recover fully, though he would spend considerable time at Armstrong Medical in the regeneration ward before he returned to duty. Jax had thought Marek was done, but Sarah had worked on him herself, and somehow she'd managed to repair enough of the nuke-inflicted damage to stabilize him.

Jax looked up at the sign above the door. Someone had scrawled I Corps by hand. He laughed to himself, but laughing still hurt, so he stopped abruptly. Someone could have gotten a better sign for the HQ of the largest ground force the Alliance ever deployed in space, he thought, still amused.

He walked up to the door, staring into the retinal scanner for clearance. After a delay of a second or two, the door popped open, allowing him to enter. He walked through, shuffling slowly down the corridor to the conference room.

"Look what just walked in!" Cain's voice was cheerful, more so than it had been since I Corps had landed on Carson's World. He glanced at Jax's cane and the heavy cast still on his right foot. "And I use the word walk loosely." He leapt up and embraced his enormous friend. "It's good to have you back, Jax."

"It's good to be back." Jax scanned the room. Seated around the table were the senior officers of the corps, at least the ones healthy enough to be there. General Gilson sat along the far wall, leaning at an odd angle, trying to keep the weight off the sorest areas of her battered body. Gilson had been another troublesome patient Sarah was only too happy to send on her way once she was out of danger.

The political officers were all there too. Most of I Corps command staff had managed to maintain better relations with their minders than Cain had, but none of them really got along, and there was an overall feeling of discomfort. Holm found the whole thing very upsetting; he'd put an enormous amount of effort into forging a team that enjoyed mutual respect and worked well together, and the assignment of the political offi-cers had stripped away that comfortable environment. He didn't appreciate the added stress on his people.

Captain Warren sat on the opposite side of the room from Cain with an expression on his face that could curdle milk. He avoided looking over at Erik and remained silent during the entire meeting. Cain simply ignored the political officer as if he didn't exist.

"I want to thank you all for coming." General Holm stood at the head of the large table and looked out at his assembled staff. He was wearing gray duty fatigues; they all were. Sarah had given the all-clear regarding the supposed pathogen that had wiped out the population. Whatever it was there was no sign of it in her multiple tests, so with combat operations ending Holm could allow his people to shed their armor. Living in a fight-ing suit for weeks on end was almost unbearable, and Holm's announcement was met with universal acclaim.

"It has been an extraordinary campaign." The general's voice was slightly hoarse. There'd been no heavy combat for over a week, but he had still been overwhelmed with tasks, and he was tired...tired to the bone. "I just wanted to assemble you all to tell you personally how proud I am of I Corps. We faced extremely difficult and unexpected conditions here, and at no time did any of our personnel perform with less than total professionalism and preparedness."

The officers in the room were grizzled veterans, but Holm's praise touched them all. They had fought together on multiple worlds, and they had become a cohesive team. Forged in the inferno of some of the most brutal fighting in history, and led by a man they trusted utterly, they had evolved into the most elite fighting force ever deployed. Their enemies had set a trap for them here, one that was foolproof on paper. But I Corps didn't cooperate; they didn't yield to the mathematics that mandated their defeat, and they overcame the odds to survive and ultimately prevail.

After Cain's stand on the plateau, and the subsequent breakthrough by the Scottish brigade, the enemy's lines were compromised, and they fell back 100 kilometers to regroup. I Corps had suffered heavy losses, but the carnage they had inflicted on the enemy was far worse. The Imperial and Europan units, mostly raw and untested, were not remotely prepared for the intensity of the fighting.

When Admiral Garret and General Holm broadcast the lenient surrender terms, it was almost impossible for their commanders to refuse. The CAC and Caliphate leaders, commanding veteran units and facing dire consequences if they failed, tried to intimidate their allies into continuing the fight. It took a tense few days of negotiations, but in the end, 55,000 Europan and Imperial troops marched out and surrendered.

The CAC and Caliphate hardcore units dug in, however, and refused to give up. No longer strong enough to take the offensive, they dared the Alliance forces to dig them out of their mountainous strongpoints. They were motivated to hold out. The officers faced harsh reprisals if they surrendered. Their orders were clear; they were to hold Epsilon Eridani IV at all costs. All costs.

The engagement transformed from a pitched battle to a series of costly search and destroy missions against scattered enemy positions. The Alliance forces were re-provisioned by the returned supply and transport fleet, while the CAC and Caliphate holdouts were cut off.

Cain commanded 1st Division, or what was left of it. General Gilson had been in the hospital and Brigadier Slavin was dead. The special action battalion was assigned to onsite security at the cave, and the rest of the division was taken out of the line and assigned to guard the prisoners until they could be loaded onto transports and shipped out.

Holm assigned 2nd Division and the Oceanian units to dig out the last of the defending units. The outcome of the battle was no longer in doubt, but there was still a month of brutal fighting before the general was able to declare combat operations concluded.

He looked out over the assembled officers, their job done, at least for now. With Garret's victory in space and the total defeat of the enemy ground forces, it was possible they had won the climactic victory of the war. Though no one dared say it out loud, everyone present wondered if the fruit of this victory might be peace.

"I Corps will be remaining here indefinitely, so we're going to start reorganizing and rebuilding. We will be expanding our facilities here significantly to accommodate a long term presence, so we have hard work ahead, though I daresay it will be a little easier than the work we have done to date." The officers around the table smiled grimly. The work they had done had been difficult indeed, and costly.

Holm reached down and picked up the cup that had been sitting on the table in front of his seat. He motioned for the other to rise and do the same. "To our fallen brothers and sisters." He raised his glass as his officers repeated his toast.

Still holding his cup aloft Holm smiled. "And to the Corps. Now and forever!"

Chapter 29

C1 Headquarters Building
Wan Chai, Hong Kong
Central Asian Combine, Earth

Li An sat at her desk, a crystal glass of bourbon sitting untouched off to the side. She was frustrated and angry. Her plans, so carefully prepared and well-conceived, had completely unraveled. "Liang, you incompetent fool. You almost succeeded in your mission and you threw it away and let Garret escape in a lifeboat?" She was taking to herself, her voice soft but dripping with anger and bitterness. "If I get my hands on you, hell itself will be a relief when I finally let you die." Garret's survival, and his subsequent actions, had turned her grand plan in Epsilon Eridani into a total disaster. They had been on the verge of a stunning success; instead, they lost the war there.

Liang was, by all accounts, a prisoner of the Alliance now. Not only had he allowed Garret to escape the trap she'd so carefully planned, he'd managed to get his task force obliterated as he withdrew. He's probably in one of Stark's dungeons, she thought, giving up every secret he has. She couldn't even take it out on his family. His parents were dead, and his wife was the daughter of a Committee member. And the last thing Li An needed now was more trouble with the Committee. She knew where enough bodies were buried to survive this, but there was no question that the series of debacles had seriously damaged her position.

The war had been a disaster. The CAC navy had been virtually destroyed, and its ground forces were sorely depleted. It would take years, and financial resources they didn't have, to recover. The Caliphate was also prostrate, crippled by the loss of the vital resource-producing worlds that had been its primary source of wealth.

Europa Federalis and the Empire had made their own peace, quickly accepting the lenient terms offered by the Alliance. But the treaty being negotiated at the Ares Metroplex was anything but lenient. The Alliance was dominant, its victory decisive. The CAC and Caliphate would pay dearly for the peace both desperately needed.

Worst of all, the Alliance had control of the alien artifact. She didn't know much about it except that it was a technology thousands of years ahead of Earth's. That game, at least wasn't over. None of the Powers would allow the Alliance to monopolize such a find, and even with Garret and Holm to fight their battles there was no way they could stand up to all of the Superpowers long enough to research and adapt the new technology. She'd never actually gotten anyone inside the facility, though, and she didn't have the proof she'd need to put together a grand coalition against the Alliance. She didn't have it now, but she was determined to get it.

She looked over at the credenza, two boxes sitting opened on its polished wood surface. The first was a case of bourbon, a very rare and expensive one. There was a card attached: With all my love, Gavin.

Stark had gotten the better of her, she had known that already. But it wasn't until she opened the second box that she realized just how he'd done it. It was a large cube of clear polymer, and inside, suspended artfully, was a head. A pale-skinned face framed with white-blond hair stared out at her, lifelessly. Carillon.

All the effort to turn a member of the Directorate and the fool gets himself caught. She figured that Carillon's death had likely not been a pleasant one. Gavin Stark did not take kindly to betrayal; she knew that much.

She hated the smug bastard, and she was determined to have her revenge. She turned her chair and leaned back, looking out over the harbor to Kowloon. "This is not over, Stark," she muttered to herself. "Enjoy your success while you can, because the wheel will turn." She reached behind her, taking the bourbon in her hand and raising it to her lips. "Yes, my friend. The wheel will definitely turn."

Thirteen thousand kilometers away, two old friends were sharing their own drink, though it was Scotch, not bourbon.

"To victory." Gavin Stark sat behind his massive mahogany desk, smiling broadly. He raised his glass, admiring the caramel color of the Scotch in the almost priceless ancient crystal glass. Stark admired antiques; his office was furnished with old and extremely valuable pieces. His desk had been salvaged from the wreckage of Langley; it had belonged to the last director of the old CIA, and before him to a U.S. president.

His companion was standing at the side table, another priceless antique, pouring his drink. He added a splash of water to his Scotch, something he had been doing more often in recent years. It brought out the flavor of the fine single malt, he felt. "To victory," he responded, raising his glass before taking a drink and walking over to one of the guest chairs. "But not arrogance," he added as he sat, slowly lowering his aching joints into the plush leather seat.

Stark laughed. "Do you think I will let success go to my head?" He leaned back, stretching out in the massive leather chair. "You know me better, my friend." He picked a small piece of lint off of his otherwise spotless tuxedo. "I am well aware of the many problems we still face."

The older man smiled. "Yes, there are always more challenges. But it is a moment for limited celebration." He ran his eyes over his companion's perfectly tailored suit. "You should be leaving soon."

"Are you sure you won't come?" Stark was looking forward to the Presidential reception, even if he was going under his cover as a megacorp executive and not the mastermind of the Alliance Intelligence services. "It should be amusing."

The old man laughed. Jack Dutton had been a power in Washbalt for seventy years. "I have been going to these things since before you were shaving. They have all been interminable. Now I am old enough to have an excuse to stay home." He took another drink. "But by all means, you enjoy watching that pompous ass take credit for the victory."

Stark smiled. "The president can do whatever he wants.

The more he struts around and plays a role, the less he interferes with our running things." He paused for a second. "When he is no longer necessary, we can deal with him."

Dutton smiled. "I suspect that will be your game, my friend. That plan is a little longer term than I am, I think."

"I'm not sure I really believe you are capable of dying. You're too grouchy." Stark smiled for a minute, then he straightened in his chair, his face suddenly serious. "You are right about having some problems, however. The war was won; there is no doubt about that. But we still have Garret and Holm to deal with, and both have become even bigger heroes." He paused, his brow furrowed in thought. "I'm not sure how to get rid of them now that we will be at peace."

"We will just have to watch for our opportunity." Dutton shifted slightly in his seat, trying to get comfortable – something that was becoming more difficult with each passing year. "We will need to be patient. And watchful. They must be carefully monitored." After a brief pause, he added, "And I would put Erik Cain on that list as well. He does not have Garret's rank, but he is enormously popular within the Corps, and he is famous on Earth too, thanks to that stupid press tour a few years ago."

Stark frowned. "I think you are right. By all accounts, he is not a fan of government authority. I have a report here from his political officer..." He sifted through a pile of data chips on his desk. "...well, it's here somewhere. Anyway, he complains quite vociferously about Cain's disrespect for him, and he urges that he be dismissed from the Corps." He looked up from his desk. "Of course, that is out of the question right now. Cain is the hero of Carson's World, and his service record is spotless."

Dutton's eyes met Stark's. "Yes. We will have to do something about that, won't we?" He put his glass down on the desk. "We need a plan to sabotage Cain's career."

Stark's eyes widened. "Alex ran into him on Carson's World. She mentioned he acted strangely around her. She thought it was odd, but she wasn't able to get anywhere with him." He hesitated, thinking. "But I know something she doesn't. Erik Cain is involved with Alex's long lost older sister, a doctor in the

Corps. Isn't that an interesting development?" His expression hardened. "I think I will assign this to our sexy little Alex. She may be able to find a way to undermine him, maybe through her sister." His mind was moving quickly now. "Indeed, if we can get control of Cain, we can get to Holm too. Cain is his protégé, and from what I hear they are almost like father and son."

"That is interesting. Very interesting." Dutton's eyes fell to the desk as he considered the possibilities.

"On the topic of Alex, do you think I should appoint our little vixen to Carillon's Seat?" Stark had usually decided what to do before he asked for advice, but this time he was really not sure.

Dutton laughed. "It might be worth it just to see Number Ten go apoplectic." He paused while Stark let out his own laugh. "I would say do it or leave the Seat vacant for now. You really can't move Samuels up, and Number Five is stretched to manage his current duties." He smiled wickedly. "Alex is a capable operative. She did very well to keep the CAC out of the facilities on Carson's World. If Li An had any evidence other than her word…" He snickered as he said word. "…she could get all the other Powers lined up against us. We cannot allow that to happen."

"No." Stark's tone became very serious. "The secrecy of the site is not what it was. If the other Powers have evidence of what is there we will face a serious crisis. We can overcome Li An's unsubstantiated claims – she's been lying to everyone for fifty years, and no one is going to believe her. But if she gets proof we are in serious trouble."

"You're planning to use Samuels to get the Marines out of there, right?" Dutton had been surprised when Stark told him he'd managed to flip a high-ranking Marine…and downright shocked when he found out just how high-ranking. It was the first time Alliance Intelligence had pulled that off, but it wasn't for lack of trying. The Marines were a fiercely independent and tight-knit organization. Stark had never shared how he'd gotten to Samuels, and Dutton didn't ask.

"Yes. We'll let them stay a while. Samuels will order the

facility sealed up. We'll have a delay, but we'll get them off-planet and move our own people back in."

"How about the colonies?" Dutton reached out for his drink, slowly lifting it to his lips.

"I plan to move forward aggressively with bringing them in line." He rubbed his temples as he spoke. "It is time they learned their place. But we will have to move carefully. The military will be resistant. Samuels will be a big help there, too."

Dutton glanced at the chronometer. "You really need to get going." He stood up, slowly and with significant effort. "So we've closed a chapter, but the book goes on." He smiled at Stark. "Enjoy the victory, but not for too long. We have a lot of work to do."

Stark looked over at his friend. "Yes, Jack. We have a lot of work to do." He stood up and shook Dutton's hand, and the two walked out of the office and down the hall. "A lot of work," Stark repeated softly to himself.

Chapter 30

Shuttle Beta-3
Henderson Landing Field
Epsilon Eridani IV

Cain sat quietly in the shuttle's small but comfortable compartment. This wasn't one of the cattlewagons he was used to riding back from an operation. He wore a platinum star on each shoulder now, and a private shuttle – and a plush one at that – was one of the perks.

He was alone, the only sound the soft whine of the ship's reactor as it powered up for liftoff. He looked out the window at the neat rows of shuttles, stretching almost as far as he could see. I Corps was staying on Carson's World indefinitely to protect the alien artifact, and the supplies to maintain a small army had started rolling in.

If he'd been in any danger of sleeping regularly, this campaign would take care of that. He'd led 3,617 soldiers down to the reddish dust of Carson's World. Only 1,397 of them were still operating under their own power when it was done, and some of these had arms in slings and legs in casts. Sarah and her people had worked wonders, saving over 1,000 seriously wounded Marines from his brigade. Most of those would eventually return to duty, though a few would probably be relegated to desk jobs or training positions. Still, 1,181 of his troops would never leave this hard won planet, more ghosts to weigh on his conscience.

He was waiting for Sarah. They both had six months' leave and a decade and a half's accumulated pay of which they'd spent only a fraction. They were going to enjoy some time together and see some of the colony worlds, and they were going to do it in style. Seven years crawling through the slums of Outer New York and sixteen more on the battlefield...it rated a vacation, and a damned good one at that.

Still, Cain had resisted. The Third Frontier War was officially over, that much was true. The Treaty of Mars had been signed, and the Powers had ceased hostilities, at least for the moment. But the peace wouldn't last, and Cain knew the smart move was to start getting ready for the next war.

But Holm had insisted that Erik and Sarah take some leave. He was very fond of them both, and he knew as well as Erik did that more trouble was coming. They would all face new dangers and challenges, and they needed to take whatever time they could have together, because the future offered no guarantees.

Holm thought it might be a good idea for Erik to take a little vacation right about now anyway. Cain had become somewhat controversial. His situation with Captain Warren had deteriorated considerably since he'd had the outraged political officer escorted from the alien facility. Warren had twice disobeyed Cain's orders to stay away from the cave, insisting that he was not in the regular marine chain of command and therefore not bound by such directives. The first time, Cain had yelled a bit and had him escorted back to camp. The second time, he'd come very close to summarily executing the political officer. While the military code technically gave Cain that right under combat conditions, it would have created a colossal mess. Anne Delacorte had likely saved Warren's life that day, for which Holm had rewarded her with her major's circlets.

Warren had filed a whole stack of complaints against Cain, but Erik was the hero of the Carson's World campaign and revered in the Corps, so he'd probably be safe from any serious consequences. Still, General Samuels was on his way to Carson's World to review the security arrangements for the cave, and Holm would be just as happy if Erik was off somewhere recreating with his beautiful doctor instead of here to face the number two officer in the Corps.

He wondered how long the peace would last. The CAC and Caliphate armed forces had been shattered, but they would rebuild…the question was how quickly. But regardless, peace couldn't last now. The alien artifact was thousands of years ahead of any technology man had dreamed of, and once the other Powers found out about it the Alliance would likely have a choice – share the amazing discovery or fight everyone else to hold on to it. Cain didn't kid himself about which choice Alliance Gov would make.

He knew the government would crack down on the colonies too, and he was just as sure the frontier worlds would resist. Alliance Gov had ruled over meek, terrified masses for far too long; they did not understand the spirit of people who'd left everything behind to tame new worlds. The early colonists had braved hostile environments, unknown pathogens, and the harshness of the untamed wild. They had starved, frozen, and fought for every day of survival. They considered the worlds they had built to be theirs, and they were not about to let them become copies of the grotesque society they had left behind.

When matters reached the breaking point he didn't know what would happen, but he was pretty sure it would be messy. He hoped his fellow Marines would refuse to fire on colonists; he knew he would disobey such an order. His worst nightmare was that some of his comrades chose one side and some the other. He'd face any horror before that...before he was forced to pull the trigger on another Marine. But that was tomorrow's problem, and he'd face it when it came.

He'd come a long way, and though it felt like he and Sarah were riding off into the sunset, he knew better. This was a temporary respite, a break in the storm. Worse trials lay ahead, of that he was sure. They would be sorely tested in the years to come, and while he mourned for the peaceful existence he knew was impossible, he was thankful for what he did have. If his life was to be filled with unending struggles, he was profoundly grateful to have found something worth fighting for...worth dying for if need be. There was a time he had fought just as hard for a crust of bread...or for nothing at all.

Cain looked toward the edge of the poured 'plast landing area, fringed with the patchy yellow fungus that grew in the dry red dirt of Carson's World. He saw her first in his peripheral vision, that familiar mane of reddish-blonde hair blowing in the gentle breeze – even redder on Carson's World where everything seemed to pick up a crimson tint. She wore a set of gray fatigues, her shiny new platinum eagles on the collar.

Most of all, he would fight for her, for a universe where they could live together one day without the pain and death and blood. He would fight to keep her safe, to insure that she never went through the suffering and misery she had survived so many years before.

He had been reborn, just as the Corps had promised when it plucked him from the executioner's chair. And he would keep fighting until they'd forged a universe where the price of rebirth wasn't war and killing and blood. He wasn't sure he believed it was possible, but he would keep fighting until he knew, however long it took.

Crimson Worlds Series

Marines (Crimson Worlds I)

The Cost of Victory (Crimson Worlds II)

A Little Rebellion (Crimson Worlds III)
(December 2012)

The First Imperium (Crimson Worlds IV)
(March 2013)

www.crimsonworlds.com

CPSIA information can be obtained at www.ICGtesting.com
Printed in the USA
LVOW07s2222301013

359308LV00001B/107/P